# DEAD OF NIGHT

## THE WATCHERS, BOOK 2

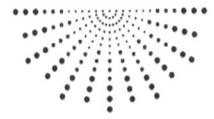

### CHRISTINE POPE

DARK VALENTINE PRESS

DEAD OF NIGHT

ISBN: 978-1-946435-02-6

Copyright © 2017 by Christine Pope

Published by Dark Valentine Press

Cover design by Christian Bentulan

Formatting by Indie Author Services

# CHAPTER ONE

THREE WORDS KEPT ECHOING IN SILAS Drake's mind.

*I've lost her. I've lost her.*

Serena's condo felt abandoned, empty. There was no sign of a struggle; he hadn't expected there to be. No, Lucius Montfort, L.A.'s vampire master, was too careful for that. He would have instructed his minions to make certain there would be no evidence of any sort of foul play. If it weren't for Serena's bag, abandoned on the dining room table, Silas himself might have thought he was imagining things. But he knew Serena. That purse, oversized and made of dark green leather, was some sort of security blanket for her. He'd never seen her leave the house without it.

Because he knew he had to be careful and not leave any trace of his intrusion behind, he'd worn tight-fitting leather gloves when he let himself into the condo, using a key she didn't know he possessed, one he'd had made years earlier. Standard protocol…just in case. He would never have used that key, except in the direst of emergencies.

He couldn't think of an emergency worse than this one.

The alarm hadn't been engaged, another sign that she'd gone in some haste. She was always very careful about setting the alarm whenever she went out, of making sure that both the top and bottom locks were secure.

He kept the gloves on as he went through her purse, hoping against hope that she might have left some clue behind. Not that he really needed one, other than her disappearance itself. She had to be with Montfort. There was no other explanation.

Even so, he mentally catalogued the items as he lifted them out one by one, and then put them back in reverse order, hoping that the careful precision of these actions would help to quell the worry rising within him. Her wallet. One of those mini packets of Kleenex tissues. A small leather case that contained lip gloss and lipstick. Another leather case, this one empty, which must have held her sunglasses. Her cell phone.

This last made him curse under his breath, because without her phone, she would have no way of calling for help. Which of course was why it remained here in her purse and wasn't with her now. Montfort—and, by extension, his lackey—wouldn't have been that careless.

Serena's keys were also missing. Montfort's half-living semivive servant must have taken them so he could secure the place properly as they left. Why he hadn't bothered with the alarm, Silas didn't know for sure. Maybe pausing to take care of that minor detail had seemed like a waste of time, especially since the alarm's main purpose was to protect Serena herself, and she was now gone.

He returned the purse to where he'd found it on the dining room table before giving the rest of the room a cursory glance. Everything appeared to be in place, in the same state of tidiness he'd come to expect from Serena. He didn't know if she was a naturally neat person, or whether that quality had been instilled in her by her parents, but he'd never seen the condo looking anything but spotless.

The kitchen was likewise in order. The dishwasher held a few plates and glasses, but that was it. When he went into the living room, he didn't see anything out of the ordinary there, either. A clock on one of the walls ticked into the silence.

Time to go upstairs.

He'd never been on the second floor of the condo before. Perhaps, if things had gone differently, he might have eventually spent the night here. His body clenched as he remembered what it was like to kiss the soft skin of her neck, to bury himself in her. To have her wrap her arms around him.

And to have her urge him to take her in his *gula* form, his wings defying gravity as he spent himself in her. The memory was still an astonishment, that she would be so open to him, so ready to accept the other side of his nature.

But Silas knew he couldn't lose himself in a reverie, no matter how pleasant. He had to do whatever he could to rescue her from Lucius Montfort. Her life was probably not in immediate danger, not when she possessed the psychic gift that made her so valuable to the vampire, but what if Montfort eventually decided that her visions were of no concrete value to him? He'd discard her like a used tissue.

Jaw set, Silas scanned the small loft area that Serena clearly had set up as her office space. On one side was a desk of pale, grayish wood and matching office chair, and on the other was a modest table, probably used for drawing, since he spotted a cup filled with pens and pencils and a few of those odd, pale gray pencil-shaped tools used for smudging.

It made sense that her sketchbook should have sat on that same table, but he saw no sign of it. Neither was it in the one low bookcase in the space, or on the desk where her closed-up laptop rested. For a moment, Silas debated taking the laptop, just in case it contained any information that might be useful, but he knew it would be missed, once it became clear that she was gone. He had a feeling Serena's absence would have to be noted at some point, despite her reclusive lifestyle. Not immediately, because her parents wouldn't be back from Santa Barbara until sometime the next day, and he couldn't think of anyone else who might notice her absence, except possibly her neighbors. But then, she spent days in her condo without ever leaving, so it might take some time before it became obvious that she had been missing for a while.

He went into her bedroom. The walls were painted a soft blue-gray, and the bed was covered in a white down comforter, with pillows in shades of blue and gray to break up all that white. The surfaces of the nightstands and the dresser were gleaming and empty. No jewelry lying out, nothing to interrupt the serenity of the space. A clock on one nightstand told him it was eight forty-two p.m.

Hating to pry, even as he knew he must check, he went to that nightstand and opened the top drawer. Serena had said she usually wrote down her visions in a little book she kept by her bedside, but he saw no sign of the book anywhere he looked. Not in either of the two nightstand drawers, nor in the other nightstand on the opposite side of the bed. He looked in the dresser as well, but found nothing except personal items like underwear and bras, socks and tank tops and yoga pants, although the drawers seemed only partly filled, as though some of their contents had been removed.

Like the sketchpad, her notebook appeared to be missing as well. It didn't take a great deal of reflection to surmise that Lucius' minion must have taken both items when he kidnapped Serena, no doubt so they could be turned over to the vampire for inspection.

The *en suite* bathroom appeared undisturbed…at first glance. Then he realized the toothbrush holder was empty. Working quickly, he opened several of the drawers, as well as the cupboard under the sink. While none of the drawers were completely empty, it appeared obvious enough to him that some of her toiletries had been taken—toothpaste and moisturizer and makeup and who knows what else. Well, her kidnapper would have had plenty of time to get whatever he thought she might need, considering how long Silas had been stuck in traffic while trying to get back to Pasadena.

The phone in his back pocket vibrated. He pulled it out, saw that the number on the screen belonged to Joseph, the senior watcher at the Humboldt compound. It was Joseph's duty to make assignments and compile reports—and it was he who had called Silas while he waited at the airport, telling him to abandon his trip to Paris and return to Pasadena as soon as possible. Emanuel had not responded to Joseph's check-in text, which signaled that something was terribly wrong.

Silas had headed to reclaim his truck from the long-term parking garage before the phone was even back in his pocket. Not that his haste had done him much good, since an accident on the 110 Freeway had backed up traffic for miles, and he'd been forced to get off on surface streets and drive away from the airport using another route. Once he'd arrived in Pasadena, he followed the tracker installed in each Watcher's vehicle so he could learn for himself what had happened to Emanuel.

His fellow *gula* had been slumped over the steering wheel of his Jeep Wrangler where it was parked on the street outside Serena's condo complex. Silas had put a hand to Emanuel's throat, but he'd known even before his fingers touched the man's cold flesh that he had been dead for at least a few hours. Thankfully, the *gula* retained their human form in death, which meant covering up Emanuel's death wasn't quite as much of a tactical problem as it might have been. Silas had texted Joseph to let him know what had happened so that a clean-up team could be dispatched to take care of their fallen Watcher, then headed up to Serena's condo, gut clenched, expecting the worst.

Which was what he'd found. No, to be fair, Serena missing wasn't the worst thing that could have happened. The worst thing would have been to discover her dead body somewhere inside her home, but of course she was nowhere to be found.

*Actually,* Silas thought, *the* very *worst thing would be to discover that Lucius had made her a vampire.*

He told himself that wouldn't happen. The transition from the mortal world to the vampire one was perilous in the extreme. Lucius wouldn't risk his prize, merely to have another undead member of his cabal.

Still, it was with his entire body braced for more bad news that Silas lifted the phone to his ear. Joseph wouldn't be calling unless something terrible had happened. "News?" he asked.

"More news, and none of it good." Joseph was never what you could call cheerful, but now his voice sounded grim enough for a funeral. Or a cancer diagnosis. "Daniel has been killed as well, and we just heard on the LAPD radio that Ms. Quinn's sister has been found murdered. Apparently, her assistant went over to her house to deliver some fabric and discovered the body."

Because it was Joseph on the other end of the line, Silas forced himself to hold back a curse. That was not professional behavior, no matter how much the news might affect him personally—and he knew he was already subject to increased scrutiny because of his involvement with Serena. Daniel gone, too. The Watchers did not number so many that they could spare anyone, and now they had lost two of their men in the space of one afternoon. Lucius Montfort was going to have a great deal to answer for, once this was all settled.

And the news about Vanessa Quinn…. The poor woman had been playing with fire and hadn't even realized how precarious her situation was. Silas had been sure that Lucius wouldn't go so far as to harm the woman, not when doing so would not only cost the vampire much of his leverage with Serena, but also because Vanessa Quinn came from such a prominent family, and her death would involve a great deal of scrutiny by the police. Apparently Silas had underestimated the vampire's rapacity...or his cunning. That he was playing some kind of long game here appeared evident enough, but what exactly was that game?

"Serena isn't here," he said, his voice tight. "I'm not sure how long she's been missing, though. Do you have a time of death for her sister?"

"They're waiting on the coroner. But it sounds as if it probably happened no more than three hours ago."

Three hours was a very long time. Serena could be anywhere. Somehow, though, Silas knew in his heart that Lucius must have taken her to his lair, to the large castle-like mansion she had seen in one of her visions. Unfortunately, even though he'd given the description of the place to Joseph so the team at the Humboldt compound could begin their search of Pasadena and its environs for a structure which matched that description, so far they'd turned up nothing. She could be literally only a mile from where Silas stood, and he would still have very little chance of finding her. The frustration of it all made him want to howl his anger at the world, but what would that accomplish?

Absolutely nothing.

"Thanks for the update," he told Joseph, voice

calm, clipped. He wasn't about to let Joseph see how disheartened he was. "I haven't found anything of any use here, so I think I'll go ahead and return to home base. Contact me if you get any new information."

"Of course," Joseph replied. A brief pause, and then he added, "I've also sent word of these recent developments to the Conclave, along with your apologies for not being able to travel to speak with them in person."

"Thank you for that as well." The words sounded stiff and formal, but Silas didn't bother to amend them. Right then, he cared very little for what the members of the Conclave might think about his involvement with Serena Quinn. The most important thing was to get her back, and as quickly as possible.

"It's nothing. Stay vigilant."

Joseph ended the call then, and Silas shoved the phone back into his pocket before heading downstairs. Another quick glance around, just to make sure he hadn't missed anything during his first pass of the condo, and then he let himself out, turning the bottom lock in the doorknob and then securing the deadbolt. No one would be able to tell that he'd ever been inside.

He was just passing the entry to the condo next to Serena's when the door opened and a man who appeared to be in his early or possibly middle forties, trim and in a white shirt and dark jeans, looked out. The man's brows drew together as his gaze met Silas', and he said, "Sorry. It's just—I'd hoped you might be Brian coming back."

Although he hadn't met the man before this, Silas immediately recognized him. Lewis Holman, one of Serena's longtime neighbors. Silas also knew that Lewis' partner Brian worked from home, just as Serena did, so it was somewhat odd that he would have gone out by himself on a Sunday evening. "No problem," Silas said, his tone neutral.

"Is Serena home?" Lewis asked.

"No," Silas replied. As Lewis shot him a surprised look, he went on, "She's at her parents' place for dinner. But she worried that she'd left the stove on, so she called and asked if I could come by and check for her. I got the key from Candace, since she's working right now and couldn't come over."

"Ah." While Lewis didn't appear completely convinced by this story, he also didn't seem inclined to question it. "Sam, right?"

"What?"

"You're Sam Willis, aren't you? The one who works for the *Times*."

Clearly, Serena had been telling a few stories of her own, probably forced into it by the need to offer some sort of explanation for his presence in her life. "Yes, that's right." Silas gave the other man a questioning glance. "Has Brian been gone a long time?"

"I don't know. I mean, I'd gone out to run a few errands, getting things for dinner, and when I got back, I found a note he'd left for me, saying he needed to go out and take care of something, but he didn't say what."

That sounded more than a little suspicious. From the few things Serena had told him about the couple who lived next door to her, it sounded as if they did almost everything together during those hours when Lewis wasn't at his job downtown. A cold, prickly sensation began to move down Silas' spine. Serena had been taken by someone, that much was clear. He had assumed the deed must have been handled by one of Lucius Montfort's semivives, his half-living slaves. Now it was beginning to sound as if that semivive had been someone close to her. She'd been wary, on her guard. How better to get near her than to suborn one of her closest friends, then send him to do the deed?

Again, Silas had to stifle a curse. He should have warned her to avoid contact with anyone, even people she trusted, but he hadn't thought that Montfort would be so bold as to go after one of her neighbors. Making a semivive required having access to a person for a decent chunk of time, long enough for the vampire antibodies to take hold in the bloodstream, allowing the vampire master to gain control of the semivive's mind. But apparently Lucius Montfort had decided the risk was worth the effort.

"I'm sure it's fine," Silas said, doing his best to sound reassuring, and hoping that the other man hadn't noticed the way he'd hesitated before replying.

"I noticed the traffic was pretty heavy for a Sunday evening as I drove over here. He probably just got hung up somewhere."

Lewis nodded, relief clear on his pleasant features. "That's what I was thinking. Traffic." He lifted his shoulders, although Silas could tell there was something forced about the movement, as if the other man was feigning an unconcern he didn't actually feel. "Well, I won't keep you. Have a good evening, Sam."

An apologetic smile, and then Lewis shut the door to his condo. Silas remained on the walkway for a second or two more, the neutral expression he'd maintained during the encounter slipping away almost at once. A wave of sadness washed over him as he made himself turn and head toward the visitor parking lot where he'd left his truck.

He knew that Serena's neighbor would never see his boyfriend again. The semivive would return, because otherwise his absence would be noted, but he wouldn't be the same man Lewis had fallen in love with, had partnered with. That man was gone just as surely as Vanessa Quinn, only this was a slow death, a death of the soul.

In that moment, Silas hated Lucius Montfort more than he ever had before.

～

It felt as if I was swimming upward from enormous

depths, attempting to claw my way through waters icier than anything I'd experienced before, as though I was drowning in an arctic ocean. My lungs labored, and my head pounded.

And then I opened my eyes.

Above me was a ceiling of dark carved wood, intricately coffered. The room wavered for a moment, came into focus. Wainscoting of more dark wood. The walls above the wainscoting were covered with wallpaper that looked like a glade of spring trees. The pattern didn't seem to repeat; I guessed, having seen similar paper in houses belonging to my parents' friends, that it must have been hand-painted. And heavy curtains of what I thought was velvet, although the space around me was dim enough that I couldn't quite make out what color the fabric actually was.

In the next instant, I realized how much my head hurt, throbbing like the worst of the migraines I'd suffered in the year after my accident before they gradually began to go away.

And at last I saw the man sitting in the chair next to the bed where I lay.

No, not a man. Lucius Montfort.

As I stirred, he offered me a smile. There was absolutely nothing reassuring about his expression, though. How could there be? The last time I'd seen him, he'd held my dead sister in his arms. His teeth looked white and perfect now, so he must have cleaned off Vanessa's blood while I was lost in a drug-induced slumber.

"You bastard," I whispered. Those two words seemed to be all I had the strength for at the moment. My voice rasped, grating against my throat.

His smile only broadened. "My dear Serena, I fear you must be angry with me. I suppose you have reason, but such hostility will gain you nothing. In the meantime—" He reached over to the nightstand, to the cut-glass pitcher of water and matching tumbler that sat there. After pouring a few inches of water into the glass, he held it out to me.

I ignored it. "Whatever you want, you're not going to get it." At least my voice sounded a bit stronger that time, not quite so hoarse.

"Ah." Lucius paused, glass still extended toward me. "It sounds as if you could use this. Drink, please, before you start making threats."

"Do you think I'm going to trust anything you give me to drink?"

He let out a somewhat theatrical sigh and put the tumbler back down on the nightstand. "I suppose you are holding that hypodermic against me. A last resort, I assure you. I had every reason to believe you wouldn't cooperate, and yet I also didn't want you to be damaged in any way. It seemed the easiest thing to do was to simply knock you out with chemicals rather than use physical force. Your head is aching, and you are dehydrated. It's better if you drink the water. Otherwise, I'll have to consider getting you an IV."

Oh, no, he wouldn't. But as I stared over at him, my expression as stony as I could make it, I realized there was very little he wouldn't dare. After all, he'd turned Brian into one of his semivives, just so he could get close to me. Brian meant nothing to him, except as a means to an end.

Which begged the question…what exactly did *I* mean to Lucius Montfort?

I pushed myself up against the pillows, shutting my eyes briefly against the flare of agony behind my temples. Yes, my head hurt, but I'd suffered far worse pain than this. I could ignore it for now.

Right then I realized that I was still fully dressed, wearing the jeans and sweater I'd had on when Brian abducted me from my home. My boots had been removed, true, but as the room came into better focus, I saw that they'd been set off to one side, placed up against the wall.

Not taking my eyes off Lucius, I reached for the glass of water and lifted it to my lips. Drank. The liquid was cool and faintly sweet, soothing against my throat. Not tap water. Something high-end, maybe Évian.

The vampire gave me an approving nod. "Good. There is nothing wrong with the water, just as there will be nothing wrong with the food I provide. I have no wish to harm you, Serena Quinn."

"You expect me to believe that?" I wrapped my hands around the glass of water and glared at him. Even though he was the one who sat there only a few feet away, I couldn't keep myself from seeing my sister's face, slack and pale, her eyes glassy, the person behind them long gone.

And the blood. Dear God, the blood. Streaking her throat, dripping down onto the pale gray shirt she'd been wearing. I didn't think I would ever be able to get that image out of my head.

Lucius was silent for a moment. The corners of his lips lifted slightly, although his eyes were as cold and silvery and inhuman as ever. "You are angry about your sister."

"Of course I am!" I burst out, then winced as another sharp pain lanced through my head, feeling as though someone had tried to drive an iron spike into my eye socket. Despite the discomfort, I went on, "You *murdered* her!"

"I suppose I did." He reached into the breast pocket of the jacket he wore and drew out a small enameled pillbox. After he opened it, he shook two small capsules into his hand and held them out to me.

"You think I'm going to take drugs from you?"

"Tylenol 3," the vampire replied, apparently unperturbed by my tone. "Not anything you need to be worried about. But I can see that you are hurting, and I wish to alleviate your pain."

"I guess you should have been more concerned about 'my pain' when you were killing my sister."

His mouth tightened. "She served her purpose."

Ignoring the throbbing in my head, I pushed myself even more upright so I could glare at him. "What purpose?"

"Nothing you need concern yourself with."

How in the world could he possibly think I wouldn't "concern myself" with my only sister's death? Maybe it was simply that he'd been a vampire for so long, had been cut off from his human self for so many years, that the concept of human grief no longer had any meaning to him. Various insults and retorts sprang to my mind, but none of them seemed strong enough to be a sufficient reply. I stared at Lucius through narrowed eyes and said, "Anything opiate-based makes me sick to my stomach. So I think I'll deal with this pain on my own, thank you very much."

"Ah," he said. "That is unfortunate." But at least he didn't seem inclined to push the issue further, and instead returned the pills to the little enamel box and put it back in his jacket pocket. "Then I think it best if you get some rest. It is early in the evening yet, but your body will need some time to recover from the drug you were given."

"Do you really think I'm going to sleep for a single second under your roof?"

This time he smiled for real, wide enough that I was given a good look at his pointed canines. "Oh, I think you had better," he replied. "After all, you are going to be here for a very long time."

Having delivered that parting shot, he got up from his chair and let himself out. I caught the briefest glimpse of a long hallway lined with oil paintings before he shut the door behind him. A second later came the unmistakable sound of a key turning in a lock.

Damn it. I pushed back the covers and then, gritting my teeth against another bolt of pain shuddering through my head, I swung my legs over the edge of the bed and stood. The room wavered around me, and I made myself stand stock still until the moment of vertigo had passed.

One step forward, then another. Each one felt as if it was pounding directly upward into my skull, but I ignored the pain. I'd had a lot of practice at that sort of thing, years of divorcing physical agony from its effects on my mind. Some days maintaining control over the pain was harder than others, but at the moment, I couldn't let my discomfort distract me.

Eventually, after an eternity or two, I reached the door. It was of the same dark wood as the ceiling and wainscoting. Mahogany, probably. The door handle was engraved brass, the lock one of those old-fashioned kinds that used a skeleton key. Even though it hurt even more to bend down, I crouched slightly and squinted so I could look through the keyhole.

Yes, a long hallway, one so long that its end was

lost in shadow. The light fixtures overhead were elaborate, aged bronze with faux candles that flickered into the darkness. They cast only enough light to show the paintings I'd noticed before—mostly landscapes, with the odd portrait here and there. The floor was wood laid in an intricate parquet pattern, bare of any rugs.

And it was quiet, so quiet that I could hear the sound of my heartbeat echoing in my ears. This place had to be enormous, if I truly was being held in the mansion I had seen in my vision. I assumed all the vampires in the coven lived here—Michael St. John, Leticia Carver, and Tristan McVey—along with Lucius, their master. Probably four vampires wouldn't make much sound, especially when scattered throughout a structure that had to be around ten thousand square feet at the very least.

If they were even here. Night had fallen, after all. Maybe they were out…hunting.

I shivered, then straightened and put a hand to my forehead until the pounding subsided somewhat. Even though every square inch of my body felt as if it had been beaten with a variety of sticks, I didn't go back to the bed. Instead, I went to the window and pushed the curtains aside. Now I was close up enough to see that the heavy velvet was dark green, no doubt chosen to coordinate with the hand-painted trees on the wallpaper.

But I wasn't here to inspect the draperies. I wanted to see something of where I was being held.

Luckily, the moon was almost full. It cast enough light that I could see the same trees from my vision, some still bare from the winter just past, others evergreens, thick with needles. From my vantage point on this upper floor, I was able to spot the paths that wound through the trees, pale in the moonlight. Off to one side, water shimmered with the moon's reflection. A pond, I thought, although I couldn't get a good idea of its size because of the trees blocking part of my view.

Everything appeared deathly still, no wind at all. My fingers found the window's latch, and I struggled with it for a moment before I realized that it must have been tampered with so it wouldn't open. That made sense, I supposed. After all, Lucius Montfort couldn't risk his captive getting away.

A wave of panic went over me then, and I clung to the windowsill. *Just breathe,* I told myself. *You're not going to do yourself any good if you start losing it this early in the game.*

Another breath, and another. That was better. I tried to reassure myself, to recall the words Lucius had said only a little while earlier. *I have no wish to harm you, Serena Quinn.*

If only I could believe what he had told me. How could I, when he'd murdered my sister, turned my friend Brian into one of his soulless minions?

In that moment, it was all too much. The tears came then, and I didn't try to stop them. I wept from sorrow, and fear, and utter frustration. Right then, I couldn't summon any hope, any reassurance that Silas would be able to find me. After all, he'd told me outright that his people had no real idea of where Lucius Montfort's stronghold was located. I had no doubt that they were already on the hunt, but would it make any difference in the end?

I didn't know. I dragged myself over to the bed and lay down, settling my aching head against the pillows. Maybe if I went to sleep, I'd wake in the morning to discover that this had all been a hideous nightmare.

# CHAPTER TWO

EVERY INCH OF HIS LOFT SEEMED TO ECHO WITH Serena's presence. She'd only spent one night here, but she'd already left an indelible imprint on the place. On his life. And now she was gone.

*Not forever,* he thought fiercely. *She's valuable to Lucius. She'll be all right until I can track her down.*

Problem was, Silas had believed the vampire wouldn't harm Vanessa. He'd thought she would be far more valuable as leverage. And yet, here Silas was, sitting in front of his police radio, listening to the conversations of the officers and the medical examiner at Vanessa's home in West Hollywood.

Time of death was set at 5:56 p.m. It made sense; that was just a little after sunset, dark enough that Lucius would have been able to venture out of his lair without risking physical harm. Vampires didn't require full dark, only that the sun be safely past the horizon.

And now that Montfort had fed, he wouldn't need to do so again for some time. Gruesome as the notion might be, Silas couldn't help thinking it would be much easier to track down vampires if they needed to feed all the time. Just follow the trail of bodies, and eventually you would be able to locate the suspect, once the vampire's patterns had been analyzed.

Not that anyone at the scene of the crime was talking about vampires. According to the preliminary inspection of the body, Vanessa Quinn's throat had been cut with some kind of a serrated implement. A way of covering up the puncture wounds, Silas guessed. Once her neck had been hacked with a jagged knife, all trace of the original cause of death would be hidden. An extremely detailed evaluation might detect some foreign antibodies in her blood, but he doubted they would dig that deeply. Standard tests, sure, to check for drugs and alcohol, and DNA analysis in an attempt to pin down the killer's identity, but he didn't think a police lab existed that had the means to test for the vampire antibodies.

Silas frowned and settled against the back of his chair. It felt wrong to be here, safe in his own home, rather than out looking for Serena. Driving aimlessly around the greater Los Angeles area wouldn't do anything except waste gas, and possibly fool himself into thinking he was doing something. Truth was, he needed a plan.

Well, for one thing, Serena had said she thought

the house from her vision must be somewhere in the San Rafael section of Pasadena. That narrowed down the search area a good bit. Even using that piece of intel, the Watchers up in Humboldt hadn't been able to find anything yet. And it wasn't as if he could simply go from house to house, knocking on doors to see which one of the homes in question was owned by a vampire. The residents would be sure to call the police before he'd gone even a block.

The police.... Silas sat up straighter then, running an abstracted hand through his hair. While he himself hadn't dealt directly with Detective Ortiz of the Pasadena P.D., Serena had. Because of their former relationship, the detective would surely be motivated to do whatever he could to help track her down, above and beyond who she was and who her family happened to be.

But whether to call now, or wait for tomorrow morning.... Yes, of course police departments were staffed twenty-four/seven, but Raoul Ortiz was one of the senior members of the force. Silas doubted he would be stuck with a Sunday night shift.

Better to wait, agonizing as the prospect sounded. He didn't feel comfortable speaking to anyone else at the department. And while things were quiet now, news of the murder being held back until the family could be notified, he knew all hell was going to break loose as soon as Serena's mother got the news of Vanessa's death...and then discovered that her other daughter was missing. A family with the sort of wealth and influence the Quinns possessed was going to be demanding answers, and soon.

He wondered what they would find.

~

I had told Lucius I wouldn't sleep, but I did. The remnants of the drug in my system, or grief, or pure exhaustion. It didn't really matter what drove me into slumber, only that I awoke many hours later, with sunlight slanting through the gap in the curtains, still pushed aside from when I had looked out the window the night before.

One good thing about the sun—with it shining so brightly outside, I didn't have to worry about a return visit from Lucius Montfort anytime soon. I'd have the whole day to get myself together, to try to come up with some sort of plan for getting out of here.

That early morning enthusiasm was tamped down slightly when I went to the window and surveyed the grounds, now brightly lit by an early spring sun. Last night, all had been still and quiet, but now I saw several men walking on the garden paths. They didn't even nod at each other as they passed, and I realized they must be semivive guards. It made sense; the vampires could keep watch during the nighttime hours, but they had to rely on their servants during the day.

I wondered how many of the semivives there actually were. Silas had killed several of them during our confrontation with Lucius' slaves in Little Tokyo on Saturday night, but since he didn't have a good idea of their numbers, neither of us knew how damaging a blow losing three or four of the semivives might be. Even if there were only a few left, that would still be too many for me. I was no martial arts expert, someone who could take on a couple of grown men — or what used to be men — at a time.

My head still hurt. I took the glass of water from the nightstand and drained the rest of it. Off to one side was a door that led to an *en suite* bathroom. Sitting on the green marble countertop was a leather case, one I recognized because it was mine. Inside were a variety of toiletries obviously taken from my bathroom.

I shivered. It seemed clear enough to me that not-Brian must have returned to my condo at some point so he could get all the necessities required for a lengthy stay. While I was forced to admit that there might be some comfort in using the soaps and lotions and cosmetics I was used to, it was still horrible to imagine him creeping around in my empty home, taking all the things he thought I might need.

Driven by an impulse, I left the bathroom and went over to the bedroom's walk-in closet. Sure enough, hanging there was a good sampling of my wardrobe — tops and skirts, sweaters and jackets. The closet's built-in drawers held lingerie and nightgowns, and socks and underwear. On the floor were arranged several pairs of shoes and boots. I even spotted the black dress Vanessa had loaned me, along with the matching shoes. What use the semivive had thought I'd have for that ensemble, I had no idea. Maybe he'd taken the dress simply because it had been hanging toward the front of my own closet, one of the last things I'd worn before my kidnapping.

Looking at the dress just brought it home all over again—my sister dead, her blood staining Lucius Montfort's mouth. Tears burned in my eyes, but I swallowed, hard, and told myself that crying now wouldn't do any good. The night before, I'd let myself weep. I had to believe that somehow, someday I'd get out of here. On that day, I would mourn. Now, however, I had to focus my energies on staying alive.

I selected a dark green sweater and a pair of jeans, along with some fresh underwear, and headed back to the bathroom. At least the door lock worked, although I knew it probably wasn't enough to keep someone sufficiently determined out. But the vampires were down for the count until sunset today, and I hadn't seen a single hint that the semivives had any sort of sexual urges remaining—not that any of them would have had the guts to go after me and risk Lucius Montfort's wrath. I decided that taking a shower was a fairly low-risk proposition, and after everything that had happened the day before, I needed to get clean. I needed to wash it all away.

So I climbed into the enormous shower enclosure, also faced with green marble, just like the vanity's countertop, and turned on the water as hot as I could stand it. Standing under the shower head and letting the pulsing jets knead away my headache felt better than I had hoped, as did lathering up my favorite shampoo and body wash. Most likely I was wasting a great deal of water, but right then I didn't care. Lucius' water bills were not my problem.

Eventually, though, I got out and dried myself off as quickly as possible, and climbed into the underwear I'd laid out. An inspection of one of the bathroom drawers showed that not-Brian had retrieved my blow dryer and curling iron as well, but I didn't bother with any of that. Instead, I scrunched some serum into my hair so it would dry wavy, its natural state. Getting dressed didn't take very long, and putting on my makeup even less, since all I did was put on some mascara and lip gloss, more because doing so made me feel marginally better than because I was trying to impress anyone.

I didn't wear a watch, unless I was going to something dressy and would get out the white gold Longines that my parents had bought me for my twenty-first birthday. And of course my phone was still, presumably, sitting in my purse where I'd left it on the dining room table, so I couldn't use that to tell me the time.

After I'd slipped into a pair of flats, I went back to the window. The sun was higher now, but I couldn't be sure of the hour. Nine, maybe closer to ten. That meant there was a long way to go before night fell and the vampires would be moving around again.

My stomach growled. I put a hand against my belly, willing it to be quiet. So far I hadn't seen any sign that Lucius planned to feed me. Up until that moment, I hadn't felt as if I wanted to eat ever again, but I realized that it had been a very long time since I'd had any kind of a meal—the morning of the day before, to be precise, when Silas fed me breakfast. True, it had been a fairly late breakfast, but still.

The image flashed into my mind of him smiling at me as he scrambled eggs and put bread in the toaster, and I immediately forgot all about my current hunger. I didn't need food—I needed *him*. I needed him to come save me.

*He will,* I told myself. *He* will. *You just have to hang on until then.*

I had to believe that was true.

Right then I couldn't see any of the semivives, but that didn't mean they weren't out there somewhere, patrolling the grounds. If I'd had access to a watch and a pen and paper, I would have made a note of the time, just in case there might be some kind of pattern to their movements. Did they have set schedules, duty rosters, that sort of thing? I really couldn't begin to guess. Not-Brian appeared to have exhibited some kind of independent thought and decision-making capabilities, but his actions must have still been guided by the commands handed down by his master.

I wondered what had happened to my erstwhile neighbor. Silas had said something about the semivives fooling their family and friends for weeks or even months before anyone began to notice a change, and yet I found that difficult to believe. I'd been able to tell almost immediately that the Brian who'd confronted me at my condo was not the same man who'd become one of my closest friends.

But then, I'd already been wary. I knew about vampires and semivives, knew there was a plot by Lucius Montfort to get his hands on me and my psychic powers. If I hadn't already been on the lookout for anything that seemed off, would I really have noticed? People's moods shifted, after all. They could get into funks. So maybe Lewis really wouldn't detect anything out of the ordinary at first. I didn't know which would be worse—realizing right away that the person you'd loved for years and years wasn't who you thought they were, or having it gradually come to you over time that a stranger slept in the bed next to you.

A chill hit me then, even though the room that currently served as my prison cell was warm enough. I moved away from the window and went over to the door, where I bent and looked through the keyhole as I had the night before. At least this time my head didn't hurt as much; the hot shower had done a good job of scrubbing away the remnants of my migraine.

The hallway outside was so dim I could barely make out anything. I realized that was because the chandeliers overhead weren't lit. Maybe there was a window at the end of the corridor, but I couldn't see it. Anyway, even if there happened to be a window, I guessed that Lucius' semivives would make sure the draperies were drawn shut.

Fighting back a sigh, I straightened up and glanced around the room. Absolutely nothing there to keep me occupied. No books, no television, no radio. And definitely not a computer. What was Lucius trying to do, drive me crazy with boredom?

*Probably,* I thought, as I went over to a small side chair of carved mahogany, then picked it up so I could take it over to the window and resume my watch of the grounds. *I could see him making sure you're left alone all day, no food, no one to talk to, so that when he shows up tonight and pretends to be all charming, feeds you dinner or whatever, you'll fall over him in gratitude.*

Well, if that was his plan, he'd be waiting a long time. I couldn't imagine myself being so desperate that I'd be grateful to him for anything.

I'd finished the water he brought me, but there was always the tap. I retrieved the glass and went into the bathroom and filled it, then took up my seat by the window once more.

The day had started out bright and sunny, but I saw a few big fluffy clouds begin to drift overhead. Had there been rain in the forecast? I couldn't remember. I might have glanced at the weather report a few days ago, but whatever I'd read had been driven right out of my head by everything that had happened over the last forty-eight hours.

I tried to imagine what might be going on out in the world. Had anyone discovered Vanessa's body yet? Probably; it was Monday morning, and she'd be having people showing up to work in the studio behind the main house. Never mind that she'd just held a show on Thursday night and should be resting on her laurels for a while…Vanessa never took a break. She was the ultimate workaholic.

Thinking about her, about her drive and her perfectionism and her way of making fabric flatter almost anyone, made me want to burst into tears all over again. Yes, there had been times when she'd driven me crazy, but she was still my sister. Even in my moments of utter frustration with her, I'd had to acknowledge what an amazing person she was. And now she was gone, all that vibrant life snuffed out by someone who'd used her only as a ploy, a way to get back at me. She'd meant nothing to the vampire.

I somehow managed to choke back my tears. Right then, I wasn't as worried about Lucius Montfort discovering me in a moment of weakness—after all, the sun was still high in the sky—as losing myself to grief, of allowing myself to wallow in despair rather than doing my very best to keep my wits about me. It wasn't that I hadn't suffered losses before; both my father's parents had died before I reached college. And yet this felt so very different. You loved your grandparents but knew they wouldn't be around forever. It was entirely different when trying to come to terms with losing a sister who was only seven years older than you.

All right. Time to take that grief and push it away into a corner of my mind for now. Perhaps one day I'd be able to mourn properly. For now, though, I had to consider my options, attempt to strategize.

How long would it be before someone missed me? Under normal circumstances, it might have been a while; I spoke to my mother once a week, sometimes even less than that, so she wouldn't have found anything strange about not hearing from me for a few days. Same with my sister, except we often weren't in contact more than once or twice a month. This Thursday's plea for me to come work her show had been something of an aberration, one driven by desperation.

Even Lewis might not notice anything out of the ordinary at first, since he was away at work for most of the day. It had been Brian whom I'd chatted and gossiped with. But of course he wouldn't mention anything about my disappearance, not now that he'd become Lucius Montfort's minion.

All that went out the window, though, since as soon as news of Vanessa's death reached my parents, my mother would be on the phone at once, trying to get hold of me. And when I didn't respond…?

Well, she'd have the police out to my place immediately, even as she and my father headed into Los Angeles to meet with the detectives who'd been assigned to Vanessa's case. At least, I assumed that was what would happen next. I didn't watch police procedurals. Would the police have my parents go to the morgue to identify Vanessa's body?

That image made the tears start to my eyes again, scalding. I pressed my palms flat against my eyelids and willed myself to stay calm, even though calm was about the last thing I felt right then. Okay, so it was very possible they'd already contacted the Pasadena police and had them go to the condo to take a look around. The police wouldn't find much evidence, though, since I'd gone calmly enough with not-Brian. No struggle at all.

But there was my purse. I never left the house without it. And also the matter of the missing keys — unless the semivive had duplicated the ones he needed and then returned mine to the pocket where I kept them in my handbag. Such a cover-up would only deepen the mystery, but it might also make it that much harder to unravel. To someone who didn't know better, the whole setup would look as if I'd been abducted from my condo by aliens or something.

Right then I thought I'd prefer aliens to Lucius Montfort and his lackeys.

Problem was, even if matters had moved quickly with the police, there would be so little evidence to go on. They would talk to Lewis and Brian, I was sure, but Lewis hadn't been home when I disappeared, and not-Brian could concoct any story he wished. In fact, I wouldn't put it past him to implicate Silas in some way...especially if he knew Silas' real name. Oh, that would look horribly suspicious, for me to have been calling him "Sam" all that time.

Damn it. I wiped my clammy palms on the knees of my jeans and looked outside again. This time I could see one of the semivives moving on that path out there. I didn't recognize him—he looked tall and well built, with sandy brown hair. Once upon a time, I probably would have considered him attractive. Now, though, I knew he was only a slave to Lucius Montfort's will.

Anyway, after the night I'd spent in Silas' arms, I knew my heart belonged to him, and only to him. It really wasn't like me to fall for someone that hard, that quickly, but then, Silas was unlike anyone I'd ever known before. Not only because he was far more than an ordinary man, but because of his strength, his integrity, his ability to do the right thing, no matter how difficult it might be.

And that was how I knew he would find me. He wouldn't give up. He'd said he loved me, and I knew it was only the simple truth. A man like Silas would never abandon the woman he loved.

All I had to do was survive until he came to take me away from this place.

# CHAPTER THREE

THE PASADENA POLICE DEPARTMENT HEADQUARTERS were located a few blocks from the distinctive domed structure that housed City Hall. Because all the metered parking spaces on the street had already been taken, Silas was forced to park in the structure at Paseo Colorado and walk over. Usually he wouldn't have minded, because walking helped to clear his head. Now, though, he could only curse the time wasted in hiking the extra distance.

The night before, he'd called the department and confirmed with the deputy taking calls that Detective Ortiz would be on duty at nine o'clock on Monday morning. Silas had left his loft downtown at seven-thirty, taking no chances that he would be late. He needn't have worried, since most of the traffic was going in the opposite direction at that hour of the morning. To fill up the time, he'd stopped at a coffee house in Old Town Pasadena and gotten an espresso. Now, though, he was regretting that small indulgence; he'd already felt on edge, nerves strained to the breaking point, and the extra caffeine only served to increase his anxiety.

He honestly wasn't sure what Raoul Ortiz could do to help, but Silas figured he needed to start somewhere.

"I need to speak with Detective Ortiz," he told the deputy in the reception area.

She looked up at him, head cocked to one side. Even behind the bulletproof glass that guarded her workstation, she wore an expression that seemed entirely too perky for that hour of the morning…or for her job at the police department. "Do you have an appointment?"

"No." He'd thought it better to come here directly, without fanfare. Also, like the rest of the Watchers, he preferred to avoid telephone contact. The phones he and his fellow *gula* used were secure, but he couldn't expect that level of security from everyone. Not even detectives with the Pasadena P.D.

"Okay. And you are?"

"Sam Willis." Silas knew he'd have to give Raoul Ortiz his real name, but he didn't want to spread it around any more than he had to. "Tell him it's about Serena Quinn."

The deputy nodded and picked up her phone, then dialed an extension. Silas listened to her give the person on the other end of the line his name and Serena's. Her dark eyes widened for a second, and she nodded. "Yes, Detective Ortiz. I'll let him know." She swiveled back toward him and said, "He'll be right out, Mr. Willis. You can take a seat over there."

Unwilling as he felt to sit down, pinging with nervous energy the way he was, Silas did as instructed and went to one of the rows of shabby-looking plastic chairs the deputy had indicated. Apparently Sunday had been a quiet day in Pasadena, because the only other person seated in the waiting area was a tired-looking Hispanic woman, barely more than a girl, with a baby in one of those portable child carriers on one of the chairs next to her. Her gaze flicked to Silas for a moment before she returned her attention to the phone she held, fingers flying as she texted away.

He was glad she had something to occupy her. He was also relieved that the baby was asleep, wasn't fussing or crying. Right then, he wasn't sure if he could have handled that kind of commotion. Yes, he was used to children, because the *gula* and their human partners all lived in a large compound—some might have called it a commune—outside Humboldt, and there were always kids of varying ages running around. He liked children. But a screaming baby when the woman he loved had been kidnapped by a very dangerous vampire was not something Silas really wanted to deal with right then.

"Mr. Willis?"

Silas looked up to see a thickset Hispanic man in a sport coat and khaki slacks standing in front of him. "You're Detective Ortiz?"

"Yes. And you're a friend of Serena Quinn's?"

It was Silas' turn to flicker a gaze at the young woman who sat across the way in the waiting area. But she appeared absorbed in her text, luckily. "Yes. Can I speak with you privately?"

The other man's dark eyes narrowed for a second, but when he spoke, his voice was neutral, pleasant. "Of course. Come with me back to my office."

Silas got up from his chair and followed the detective down a hallway with dingy linoleum underfoot that probably should have been replaced years ago. Before they got to the end, Ortiz turned into a room on the left, then closed the door after Silas had entered.

"Have a seat, Mr. Willis."

There was a metal-framed chair with shabby blue vinyl upholstery immediately in front of the desk. Silas pulled it out and sat down, then waited until the detective had settled himself in a much nicer rolling office chair.

"Actually, it's Silas Drake."

Ortiz's sparse eyebrows lifted slightly. "Why the fake name?"

"It's better if no one except you knows who I am."

The detective leaned back in his chair, expression almost too neutral. "And who are you, Mr. Drake?"

"A friend of Serena Quinn's."

"Yeah, I got that part. Why the cloak-and-dagger?"

"Did you know that she's missing?"

At once the bland look Ortiz had been wearing disappeared. His dark eyes grew hard, and he sat up so he could lay his palms flat on his desktop. A plain gold band gleamed on the fourth finger of his left hand. "What do you know about that?"

"Enough. I assume her parents must have contacted you sometime either last night or early this morning, once they'd gotten word of their daughter's murder."

The detective didn't reply for a moment. For someone with such a round, pleasant face, his expression was very grim. "Vanessa Quinn's death hasn't been made public knowledge yet. It's not every day that the sister of a presidential candidate is found murdered."

No, it wasn't. Once again, Silas wished he could be with Serena, could take her in his arms and hold her while she grieved. That she would have to suffer such a loss and then be stolen away by someone without a shred of compassion, who instead was the one responsible for that death, was intolerable.

"So how do you know about this, Mr. Drake?" Ortiz's tone had lost any semblance at friendliness.

"I know because I'm a friend of Serena's, as I told you. I came here because she told me that she'd worked with you in the past. Unlike most people, you're aware of her…special abilities."

The detective didn't blink. "Abilities?"

While Silas understood Ortiz's need to play coy, he still couldn't prevent a flare of caffeine-fueled irritation. "Yes, abilities. Her visions. She just helped you rescue a girl being held captive by an ex-boyfriend, correct? The house on Daine Drive?"

"That isn't public knowledge, either."

"No, it's not. I'm telling you in order to establish my bona fides, as it were."

A silence. Ortiz stared across the desk at him, tired brown eyes seeming to take in every detail of his appearance. Silas wondered if he looked as weary as the detective did. That morning he hadn't bothered to shave, had barely glanced in the mirror as he brushed his teeth. Right then he knew he felt about a hundred years old. If he'd gotten three hours of sleep the night before, that was being generous. It had taken all his strength of will not to transform, not to take to the skies and begin flying over the San Rafael area, desperately trying to determine which house was Lucius Montfort's lair. Unfortunately, the *gula* didn't have the same powers of stealth as vampires. All it would have taken was one insomniac spotting the strange winged creature moving overhead, one person out to do a little stargazing and instead seeing something impossible in the skies above him, and the game would have been up.

At last the detective let out a breath. "When was the last time you saw Serena Quinn?"

"Yesterday afternoon. I dropped her off at her condo around two, then went home."

"And where is home?"

"Downtown, just outside Little Tokyo."

"How do you know Ms. Quinn? Boyfriend?"

The detective's question made it sound so simple and uncomplicated, as if they were a couple of high school kids making plans for the prom. Not that Silas knew much about proms; no child of the *gula* attended public school. "Something like that," he allowed.

To his surprise, Detective Ortiz said, "Good."

It was Silas' turn for his eyebrows to lift.

"She always seemed…alone," Ortiz went on. "It didn't matter that she came from such a prominent family, or that she could have had anything she wanted. Her gift, her talent…it's as if it isolated her."

That it most certainly did. The Quinns wanted to pretend that their daughter was completely normal, and she wasn't. No, she was better than normal, a gift to the world, even if her family didn't want to acknowledge the importance of her visions. "She was…careful…around people," Silas said.

"That's one word for it. So you last saw her at two o'clock yesterday. Her neighbor says he talked to her at four, so she had to have disappeared after that."

"Which neighbor? Brian?"

"Why would it be Brian specifically?"

Silas gave what he hoped was an unconcerned shrug. At the moment he didn't feel like going into the whole semivive thing with the detective. "Serena was closer to him than most people."

"I'd have to look it up. I didn't take the report—so far this is a missing persons case, and I work homicide. But the detective who's handling the investigation is my former partner, and he remembered that I knew Ms. Quinn. So he passed some of the information along to me, knowing I would be concerned." Ortiz paused there and gave Silas a penetrating look. "This *is* just a missing persons case, isn't it?"

"It's a kidnapping," Silas replied, his tone flat.

"You sound very certain."

"It's because I am. I know who took her. Just like I know who murdered Vanessa Quinn. It's the same man. Lucius Montfort."

Silas hadn't expected the name to register with Ortiz, and it didn't. The man frowned faintly, but that was all. "Who is he?" But even as he asked the question, the detective turned toward his computer and began typing the name.

"Don't bother to look. You won't find much of anything. He won't have any kind of public record…if you can find any information on him at all. I doubt he has a driver's license. His home would have been purchased by a trust. And he definitely doesn't have a criminal history. On the surface, he's a model citizen."

"But you think he's a kidnapper and a murderer."

A bitter smile touched Silas' lips. "Oh, he's far worse than that."

"How so?"

Silas hesitated. This was the moment when he would have to decide whether to tell Raoul Ortiz the whole truth, that the man they sought was no man at all, but a vampire who had made mankind his prey for centuries. With anyone else, Silas wouldn't have bothered, knowing that some realities were too difficult for the majority of the public to accept. But Detective Ortiz had worked with Serena, had believed in her visions. If he had been willing to take that particular leap of faith, then Silas could only hope he'd be able to take one more.

"He's a vampire."

For one long moment, Ortiz didn't respond, only sat there wearing a faintly quizzical expression on his features. But then he chuckled, and Silas' heart sank. "This is a joke, right? A vampire? As in a blood-sucker who sleeps in a coffin?"

"He doesn't need to sleep in a coffin," Silas replied. "That's just folklore. He sleeps in a bed like a normal person, only in a room with the windows blacked out so he doesn't risk being touched by sunlight. That part is like the movies—he'll start to burn and smoke if even a single sunbeam touches him."

Again, the detective didn't respond right away. "You're serious."

"Yes. Look, I know it sounds crazy. But if you

tried to explain Serena's visions to a so-called 'rational' person, they'd probably think you were crazy, too. You know they're real, though. You know they've saved lives. So if you can accept the reality of a woman who has visions that are true, that are accurate, then you should also be able to accept the reality of a vampire."

"I don't know." Ortiz reached up to run a hand through his thinning hair, ruffling the gray-speckled fringe around his ears. His shoulders lifted, and he went on, "I think if you gave a random quiz, you'd probably get more people who're willing to believe in psychics than they are in vampires."

"That may be true. But I can tell you now that they're both real."

"And how do you know so much about vampires, Mr. Drake?"

"Let's just say that my…family…has been tracking vampires for a long time."

The detective appeared to digest that statement for a moment. Silas worried that he'd attempt to probe deeper, but instead Ortiz asked, "What about were-wolves? Witches? Mummies?"

"Definitely no werewolves or mummies. Witches?" Silas shrugged. "There are many who claim to be witches. I haven't investigated their claims for possessing psychic or supernatural powers, so I can't say one way or another."

"Aliens?"

Silas could only lift his shoulders again. "Probably not. But believe me, vampires are real. I've met them, spoken with them. I've seen the evidence of their crimes."

"So you say. But I've been on the force for twenty years, and I can safely say I've never seen any evidence to suggest that a vampire was responsible for any of the murders I've investigated."

"No, you wouldn't, because you don't know what to look for, and they're very good at covering their tracks. Just because you personally haven't witnessed something doesn't mean it doesn't exist."

Ortiz drummed his fingers on the tabletop. From the way his brows had pulled together, and the worried pucker that had formed between them, Silas had a feeling the detective was doing his best to reconcile what he'd just been told with everything his rational mind was convinced it knew.

"Believe me, I know it must sound mad to you. And the thing is, unless you've seen a vampire in action, or seen the way they burn up in sunlight, they would look like normal people to you."

"No fangs?"

"Not really. Slightly pointed canines, but no more than you might see in certain individuals—David Bowie, or Ricky Gervais."

This time the detective almost smiled. "Are you saying Ricky Gervais is a vampire?"

"No, I'm just saying that if you stood him next to a

vampire, you'd think that their teeth were remarkably similar. That's all."

Ortiz's gaze slid over to his computer screen, and he frowned again. Silas got the impression that he was distracting himself with his online search because he didn't want to come out and admit that vampires just might be real. "You were right. I'm not finding anything."

"You won't. That is, I know he entered into a business partnership with Vanessa Quinn, and so there were reports on several fashion blogs about the arrangement. But if you really tried to dig any farther past that, to locate anything about his history or his background, you wouldn't find very much."

"And no one thinks that's a little strange?"

Silas shrugged. "People think what they want to think. Lucius Montfort presents himself as a wealthy man, someone with a large fortune. These days, no one thinks it all that unusual when wealthy individuals hide their money and property in trusts and offshore accounts, that sort of thing."

"I suppose you're right." His gaze flickered over to the computer one last time before he appeared to fix his attention solely on Silas. "You'd think if this Montfort character was a vampire responsible for Vanessa Quinn's death, you'd see some evidence of the attack."

"Her throat was cut precisely to cover up the puncture marks that Lucius Montfort left behind."

A humorless chuckle, and Ortiz shifted in his seat.

"Sounds like you've got this whole thing figured out, Mr. Drake."

"Silas. It's not so much that I have it figured out, only that I've been keeping track of Lucius Montfort for some years. And even with all that surveillance, I still haven't been able to determine exactly where he's been hiding. Vampires are very good at stealth, Detective Ortiz."

"Raoul," the other man said. "If we're going to be on a first-name basis here."

"All right, Raoul," Silas amended. "Anyway, all we—"

"We who?" the detective cut in, his gaze sharpening.

Silas wanted to curse his carelessness, but doing so would only bring more attention to his slip-up. Yes, he'd decided that bringing Raoul Ortiz in to help with the search for Serena was his best and only option, but he also knew that he had to be careful about what he said. The Watchers needed to be kept out of it. The mistake could be blamed on stress and lack of sleep, but that wasn't a good enough excuse. He needed to remain mindful of what he was doing, no matter what happened. "Sorry, I. I suppose I was already thinking of you and I working together on this. Anyway, I knew Lucius Montfort was somewhere in Southern California, but it wasn't until Serena had a vision about his home that I realized he was right here in Pasadena."

"A vision, hm?" Ortiz steepled his fingers under his chin and pursed his lips slightly. "What did she see?"

"A mansion, probably in the San Rafael area, or maybe Linda Vista. Very large, sort of castle or chateau style, made of stone."

At those words, the detective straightened up, his brow furrowing once again. "Gray stone?"

"Yes, that's what she said. As far as she could see from the vision, it seemed to be built on the edge of the arroyo, looking east. It—"

"So it's not his," Ortiz murmured, and Silas sent him a questioning look.

"His who?"

"No one," the detective replied. "That is…someone from a case I worked on, some five years back. A very unusual man, but not, one would think, a vampire. His home sounds very similar to what you just described, but it's on the north side of the 210 Freeway. Still the western part of town, but a completely different section, up in Linda Vista. But I suppose it's not that strange. Back in the building boom of the early twenties, 'Norman chateau' was one architectural style that a lot of the wealthy East Coast transplants were into. But it should still help to narrow things down, especially if, as you said, the place was built on the edge of the arroyo. There aren't too many of those view lots. Did Serena draw it?"

Silas startled slightly at the question, then realized

that if Ortiz had worked with her on several cases, then he would have known about her habit of sketching out her visions. "She did," he replied. "But her sketchbook is missing, as is the notebook where she wrote down her visions. I noticed that when I returned to her condo—she'd given me a key, so I had permission to enter. Anyway, whoever took her took the sketchbook and notebook as well."

"Why would they do that?"

A fair question. Silas had to pause for a second, attempting to decide once again how much he felt comfortable telling the detective. But they'd come this far, so it seemed foolish to equivocate now. Besides, all he had to go on were suspicions. Nothing concrete. The more information Raoul Ortiz possessed, the more he might be able to help. "Lucius Montfort took Serena specifically because of her powers. This isn't a case of him wanting her because he needed a victim to feed on. Vampires can actually go quite a long time in between infusions of human blood. In fact, they can drink blood on its own, obtained from a blood bank or hospital, rather than taking it from their victims. Yes, it's more exciting for them to hunt, to see humans as their prey, but it's not necessary."

"Well, that's reassuring," Ortiz said dryly.

"I didn't intend it to be. I just wanted to let you know what you were up against. And I can tell you now that the medical examiner's investigation won't find any sign of bite marks."

"All signs so far point to a robbery. Yes, the wound was horrific, but it's also the sort of the thing you might see if someone used a hunting knife with a serrated edge." The detective stopped there and gave Silas another of those shrewd, searching looks, as if he was carefully weighing everything that had been said so far, matching it against what he himself knew, and performing the necessary mental arithmetic. "You're in possession of a lot of details about Ms. Quinn's murder, all things considered. Some might say that points to you being the prime suspect."

"I'm not a suspect."

"You have an alibi?"

In fact, Silas didn't, because he'd gone directly home after saying goodbye to Serena, and hadn't interacted with anyone once he got to the complex where his loft was located. There was a slim chance that one of the other residents might have seen him park his truck, or walk to his unit, but such a thing certainly couldn't be guaranteed.

Except....

"I was at LAX at the time of her murder. I have the time-stamped receipt from a parking garage there to prove my whereabouts. There's no way I could have gotten all the way from El Segundo to West Hollywood in the timeframe we're talking about."

"What were you doing at the airport?"

"I was going to take a short trip. I canceled it when I found out that Serena had disappeared."

"And how did you find out? She wasn't reported missing until late last night."

Damn. Silas hadn't thought this would turn into an interrogation, that he might be suspected of Vanessa Quinn's murder simply because he knew too much. However, he stilled the annoyance within him as best he could. After all, Ortiz was just doing his job. "She wasn't answering her phone."

"You thought she'd disappeared just because she didn't answer a call right away?"

"It's not like Serena to ignore me like that. I knew something had to be wrong. So I canceled my flight and headed up to Pasadena to see what was going on."

Ortiz didn't say anything for a long moment. He only sat there behind his desk, a powder-coated steel monstrosity that had probably been the height of police department decor back in the nineties but was looking a little worse for wear by now. At last he said, his tone so noncommittal that it could have meant anything, "You realize how crazy this all sounds."

"Yes. That doesn't change the fact that it's true."

"You have the receipt from the parking garage?"

Luckily, Silas did. He dug it out of the pocket of his leather jacket and handed it over to the detective, who scanned it briefly, then gave a reluctant nod.

"I suppose this could be an elaborate forgery, but I have a feeling it probably isn't. You want to tell me how you know all this about Vanessa Quinn, though?"

"Let's just say your communications equipment isn't quite as secure as you might think."

The other man didn't blink. "So...what are you exactly, Silas? NSA? Secret Service? I could see that, considering the connection with Senator Quinn, although I wouldn't say that hair was exactly regulation."

Silas didn't crack a smile. "No, I suppose it isn't. I'm just an ordinary private citizen with a background in paranormal investigations."

"You may be a private citizen, but I don't think there's anything particularly 'ordinary' about you. But...." Ortiz let the words trail off there, as if pondering the best way to continue. Then he shook his head, and reached for the coffee cup that sat to one side of the desk. He took a large swallow, wincing slightly as if the liquid it contained was either cold or bitter, or both. "But at the end of the day, the important thing is that Serena is missing and we need to find her. So I'll help you as best I can. I'm not assigned to the case, but Kosky shouldn't mind me participating, once I've talked to him and let him know what's going on."

"Kosky?"

"My former partner. His wife wanted him off homicide because it was giving him nightmares. So he transferred, but we still talk, trade ideas. We'll be on it."

"Thank you," Silas said. Yes, that was some relief,

but only a little. Having Ortiz's assistance—and this Detective Kosky, too—would be a big help. That didn't mean they wouldn't still be looking for a needle in a haystack.

A very big needle. A mansion-sized needle. Even so, Lucius Montfort had managed to stay hidden for a very long time. Would the resources of the Pasadena police department finally be enough to smoke him out from his lair?

Silas could only hope. A clock on the wall above Ortiz's head ticked loudly, telling him they didn't have forever. That time might be running out even now. About all he could do was pray that Serena's clock wouldn't tick to a stop before they found her.

# CHAPTER FOUR

Dusk came at last, stealing over the garden, shrouding the trees in gloom as the sun sank below the western horizon. Or at least I assumed it did so at the appointed time; my room — my prison — seemed to be on the east side of the house, and so I couldn't actually watch the sun go down.

By then I was ravenously, achingly hungry. Sure, I would skip meals from time to time if I was busy or if I simply wasn't in the mood to eat. But by that point, I hadn't consumed anything for nearly thirty-six hours, a fast that extended far beyond anything I'd ever experienced before, except for the days I'd been lost in a coma following my accident...and at least then I'd been given intravenous nutrients. Now, though, for all I knew, the drug that not-Brian had given me the evening before to knock me out was also doing a number on my system, its traces still lurking in my bloodstream, making me weak and tired and hungry as a bear waking from its winter nap.

No one had come near my room all that endless day. I'd drunk water almost obsessively, trying to fill my stomach with that since I didn't have anything else. It wasn't enough, though. And while I saw the semi-vives moving through the gardens at more or less regular intervals, I hadn't heard a thing within the house itself, except faint creaks here and there as the structure expanded with the warmth of the day. Now it was doing the same thing in reverse as the air outside began to cool, and still I was left alone.

What the hell was Lucius Montfort doing? Waiting until I was so weak with hunger that I couldn't fight back against him, would welcome him with open arms?

I was wondering whether I should just say the hell with it and crawl back into bed when the door opened.

No knock first, of course. No warning. I turned and saw Lucius Montfort standing at the entrance to the room. Naturally, he wore a particularly loathsome smile.

"And how are you this evening, Ms. Quinn?"

"Lovely," I said, the word caustic enough to eat through metal. "Thanks for checking in on me. I was beginning to wonder if you'd forgotten I was here."

He affected not to notice my tone. "My apologies. As you know, I'm not a day person."

"And you couldn't have one of your minions bring me a sandwich?"

"I wasn't sure you would have accepted one from me, considering how suspicious you were of the water I provided last night." His smile relaxed somewhat, but even in the dim light, I could see the sardonic twitch at the corner of his mouth. "Can I assume that you might be willing to eat something now?"

"I might," I replied grudgingly. It would have been nice if I'd had the willpower to fast indefinitely, but I knew that wouldn't work. Anyway, my chances of making a break for it would be diminished considerably if I was so weak from hunger that I couldn't function at a normal level.

"Then let us go downstairs. I fear I don't have much household staff, much less a cook, but I had one of my servants get some takeout."

I did my best to quash the incongruous vision of one of his semivives pulling up to the drive-through at a McDonald's and ordering both of us Big Macs and fries. Not that vampires needed such things to survive, but Silas had told me they would eat normal food, if it helped to maintain the façade that they were just ordinary mortals like the rest of us.

I had to wonder if Lucius would share a meal with me, or whether he'd simply sit there and watch me as I ate, rather like someone at the zoo hanging around to see the lions get fed.

Or, in my case, one of the gazelles. Predator I certainly was not.

"All right," I said, with obvious reluctance. Yes, I'd go with him, because I was dying to get out of that room, and I was starving enough that even a luke-warm burger sounded heavenly right then.

He offered me another of those malignant smiles, and stepped out of the way so I could move past him and into the corridor.

Since I'd seen it the night before when I looked through the keyhole, the hallway didn't seem all that unfamiliar. I walked past the paintings, many of which I guessed were imitations of original English landscape oils by Turner or Reynolds. Or were they originals? Lucius was, according to Silas, old enough to have encountered the original painters, in which case the landscapes I saw now were priceless and should have been in a museum. Even if they were knockoffs, they wouldn't have been cheap. Good imitations were still worth a lot, and I thought these had probably been painted in the twenties, around the same time the house was built. If, of course, I'd guessed correctly as to its vintage. The house I'd grown up in was also about that old, although the Quinn homestead took its inspiration from the neoclassical and Federal architec-ture of the early nineteenth century, rather than the style of the gloomy gothic mansion where I was currently being held prisoner.

I knew I was trying to distract myself by thinking

about the architecture and the décor, neither of which had much bearing on my immediate future. Better to occupy myself with attempting to decide whether the heavy furniture I saw around me was more knockoffs, or actual antiques brought over from England and the rest of Europe. The pieces definitely fit the house, which basically looked as if it had been put together for the express purpose of providing a suitable domicile for a vampire master and his—what did vampires call the other vampires they made? Children? Servants? Puppies?

That last thought almost made me chuckle, dire as my current circumstances were. I noticed that Lucius didn't bother to speak as we walked along, although I saw that he never ranged more than a foot in front of me, as if worried that I might try to make a break for it if a greater distance separated us. Much as I would have liked to attempt such a thing, I knew better. Silas had told me that vampires were inhumanly fast, so my chances of getting away while in Lucius Montfort's presence were basically zero. No, if I was going to escape, I'd have to find a way to do it during the daylight hours, while Lucius and his three cohorts were safely asleep. I'd have to deal with the semivives —and I didn't know for sure how many of them there might be loitering around the property—but I'd still prefer to take those chances, rather than going up against four angry vampires.

We passed a formal dining room and kept going.

Despite myself, I could feel my eyebrows lifting slightly, because I supposed I'd assumed that Lucius would be playing lord of the manor with me, and intended to consume our takeout meal on the kind of huge dining room table most people had only seen in the movies, but which I'd grown up with.

Did vampires have eyes in the backs of their heads? I didn't detect any peering out at me from beneath Lucius' pale hair, but even though he was in front of me and shouldn't have been able to see my expression, he said, "I thought we would eat in the game room. The setting is much more...intimate."

I didn't like the sound of that at all, but I also knew this was not the time to argue. I only said, "All right," and continued to follow him down the long hallway, until we passed a room that must be the library—all those books! I'd have to summon the courage to ask to borrow a few, if I was going to be locked in that damned room all day—and finally came to the game room, a chamber not that much larger than my bedroom, with a round table in one corner and a large Persian rug covering the wooden floor. On one wall was a fireplace. I was a little surprised to see a fire crackling away in the hearth, since, from what I could tell, the day hadn't been all that chilly. Yes, the temperatures always dropped fast after sunset at this time of year, but....

Well, maybe vampires were cold-blooded. Or

maybe this was his way of making things more "intimate."

*Good luck with that, you bastard,* I thought. *Do you think I'll ever forget what you did to my sister?*

On the table sat two place settings, with old-fashioned silver warmers protecting the plates beneath them.

"Do you like Indian food?" Lucius said, his tone so pleasant that an observer who didn't know better would think we were about to sit down and share a civilized meal. "There's a place in old town that's very good, so that's what I ordered."

"What the hell do you know about real food?" I asked, not caring how rude I sounded.

Of course he didn't take offense, but only sent another of those unpleasant smiles in my direction. "Just because my kind has its preferences doesn't mean it can't find other pleasures elsewhere."

I didn't like the sound of that at all. But since we were talking about food, I knew better than to say anything that might send the conversation in an uncomfortable direction. "I like Indian food. Did you get this from Masala?"

"As a matter of fact, I did." He lifted the cover off one plate, then the other. The savory aroma of korma drifted to my nostrils, and I actually salivated, I was so hungry. "My...research...told me that you aren't vegetarian. So I thought lamb korma would be appropriate."

"Sure," I said, my tone guarded. Lamb korma was actually one of my favorite Indian dishes, but I sure wasn't going to give Lucius Montfort the satisfaction of knowing that. Since there didn't seem to be anything else I could do, I sat down in one of the two leather-upholstered chairs and settled a napkin in my lap. Fabric, naturally. We might be dining on takeout, but clearly the vampire didn't want to sully his pseudo-Norman chateau with paper napkins.

He seated himself as well, disposing a napkin on his lap. Off to one side was a silver basket with another napkin covering its contents; he moved the fabric out of the way so he could put a piece of naan on my plate, then did the same for himself.

I also noticed a wine bottle sat on the table. Disquieted, I watched as Lucius removed the cork and poured some for the both of us. All right, I supposed it was a good thing that he had to uncork the wine, that it hadn't been sitting exposed in a decanter, but the last thing I wanted was to share a bottle of wine with the —the *thing*—that had murdered my sister.

Making him angry didn't seem like a very good strategy, although I had a feeling I wouldn't be able to keep my mouth shut for very long. For the moment, however, I forced myself to take a tiny sip of the wine, and then tore off a piece of the naan to soak up the alcohol before it could inflict too much abuse on my desperately empty, aching stomach.

Lucius drank as well, a much larger swallow than

the one I'd just consumed. To my surprise, he lifted his fork and ate a bite of the lamb korma after he set down his wine glass. For some reason, I'd thought the food on his plate was only a prop, something put there to try to trick me into thinking he was just a regular man.

Possibly I looked surprised again, because he said, "Is it so unbelievable to see me eating actual food?"

"Yes."

"Vampires in real life aren't quite the same as those in books or movies or television. You'll grow accustomed to our habits."

*Like hell I will,* I thought fiercely. *I'm not going to get "used" to anything. I'm going to get the hell out of here just as soon as I can.*

"I suppose," I said, the words noncommittal. "So tell me, if you can eat food like a regular person, what the fuck were you doing taking a chunk out of my sister's throat?"

Normally, I didn't swear very much. Too many years of having my mother frown fiercely and tell me ladies didn't talk that way, I supposed. In this instance, I'd used the profanity on purpose, to see if I could get any kind of a reaction out of Lucius. So far, he'd been smug and falsely courteous, the very epitome of someone who knew he held all the cards.

At first he didn't say anything, but merely held his glass of wine up toward the light, as if he was inspecting the color. I couldn't tell exactly what it was

—I thought it might be a pinot noir—but it gleamed a deep garnet hue, far darker than the blood that had traced its way down the pale skin of my sister's neck.

"It wasn't a chunk," he replied at last. "Our teeth puncture, not tear. As to the rest...." His shoulders lifted, and he drank some of his wine before replacing the fine crystal goblet on the tabletop. "We must have our sustenance, just as you must."

I opened my mouth to say he could have chosen another victim. Anyone, as long as it wasn't my sister. But a wave of shame went over me then, and I told myself that I shouldn't ask someone else to deal with such a loss when I didn't want to do the same. Was one person's life of more value than another's? Maybe if I could guarantee that Lucius was getting his blood from someone on death row, or an admitted child molester or rapist. Even so, I realized I shouldn't be asking the universe to barter one life for another. That wasn't my place.

Apparently he realized that I didn't have a ready answer to his words, because he went on, "I am not asking you to understand. Perhaps with time...." He stopped there and tore off a piece of naan, although he didn't eat it. "Imagine what it would be like to have a rare disease, one that can only be held at bay by regular doses of a very rare element. Then imagine that the element you need is found only in human blood, specifically the blood of the living. What would you do?"

"I'd let myself die before I took someone else's life," I told him. A good show of bravado, although I wasn't sure if I really had the strength to make that kind of choice. God willing, I would never have to.

But a vampire? I didn't know about that one. Technically, one could say they weren't really alive, so what did it take to kill them?

"Very brave words," Lucius said. His silvery eyes glinted, taking on a strange golden tinge from the light of the bronze chandelier that hung above the game table. "And noble. Well, then, I will tell you outright that I am not quite so noble. I have done what I must to survive. Yes, I can go quite a while without taking a life, and even longer if I drink blood supplied in a much more civilized way, bought legally from a blood bank. Sooner or later, however, I must have living blood. Without it, I will die."

"And I'm supposed to feel sorry for you? According to what Silas has told me, you've already been alive for centuries. If you dropped dead right now, you would still have had far more life than anyone deserves to."

Again I'd been hoping for some kind of a reaction, that my words would goad him into saying more than he intended, but I should have known. As I'd just pointed out to him, Lucius Montfort was very, very old. He'd had ample time to learn how to school his emotions…if he even had any. He popped the piece of naan he held into his mouth, chewed, then said, "I suppose some might see it that way. I, however, do not. And neither, I'm fairly certain, do my compatriots."

"Yes, and where are they? I'm surprised you didn't invite them to this lovely little dinner party."

"They are occupied with their own business. I made them, but I do not control their every movement. They are young enough to enjoy spending their evenings out, while I've grown to prefer the comforts of home." He paused for a moment, pale eyes fixed on me. That cool, inhuman regard made me want to shiver, although his next words were innocuous enough. "You need to eat, Serena. You must keep up your strength."

"Why?"

"Because, although I know you won't believe me, I don't wish any harm to come to you. We held off giving you food earlier because we needed to make sure all the drugs were out of your system. Now you need to replenish your energy. And tomorrow, you will have both breakfast and lunch."

"How very kind of you," I said, my tone falsely sweet. "I don't want to be a bother, though. Maybe you should just let me go."

Lucius chuckled. "Oh, no, I think not. All that trouble to get you, only to release you the next day? I'm afraid that wasn't my plan at all."

"What *is* your plan?" Even as I asked the question, I realized how desperate those words sounded. Of course the vampire master would never tell me what he was plotting. He was far too smart for that.

"Nothing that involves causing you any harm. Now eat." An edge entered his voice as he added, "I must insist."

Since I knew that protesting would be futile—and because I wasn't brave enough, or strong enough, to go on a hunger strike—I picked up my fork and put a piece of lamb in my mouth. It practically melted, the korma sauce rich and slightly sweet. By that point it was only lukewarm, but my stomach didn't care. It wanted more.

So I ate another piece, then a forkful of rice, and continued until I'd made short work of the food on my plate. The whole time, Lucius Montfort watched me closely, the corners of his mouth curled up slightly. Not enough for a smile, but a definite smirk. Yes, he ate as well, but slowly, as if he only did so to keep me company, and not because he actually needed to.

Well, I already knew that about him. What I couldn't help wondering during the entire meal was exactly what he did have planned for me. *Nothing that would bring you any harm.* That was all well and good, but I couldn't allow myself to believe him. Was he just waiting for me to have a vision so he could pick my brain about it afterward? That was the only explanation which made any sense. Had his "research" about me also told him that my visions didn't come on demand, that they often didn't make much sense? The chances of my seeing anything which might help him with his apparent plans for world domination were really very low. And yet Silas had worried that Lucius would want me for that very thing.

I supposed I would find out what he wanted soon enough. Problem was, I doubted I would like the answer very much.

# CHAPTER FIVE

A<small>LTHOUGH</small> R<small>AOUL</small> O<small>RTIZ</small> <small>HAD</small> <small>SAID</small> <small>HE</small> <small>WOULD</small> start digging into the problem as soon as he could, Silas knew he couldn't sit idly by and wait to hear if the detective had found anything of value. No, he intended to be as proactive as he could—which meant that he needed to get out and do some old-fashioned legwork.

Well, somewhat old-fashioned. He'd used Google's street-view function to get a better idea of the neighborhood where Serena had thought Lucius Montfort's hideout might be located, and was struck at once by the obvious wealth of the area. Different from Bel Air or Beverly Hills, because these homes in general were older. But then, if Southern California had any locales that could be thought of as "old money," it would be these more rarefied areas of Pasadena, or the smaller community of San Marino where Serena herself had grown up.

His truck was a newer model, but even if he went to wash off the muddy spots left behind from the last rain storm, Silas had a feeling it would stand out too much there, especially if he drove back and forth on the same streets a number of times in order to get the lay of the land. Better to have something more upscale, although not too flashy or conspicuous. He knew of a car rental place in West L.A. that loaned out luxury and exotic cars, and so he drove there and agreed to pay $500 a day for the honor of driving a current-year Mercedes S-class convertible.

"Sure you don't want the Ferrari?" the manager asked as he took Silas' black American Express card from him. "It's only a hundred fifty more per day."

A canary-yellow Ferrari wasn't exactly a good idea if you wanted to be inconspicuous. Silas shook his head. "No, the Mercedes is fine. I assume it takes premium?"

"Of course," the man replied as he handed Silas' charge card back to him. "But you don't have to worry about refilling it. That's part of the service."

"I thought I'd better ask, though, in case I need to fill it up."

"Going far?" the man asked, eyes narrowing slightly. "Remember, the contract states that you have to stay in California."

"No worries," Silas assured him. "I'm just going to Pasadena."

With that, he scooped up the keys and headed out to his rented car, which had already been positioned so he could make an easy getaway from the lot. The scent of rich leather surrounded him as soon as he shut the door.

*Don't get too used to it,* he told himself as he eased the Mercedes out into traffic and began heading east on Sunset. *I doubt the Conclave would approve the purchase of a vehicle like this.*

The rental, of course. That American Express Centurion card guaranteed Silas could take care of whatever incidentals might occur during the course of his investigations. But $100K of the latest German engineering? Probably not.

Although the day was warm and sunny, he didn't lower the convertible's top. The car's windows were tinted slightly, just enough that anyone looking at the vehicle would probably have a hard time getting a clear view of the person inside. And that was just how he wanted it. The convertible top was more for show than anything else.

Since he was already on Sunset Boulevard, he decided to take that route all the way into Hollywood, then up and over the hill at Universal City so he could pick up the 134 Freeway there. That would guide him into the western edge of Pasadena, where he'd exit at Colorado Boulevard and then backtrack into the upscale San Rafael neighborhood where Lucius was apparently holed up.

As Silas prowled the surface streets, the homes he passed grew increasingly larger and more expensive-looking. He couldn't help wondering what Lucius' neighbors thought of him. After all, someone who only came and went during the nighttime hours might arouse some suspicion. But after Silas turned onto San Rafael Avenue and realized how private most of the houses were, how they were set back from the street behind hedges and electronic gates, he guessed that most of the people who lived there probably never even saw the neighbors who shared property lines with them.

The setup of the area also made it much more diffi-cult for him to get a good look at a number of the houses. He couldn't get out and start walking around, not without calling far more attention to himself than he desired. Someone would be sure to notice, and probably would call the police. With his shaggy hair and T-shirt and work boots, he didn't precisely look like the sort of person who lived anywhere near here. Maybe he should have attempted to clean himself up before he embarked on this mission, but this was only a preliminary fact-finding operation, and he hadn't planned on getting out of the car at all.

At any rate, even though he saw places that were certainly worth multiple millions of dollars, and even a few that fit Serena's general description of a chateau-like structure, none of the houses he passed had the distinctive wrought-iron fence with the fleur-de-lis spikes at the top that she'd sketched for him. He supposed it was possible she'd gotten that particular detail wrong, but he didn't think so.

It was far more likely that the house he sought was one of those set far back from the street on a private driveway, one guarded by a gate. Her vision of the home had been from the arroyo side, not entering from the street itself. So he could narrow his selection down to the residences that backed up to the Arroyo Seco.

Which meant that what he should really do was drive back out of this neighborhood, then maneuver down to the trail head that led into this section of the shallow canyon. He'd read up on the area a bit, so he knew there was a parking area where the Tad Williams trail began.

Since it was early afternoon on a weekday, parking spaces were still available, even though Silas guessed this area must be overrun on a Saturday or Sunday. He parked the Mercedes, which looked slightly out of place next to the Toyota Land Cruiser and Subaru Outback that also occupied the lot, and climbed out, following the signs leading to the trailhead.

At this time of year, after an unusually wet February, the arroyo itself was quite green and lush, giving the lie to its name, which translated as "Dry Canyon." However, Silas wouldn't allow himself to relax and enjoy the walk, not when so much was at stake.

From down on the trail, he could see the way some of the homes had been built almost at the edge of the canyon wall. The views must be spectacular, but he wasn't interested in views. He only wanted to see if any of the houses lining the edge of the arroyo matched the drawing Serena had shown him.

So far, they didn't. Yes, a number of them had trees crowding on every side, so it was very difficult to get a good look at the structures they hid. And yes, Serena had said there were a lot of trees surrounding the property in her vision, but still he couldn't see a single fence that looked like the one she'd described.

Frustration mounting, Silas continued along the trail. From time to time he'd pass someone out for a midday walk—this trail wasn't challenging enough to call it a hike—and he'd nod so as not to appear completely antisocial, while at the same time hoping that none of the people he saw would recall much of him. At least he'd remembered to put on his sunglasses, which he hoped would disguise his appearance somewhat. The *gula* didn't really need eyewear to protect them from the sun, but sunglasses had their other uses.

He walked a good distance, at one point going under a bridge that connected the east and west sides of the arroyo, and then under yet another one about a quarter-mile from the first. At that point, the trail curved, following the path of the dry creek bed, and the houses he was able to see began to grow smaller, not nearly as ostentatious as the ones farther up the arroyo. Silas stopped, realizing that there probably was no reason to go any farther. The house Serena had described couldn't be down here, which meant....

What? That it didn't exist at all? That her vision, for whatever reason, had shown her the wrong thing?

*You don't know that,* he told himself as he turned around and began to retrace his steps. *There are at least ten properties that are so secluded, you couldn't see anything of them either from the road or from down here on the trail.*

True, but where did that leave him? Purchase a drone and camera setup to do a little aerial spying? He had a feeling that wouldn't end very well; there had already been some well-publicized attempts to curb the use of those things in residential areas due to privacy issues. Or was it time to whip out the American Express card again and charter a helicopter so he could get an aerial view of things? Yes, he'd done some surveying online with Google Maps, but even the most zoomed-in images wouldn't be close to what he might be able to see out of a helicopter. Problem was, he had a feeling that the people who lived in those multimillion-dollar mansions might not be very happy about a helicopter buzzing them at low altitudes.

Maybe it was worth the risk, though. Every

moment Lucius Montfort had Serena in his custody was a moment that her life could be in danger. His training told him he should be cautious, but could he allow caution to override Serena's safety? Anyway, Silas thought he still might be able to see a lot before the Pasadena P.D. sent one of its own choppers after him. If the Pasadena P.D. even had helicopters. Silas didn't know for sure; they were a good-sized police department, but they also weren't exactly the LAPD. He supposed he could call Raoul Ortiz to find out, although he could only imagine what Ortiz's reaction would be if he proposed doing strafing runs on the ritzy San Rafael neighborhood.

Well, a call couldn't hurt. If nothing else, Silas would be able to find out if the detective had had time to dig into the property records for the area and find anything that came close to Serena's description of the vampire's home. That might help to narrow their search if nothing else.

And if Ortiz shot down Silas' idea about the helicopter…well, they'd think of something else. Because he was damned if he was going to give up this easily.

Lucius had allowed me to take some books back up to my room. The library seemed heavily focused on the classics, in pretty leather-bound editions that had probably been purchased more for their aesthetic value than their actual contents. Whether I'd be able to concentrate on reading any of the books I'd selected, I had no idea, but I had to do my best to while away the idle hours. After dinner, he'd walked me back upstairs, said good night, and locked the door behind me. Clearly, he could tell that I'd had enough of his company. It also seemed clear enough to me that he didn't intend for me to share his nocturnal schedule.

At least, not right away.

I glanced out the window but didn't see much of anything, since the moon hadn't risen yet. In a way, I was feeling far better than I had just an hour earlier, because at least I'd eaten. Only one glass of wine, though, drunk slowly, even as I wondered the whole time whether Lucius had found some way to spike it, despite my having watched as he uncorked the bottle.

More than twenty-four hours since my sister's murder, since I'd gone missing. Was the whole horrible situation all over the news, or was my family attempting to keep things quiet? To be honest, I didn't know for sure which angle they'd take. Vanessa's violent death would no doubt increase support for Jackson and his campaign; people loved to rally around those who were seen as having suffered a terrible loss, as much as the mere thought of such exploitation made me want to shudder.

My disappearance, on the other hand, might only cause trouble. I didn't find it too outside the bounds of possibility that some of the more unsavory news outlets might try to tie the two crimes together somehow, especially if there was even the slightest whiff of a connection between Lucius Montfort and me. People would have seen us talking at the reception. And there was that lie I'd told Vanessa over the phone, that he'd made a pass at me first before moving on to her. Yes, as far as I knew, no one had been around to overhear our conversation, but was that the sort of thing the authorities could somehow dig up? I assumed they'd have no problem getting access to Vanessa's phone records, so they'd know that I talked to her on Friday, but whether they'd be able to hear the actual content of the call was another matter. It wasn't as if they'd had legal permission to record our calls.

No doubt those phone calls were all stored on an NSA server somewhere, but good luck with that. Even though both the people involved happened to be the sisters of a U.S. Senator's, I didn't think the intelligence agency would provide any of that data, even if asked nicely.

As to what my parents must be going through — my mind shied away from that topic, because I knew if I tried too hard to imagine their reactions, then it would feel as if I were experiencing those reactions myself. I couldn't lose myself to grief now. Maybe someday I'd have the leisure to mourn. In the meantime…

…in the meantime, I had to do what was necessary to survive. Yes, Lucius had been all politeness at dinner, but he was too polite. He knew he held all the power in our relationship. No doubt it amused him to treat me like an honored guest rather than a prisoner.

*He doesn't hold all the power,* I thought then. *Since it's your powers he wants. But because I can't control them, I'm not sure how much good that does me.*

Scowling, I went into the bathroom and readied myself for bed. I found it a tiny bit comforting that at least I did have my familiar toiletries, the oversized T-shirt and leggings that I usually wore to bed. There was something here in this strange, dark house that was mine, and so I wasn't completely surrounded by unfamiliar things.

Still, it was difficult to climb into the oversized antique bed and attempt to go to sleep. Last night, I'd been knocked out when they brought me here, so this was a new experience for me. Everything felt off, from the weight of the heavy cut-velvet duvet to the firmness of the mattress beneath my body. And the house was far too quiet. Back at my condo, I slept with one of those white-noise generators going because there was enough traffic on Cordova Street that I needed the help.

I'd had no problem falling asleep at Silas' loft, even though I could hear the cars moving on the rain-slick streets outside, because he'd held me in his arms, and the strong, heavy beat of his heart had been enough to lull me into slumber.

The memory was sharp and painful enough that it was almost like a knife lancing through my body. I clutched one of the bed's spare pillows and pressed it against me, needing something to hold on to. I needed *him,* needed his strength and his quietly reassuring presence. How could I ever get through this without Silas to help me?

The world blurred then, going hazy in the prelude to one of my visions.

No. *No.*

But I couldn't stop it. I'd never been able to prevent a vision from happening. All I could do was hold on and pray it wouldn't last for very long.

I saw a gray day, rain falling. A warehouse of some sort, although I couldn't make out any details about the structure, except that it was large and square and just as gray as the day itself. People standing in a line, while men in dark uniforms I didn't recognize looked at their driver's licenses or some other form of I.D. — I couldn't tell for sure, because I appeared to be observing from some ways off, although it seemed that I stood on the ground like everyone else and wasn't floating overhead the way I had when I'd seen Lucius Montfort's mansion in a vision.

A dark, sleek car — a Mercedes limo — with deeply tinted windows pulled up to the warehouse, and a man wearing the same dark uniform as the ones I'd first spotted got out of the passenger side of the vehicle and went to open one of the rear doors. From inside the vehicle emerged a tall man, his pale hair pulled back into a sleek ponytail.

Lucius.

No, that wasn't possible. I could tell from the quality of the light in the vision that it was daytime, albeit a dreary day. The vampire shouldn't have been able to be outside at all, and yet there he was, striding briskly from the Mercedes toward the warehouse, the man who'd opened the car door following a few paces behind.

They went to the entrance of the building, where one of the uniformed men bowed slightly to Lucius and handed him a clipboard with some sort of paperwork on it. Lucius appeared to glance over the papers briefly before he disappeared into the warehouse.

The vision wavered then before melting away into the recesses of my consciousness. I blinked and pushed myself up to a sitting position. Usually, I was glad when a vision hit while I was lying down, rather than walking or even simply standing still. I'd stumbled and given myself a nasty bruise on more than one occasion while in the throes of a vision. This time, though, I couldn't keep myself from shaking.

Lucius Montfort, walking around in the daytime as if doing so was the most natural thing in the world. What was going on in that warehouse? I was halfway relieved that the vision had ended before I was able to see anything more. And yet, I somehow knew it was something I needed to see, something which might give me a clue as to exactly why the vampire wanted control of me and my visions.

A very brief knock, and the door opened and the overhead light turned on. Despite the disorientation which tended to visit me after I'd had a vision, I went stiff with outrage, because Lucius walked in and then closed the door behind him.

"What the hell do you think you're doing?" I demanded, clutching the covers against me. Truthfully, I was almost as covered up in my makeshift pajamas as I was in my day clothes, but that didn't seem to matter right then. Something about being caught in bed like that made me feel far too vulnerable.

He didn't directly respond, only came closer so he could loom over me. An unpleasant smile pulled at his mouth. "You had a vision, didn't you?"

"I—" Alarm spiked through me. How could he have known that? According to the few comments my mother had made on the subject, I really didn't give many outward clues that I was lost in a vision. My eyes might get a little glassy, and it might look as if I wasn't really focusing on any one thing in particular, but it wasn't as if I began to have convulsions or something. Was there some kind of surveillance system installed in my room? Voice sharp, I said, "I don't know what you're talking about."

A small flicker of annoyance might have shown in

his eyes, but his smile didn't budge. "Don't bother to lie to me, Serena. You were suddenly staring at nothing, and your entire body went stiff. It wasn't that difficult to tell something was happening. So what was it? What did you see?"

"How did you see *me?*" I shot back. "Hidden camera?"

"Of course," he replied without blinking. "You didn't really think I would leave such a valuable prize completely unguarded, did you?"

I'd thought I was angry before, but that was nothing compared to the rage that boiled through me at his response. I flung back the covers and pushed myself out of the bed, my entire body shaking. Right then, I didn't even care that I was in my sleeping attire, or that barely a foot separated us, or even that he was a vampire with hundreds of deaths on his soul. "You've been *spying* on me?"

"Yes," he said, apparently unmoved by my outrage. "Oh, only in this room. I'm not so ill-mannered that I would put surveillance devices in the bathroom. But since it lacks a window, the bathroom is safe enough."

Those words didn't do much to mollify me, especially when I thought of how I'd changed into fresh clothes in this room, how I'd been naked except for my underpants. True, that had happened this morning, while Lucius had probably been asleep in his coffin— or whatever it was that latter-day vampires did during the daylight hours—but that didn't mean his semivive slaves couldn't have seen far more than I would have ever wanted them to.

"Oh, well, that makes it all better," I snapped. "You had better get those cameras out of here now, or I won't tell you a single damn thing about my vision."

"I think you will," he said, his voice turning silky. Before I could really react to what was happening, his hand shot out and took me by the wrist. His fingers were cold and hard, like steel against my flesh. They tightened slightly, and I forced myself not to wince. "Serena, you are valuable to me, it is true. But don't think I won't hurt you if it becomes necessary. You can be injured and still have your visions."

That remark, uttered in a tone so dispassionate that it was far more frightening than a shouted threat, made a chill go through my body. Or maybe it was simply the cold which seemed to flow from his inhuman fingertips. I didn't respond, however, and he continued,

"I do not appreciate impertinence, or rudeness. But…." The words trailed off, and he bent closer to me, so close that his lips almost brushed my cheek. This time I couldn't help shivering, and he smiled again, a slow smile that showed off his sharp canines. "But it does not need to be war between us. You will work with me, and I will make sure that no harm comes to you."

"Get away from me," I whispered.

"Does it bother you, to have me so close?" He

shifted so I could feel his cold breath against my flesh, even as he lowered his head toward my throat. "Does it bother you to know that I could break your skin in the next second?"

I didn't dare move. In fact, it almost felt as if my heart wanted to stop beating, because its pounding would surely draw his attention to the blood that moved in my veins. But somehow I managed to say, "Everything about you bothers me, Lucius Montfort."

To my surprise, he chuckled. And then, thank God, he straightened and pulled away, although he didn't relinquish his grip on my wrist. "Yes, I suppose it would. Thank you for your honesty, Serena. Now, I want you to continue to be honest, and tell me what you saw."

I wanted to lie, to fabricate something. Anything. A story so far from the truth that he'd never be able to guess what it actually was. Somehow, though, I guessed that he'd be able to smell the lie, and would find some way to extract it from me despite my best efforts to conceal the truth from him. "I saw you."

His dark brows, such a contrast to the white hair, lifted, even as his gray eyes narrowed slightly. "Doing what?"

"I don't know for sure. You got out of a car and walked into a warehouse."

"A warehouse? Where was it?"

"I couldn't tell. There wasn't any signage, and I didn't see anything of its surroundings. Just the building, sitting on a large patch of asphalt. No trees. And…." I hesitated, because I knew the key element of my vision had been the astounding image of him walking around in the daylight with no apparent ill consequences. If I provided him with that information, then he would want to know how such a thing was possible, and of course I had no idea.

"And what?" His fingers tightened on my wrist, but I didn't move. However, I also didn't misunderstand the threat.

"And it was daytime. A gray, cloudy day, but it wasn't night. I could see that very clearly."

He went very still. "Daytime."

"Yes."

Slowly, he released me from his grip. My flesh ached where he'd held me, and I wondered if I would have bruises the next day, but at least he had let me go.

A long pause. His gaze was like a weight on me, but I told myself to stay still, to do my utter best to act as if being subjected to that pale, inhuman stare wasn't of any great import. Finally he asked, "Do your visions always come true?"

"I don't know," I said honestly.

He didn't like that answer, I could tell. His mouth compressed, and his nostrils flared. "What do you mean, you don't know?"

But I stood my ground and replied, arms crossed, "I mean that I *don't know.* Most of them, yes, they've come true, in one form or another. But I've had others that I was never able to connect to anything that seemed to occur in real life, whether my own or someone else's. So I can't tell you if the vision I had tonight was one of those, or whether it will eventually happen. Time will tell, I suppose."

"'Time will tell,'" he repeated, his tone musing. Abruptly, he moved away from me so he could stand by the window. He pulled the curtains aside and looked out into the moonlit gardens, although it seemed to me that he wasn't focused on any one thing in particular. "To see the sun again…."

As much as I hated him, I couldn't help being slightly moved by the wistfulness in his voice. What would it have been like, to go centuries always in the dark, to never look on a blue sky or feel the warmth of the sun on your skin? Even I, who admittedly spent a great deal of time holed up in my house, couldn't imagine that kind of deprivation. Had Lucius become a vampire willingly, or had some master vampire thought he would make a good disciple, and so turned him to this unnatural life?

Of course I would never ask him that. I wasn't sure if I really wanted to know, just in case the answer might make me want to pity him.

He closed the curtains and turned back toward me. "Thank you, Serena. Thank you for telling me the truth…and for giving me some hope. A very good night to you."

Before I could reply, he had moved across the room and let himself out. A key clicked in the lock, and I was alone again.

However, I didn't know if I could allow myself to be relieved. One hand went to my neck, to touch the sensitive skin of my throat. I felt his cold breath again, the threat in those sharp canines. He could have bitten me then. There was nothing I could have done to stop him.

A shudder went through me, and another, and suddenly I was shivering violently, overcome by the aftermath of what had just occurred. I hurried back to the bed and pulled the covers up to my chin, hoping they would be enough to dispel the chill that had overtaken my body.

I knew it would take me a very long time to fall asleep that night.

# CHAPTER SIX

THE DETECTIVE DIDN'T SEEM VERY HAPPY TO SEE Silas the next morning. Yes, he hadn't told him to leave and come back later, but the flash of irritation that deepened the lines between Ortiz's brows was obvious enough. He shut the door to his office, then said, "This kidnapping isn't anything that's going be solved instantaneously. And it doesn't help that all hell has been breaking loose around here."

Silas had seen the news van with the local NBC affiliate logo pulling away from the curb in front of the police department building, so he'd already guessed something must have occurred at the station that morning. Although normally he didn't pay much attention to television news, preferring to get his information about the outside world from places like NPR's website, he'd gone home the day before after dropping off his rented Mercedes and had flipped through the local channels, trying to see if anyone had reported on Vanessa Quinn's murder yet. The late afternoon and evening news had been quiet on the subject, but then the story finally broke in the 11 p.m. broadcasts. Why they'd waited so long, he didn't know for sure. To get input from the family?

That seemed to be the case, because the news showed a press conference with no lesser a personage than the chief of police himself, with a handsome couple Silas recognized from photographs as Serena's parents standing to the side. William Quinn wore a gray tweed sport jacket and a white shirt, and even though he looked tired, he stood straight and tall, looking like he should be the senator in the family, rather than his son. Next to him was Barbara Quinn, dark hair expertly tinted, makeup flawless, even though her eyes appeared puffy, as if she'd been weeping. Silas couldn't fault her for that; she'd lost one daughter, most likely thought she'd lost both of them. There was no way she could know Serena was still alive.

Actually, Silas couldn't be sure of that, either, although he felt in his bones that the woman he loved hadn't suffered her sister's fate. How long she would survive in Lucius Montfort's clutches...well, that was a question Silas didn't want to contemplate right then. Serena was intelligent and resourceful, but Lucius was a vampire master who had centuries of killing behind him. He definitely couldn't be trusted.

The chief of police released the information that the woman who'd been found murdered early Sunday evening was in fact Vanessa Quinn, noted designer and sister of U.S. Senator Jackson Quinn. Chief Villareal went on to say that Ms. Quinn's sister had also been reported missing around the same time.

"We're not sure if there's a connection between the two crimes," Villareal went on. "We are asking for the public's help. If you've seen Serena Quinn or someone who matches her description, please call the LAPD's tip line at 877-ASK-LAPD, or send a text to CRIMES (274637). We wanted to show everyone a recent picture of Ms. Quinn as well."

From behind the podium, he pulled out a large color photo of Serena, one that had been mounted on foam-core to keep it rigid. At the sight of her face, smiling uncertainly at the camera, Silas felt himself tense. It all seemed to come back to him full force as he looked at her big hazel eyes, the delicate outlines of her features. The cold shock he'd felt as he stood in her condo and realized that, despite all his precautions and the precautions of the rest of the Watchers, Lucius had still been able to steal her from him.

The chief continued, "Several witnesses have reported that they saw Serena Quinn in the company of a man who might have been involved in her disappearance. He gave the name of Sam Willis, but we believe this to be an alias. He is approximately thirty years old, six foot three, with longish dark hair. He may be armed and dangerous. If you see this man, do not confront or engage him. Again, call the LAPD at 877-ASK-LAPD, or call 9-1-1."

Hearing that little tidbit, Silas wanted to curse, although he made himself remain silent as the news conference continued. Who had provided the LAPD with that particular piece of information? Probably Lucius Montfort's latest semivive, Serena's former neighbor Brian. At least they didn't have an actual photograph of him, but Silas found that cold comfort. If people were on the lookout for anyone matching his description, that meant he would have a much more difficult time returning to Serena's condo to see if he could dig up any evidence he might have overlooked.

It also meant that he was at risk by merely coming back to Pasadena P.D.'s headquarters. He'd done what he could to alter his appearance slightly by slicking his hair back into a short ponytail rather than wearing it loose as he usually did, and he'd shaved off his scruff of a beard and traded his regular T-shirt for a dark button-down, but he wasn't sure if that would be enough.

Judging by the frown Raoul Ortiz now wore, Silas had a feeling it wasn't. "I saw the LAPD press conference last night. I've been doing what I can to lie low."

"Including coming here, I suppose."

Silas shrugged. "Calculated risk. Needless to say, I don't feel comfortable discussing our own independent investigation on the phone, or via email."

"No, I suppose you don't." Ortiz went to his desk and sat down, then picked up the coffee mug that always seemed to occupy a spot on the upper right-hand side of the blotter on the desktop. "I'd offer you some coffee, but trust me, you don't want to get poisoned. I'm just immune to it after all these years."

"I'm fine," Silas told him. Not wanting a repeat of the espresso incident of the day before, he'd had a single cup of French roast at home before setting out this morning, but nothing else.

"Anyway," the detective went on, "we had the Quinns visit this morning. They're gone now," he added, probably in response to the expression of alarm Silas felt creep onto his face. "Left about twenty minutes ago. They basically wanted to know why the entire department wasn't working on finding out what happened to their daughter. Kosky was sweating bullets…and he's their people."

"'Their people'?" Silas echoed, not sure what Ortiz had meant by that remark.

"Pasadena money. Well, true, the Quinns are from San Marino, but close enough. For all I know, Kosky's father and William Quinn play golf together. Even so, he looked like the Grim Reaper had been after him by the time he was done with that interview."

"No leads?" The question, he knew, was basically useless. Of course there were no leads. Lucius Mont-fort had made quite sure there would be no evidence left behind in Serena's condo to go on. The one real

lead they had was the one Serena herself had provided
—the description of Montfort's home.

"None. The house is clean. They swept it for
prints, for hair samples. Most of what came back
belonged to Serena herself, naturally. A few random
hairs and prints they couldn't track down." The detective stopped there and shot Silas an amused glance.
"Yours, I'm assuming."

"Probably," he replied. "You won't find my prints
in any database, though."

"Well, that's something. At least they won't be able
to make any kind of a concrete connection between
you two."

"No. We're careful about that sort of thing."

Ortiz swallowed some coffee, although he kept his
gaze fixed on Silas the whole time. "You going to tell
me anything about this secret society or organization
or whatever it is that you belong to?"

"I'm not at liberty to do that."

"And yet you expect me to run a secondary investigation behind the department's back. Trust is a two-
way street, you know."

Maybe it was, but Silas knew he couldn't put the
*gula* in jeopardy, just to satisfy Raoul Ortiz's curiosity.
"I understand that, but I'm not in a position to give out
that information. It's nothing illegal, I assure you. But
there's a reason why they need to maintain their
privacy."

"I'm sure there is." The detective's mouth twisted

slightly, seeming to signal his dislike of all the secrecy. Then he swiveled his office chair so he was facing his computer's screen, and typed in a couple of commands. "Because of its possible connection to her sister's murder, the investigation into Serena's disappearance has been given top priority. So that's something."

"I'm sure the Quinns' visit had something to do with that as well."

Ortiz shrugged. "Yes. That goes without saying. But at least we've got an expanded team on it."

"Doesn't matter. They won't be able to find anything."

"Even with the connection between this Lucius Montfort and Vanessa Quinn?"

"It's a long shot. Vanessa Quinn had a fairly wide network of business acquaintances. Montfort was one of the most recent, but from what Serena told me, it sounded as her sister had made more than one connection at the reception after her latest show, had begun to negotiate with several of those connections. Any one of them could also be implicated."

"Yes, but she wasn't sleeping with any of them, just Lucius Montfort."

That remark made Silas shoot a surprised look at the detective. "You knew about that? Pretty quick work."

Another lift of the detective's chubby shoulders. "Her parents gave us permission to get into her laptop.

According to the calendar on her computer, and a receipt that was sent to her personal email account, she had a dinner date with Lucius Montfort on Friday evening, a dinner date that apparently turned into a night at the Mondrian Hotel in West Los Angeles. It wasn't too hard to put two and two together."

A night that she'd shared with Lucius. When had the vampire slipped away...three in the morning? Four? He'd have to allow himself enough time to get back to Pasadena before the sun rose; Silas guessed that the vampire would have driven to the hotel, to keep up appearances. But leaving Vanessa to foot the bill, too? No wonder she'd been so short when she spoke with Serena the next day.

It also explained why Lucius was missing when Silas and Serena had their encounter with the vampire trio in Little Tokyo. He'd been off halfway across town, wining and dining his next victim, his orders to his semivives already given.

Well, if nothing else, Silas had to give him credit for some masterful multitasking.

"Even with a connection between the two of them established, you won't be able to get close to his house through regular detective work," he said. "I don't know how long he's been in his current residence, although my best guess is around ten years. He might have had a different name when he first came to Southern California. But I absolutely guarantee that the real truth of who owns his house will be buried so deep you'll never find it. Which is why we need to focus on the description Serena gave us." He drew in a breath and added, "I think we're going to need a helicopter."

Ortiz's slightly protuberant dark eyes appeared to bulge even more as he took in that remark. "Excuse me?"

"I went to San Rafael yesterday, drove around, tried to get the lay of the land. I didn't see anything that matched the drawing Serena made of the place, but, as I'm sure you already know, a lot of those houses are so set back from the road that it's hard to get a good look at them. Google maps don't provide enough resolution, so I thought a helicopter—"

"Oh, hell no," the detective broke in. "For one thing, I can't just request a chopper out of the blue to go joyriding. We've only got three, and they're assigned to traffic control and routine patrols."

Well, that answered one question. Pasadena P.D. did have air support, even if Ortiz made it sound as though it wasn't exactly accessible to all members of the force. "I was thinking about chartering a helicopter."

"Worse. We might be able to explain low-altitude surveillance by telling the people in the neighborhood that we were pursuing a subject. But you can't just go buzzing around, staring down into the backyards of people with million-dollar houses while they're out sunbathing or whatever. You'd have one of our choppers out there to investigate in nothing flat."

That was exactly what Silas had been afraid of. "There's got to be some way to get closer to some of those houses."

"Short of taking a stack of Bibles and going door to door, pretending you're a Seventh Day Adventist or something, I don't see how. And," Ortiz continued, a note of warning in his voice, "I don't advise that, either. A lot of those places have guard dogs. People with money like their privacy."

The best privacy money could buy, apparently. He'd already had to deal with some of these limitations during the past three years as he'd maintained his constant watch over Serena, even though he'd kept his distance. It was far easier to keep track of her at her condo, where she only had an alarm system in the unit itself. The rest of the complex was open, although Silas had known better than to let himself be observed by the other residents. When Serena went to visit her parents, however, he'd been faced with much the same restrictions—the Quinn mansion in San Marino was hidden behind a large stucco wall that encircled the entire property. He'd also noted the patrols that performed a sweep of the neighborhood on a regular basis. So he'd never been able to see much of the house, except brief glimpses here and there when the gates opened to let her car in. Not that she drove there herself, of course; she always took a taxi or an Uber, except for the rare occasions when Vanessa would pick her up for a family function. Even when the gates had been open, Silas hadn't been able to pause and really get a good look at the grounds of the property, because he had to act like a casual driver just passing through on his way to someplace else.

"There's the assessor's office website," Ortiz added, his tone somewhat gentler. Maybe he'd seen defeat in Silas' face, although Silas did his best to remain impassive at all times. Unfortunately, it was much more difficult to be stoic when the woman you loved had been kidnapped by a bloodthirsty, power-hungry vampire. "I'd suggest starting there, if you haven't already."

"And how am I supposed to narrow it down when I don't know the parcel number, or the street number, or the name of the person who owns the property?"

"You can still pull up all the parcels for the area. It's someplace to start."

There was a brush-off if Silas had ever heard of one. Yes, he understood that the detective had other work to do, other cases to pursue, while he had nothing, now that his charge had been stolen from under his nose, but….

But nothing. This was grunt work, but he was used to that. He might not have had the aptitude to be one of the Watchers who sifted through information on a daily basis, hacking in to secure systems to procure what couldn't be acquired legally, but even so, he'd been trained to spend long hours poring over the information those hackers procured, looking for anomalies, searching for patterns. At least this was something he could do from home.

"All right," he said. "I'll get on it."

"Good. And Silas—"

He'd been about to put his hand on the doorknob and let himself out of Ortiz's office. "What?"

"Next time you want to talk in person, text me and we'll meet someplace. Better if you don't come around here for a while."

Anger flared, even as Silas understood the reason behind the request. The last thing Ortiz needed was for someone who matched the description of Serena Quinn's would-be kidnapper to be seen hanging around his office. "Of course," he replied, and left.

He told himself to calm down. Impatience only led to mistakes. At least it was morning, hours and hours before the sun set and Lucius would have a chance to interact with Serena again. The problem was…what would happen once he did?

Yoga helped a little. Whoever had taken my clothes from the condo hadn't bothered with any of my workout gear, but I could do all right in the oversized T-shirt and leggings that I slept in. Somehow I'd finally had managed to fall asleep, and had woken up this next morning determined to make the best of my captivity, to show Lucius that he might frighten me, but he would never beat me down.

So...sun salutations—more than ever I was happy to greet the sun, knowing that I wouldn't have to face the vampire again for another eight hours—cat-cow pose, downward-facing dog, and the rest of my morning routine. I missed the soft new age music I would play in the background, but I tried not to focus on that lack, instead letting the slow, steady beat of my heart guide me through the movements.

Just as I was about to conclude things with a *savasana,* releasing the energy I'd built up during the routine, someone knocked at the door. At once I went rigid, terrified that somehow Lucius had acquired the power of day walking that I'd seen in my vision. But when I went to answer the knock, I only saw one of the semivives outside, the good-looking one I'd noticed the day before as I stared out the window.

"Breakfast," he said shortly, and I realized he carried a tray with a bowl of fruit, a poached egg, and what looked like a raisin bran muffin. Off to one side was a mug of coffee.

"Um...thanks," I replied. "I guess you can put that on the dresser."

Without saying anything else, he came inside my bedroom, crossed over the dresser, and set down the tray. Still silent, he turned around and headed back to the door.

"Wait," I said, just as he was about to shut the door and lock me back in. "Who sent the food?"

"The master requested that you get breakfast and lunch each day. Lunch will be at one o'clock."

The words came out so lifeless and mechanical, I would have thought the guy was an android...if I hadn't known better. He must have been under Lucius' control for a very long time. Because of that, I knew it was probably pointless to attempt to get any useful information out of him, but I had to try.

"Did he say how many days he planned to feed me? Have you bought a lot of groceries?"

The semivive's dark brows drew together, even as his eyes remained blank. "We always buy groceries to feed all of us. We cannot live as the master does. Have a good day."

And then he shut the door. A second later, I heard the key turn in the lock.

So much for that. I supposed I should have realized that of course the semivives weren't vampires — they needed real food to sustain their bodies, even if their minds weren't truly their own. And even Lucius and Co. could eat...if they felt like it.

I glanced over at the breakfast tray. Because we'd eaten takeout the evening before, I'd just assumed that no one here had the ability to cook. Apparently someone did, although a poached egg wasn't exactly on the same level as having to prepare a real meal, especially one that would require a level of skill like making last night's excellent korma.

My stomach told me I needed to start eating the food I'd been brought, rather than just stand there and stare at it. I went over and picked up the fork that had been placed on the tray, then dug into the poached egg. It was bland and could have used some salt, but at least it was nourishing. I ate all of it, then the fruit, and finally the muffin, interspersing bites with sips of strong but excellent coffee. Maybe the semivive who'd prepared all this had retained enough of himself that he wanted to have good coffee around, even if his mind was no longer his own.

Between the yoga and the food, I felt far better physically than I had the morning before. Mentally, though, I couldn't stop thinking about the vision that had visited me last night, of the horrible revelation that Lucius had cameras hidden in this room. I'd done my best to try to discover where they'd been placed, but, lacking a ladder or any real means of getting close enough to the ceiling to inspect the light fixture, I was more or less stymied. But I did know that the bathroom was safe, so I would simply change in there from here on out.

Avoiding cameras was the least of my problems, however. Over and over I'd played back my vision, trying to glean every last detail from it that I could. Unfortunately, there hadn't been a tremendous amount of information to recall. I hadn't noticed the license plates on the limo—if it even had any—so I couldn't tell exactly where the events of the vision were taking place. I hadn't noticed a skyline, or mountains, or any sort of distinguishing landmark.

The uniforms the men had worn were similarly featureless. High-collared and plain, almost like the Imperial uniforms from the *Star Wars* movies, if you took away the rank insignia and the silver belt buckles.

And what was going on with that line of people heading into the warehouse? Belatedly, I realized that they had all looked young, probably under thirty. There weren't any children. It was as if everyone there was somewhere between twenty and thirty.

Which meant...what? The vision had stopped before Lucius entered the building, so I wasn't given the chance to see exactly what was going on inside. A factory for extracting fresh, young blood? I wouldn't put it past him, not for a second, but even a vampire given regular feedings of prime grade-A plasma shouldn't be able to walk around in daylight. At least not according to what Silas had told me about vampires.

I took a shower, washed my hair, put on makeup. Why, I couldn't really say—it wasn't as if I cared about impressing Lucius Montfort. But that was fifteen minutes where I didn't have to stare moodily out the window, or try to read a book when I couldn't keep my mind from racing with worry about my parents, about Silas, about…well, about everything, actually.

Eventually, though, I had to go back out and try to do something with myself. I pulled the carved wooden chair over to the window so the light would be better, and sat down with the book I'd selected earlier, a leather-bound edition of Jane Austen's *Persuasion*. There was actually an entire set of Austen on the shelves in the library downstairs, all with the same handsome leather covers and gold lettering. No doubt purchased more for the way they looked on a shelf than because Lucius intended to read any of them, but I wouldn't let myself dwell on that. At least they were there, which meant I'd have enough to occupy me for about a week before I had to range farther afield in my reading materials.

I had to stop myself there. I couldn't be here for an entire week. I just couldn't. I had to believe that Silas would come for me before then, or I'd find some way to escape, cameras or no. That semivive who'd brought me my breakfast definitely wasn't the sharpest tack in the box. If the rest of them were anything like that, then maybe I had a better chance of getting away than I'd originally thought.

In the meantime, though, I figured I might as well let Lucius believe he had me beaten. I sat in the hard little chair and read of the travails of Anne Eliot, pausing only when the same slow-witted semivive brought me a lunch of chicken salad and more fruit.

Good chicken salad, too, with cut-up grapes and raisins and nuts in it. At least I wouldn't have to worry about starving.

Eventually, the light began to fail. It had been a clear day, with no clouds at all, and so the glow of sunset lingered for a long time. Even so, there came a time when I had to set down my book and go turn on a lamp, then close the curtains against the night.

I'd been halfway expecting the knock, but I still startled when it came. Then I pulled in a breath, smoothed my hands over the skirt I wore, and went to the door. Lucius Montfort stood outside, impeccable as always in a dark suit and dark shirt, pale eyes glittering in the faint light from the chandelier overhead.

"Dinner?" he asked. At least he'd knocked this time instead of barging in.

I nodded. For now, I had to play along.

# CHAPTER SEVEN

THE HOUSE LOOKED THE SAME, DIM LAMPS, shadows hiding in the corners. Thank God Lucius didn't offer his arm, because I didn't know how I would have reacted. Playing along with these dinners was one thing, but touching him voluntarily? I had to repress a shudder at the very thought.

I'd halfway expected him to take me back to the game room where we'd shared Indian takeout the night before, but that didn't appear to be his plan. Instead, he stopped at the dining room, where five place settings were laid out on the long table and candles gleamed in candelabras everywhere I looked, from the middle of the table to the sideboards.

"I thought we should all share a meal," Lucius said, pointing me toward the chair to the left of the head of the table.

"'All'?" I repeated dubiously, not liking the sound of that very much.

"You and I, and Michael and Leticia and Tristan. Since we are sharing this house, I felt it a good idea for us to spend some time together."

Okay, I *really* didn't like that idea. Lucius on his own was bad enough, but to have his three vampire "children"—or whatever they called themselves—sitting down to dinner with us was enough to curdle my stomach, and I hadn't even had anything to eat yet.

Somehow, though, I managed to summon a smile and said, "That sounds great. I didn't get much of a chance to visit with them the last time we met."

My response made Lucius laugh outright. Not that I found anything particularly appealing about the sound, because I knew he had to be laughing at me, at my false bravado. "You are an amusing young woman, Serena Quinn," he said as he reached for a decanter that had been sitting near his place setting. "I know you must be frightened out of your mind, and yet you make jokes."

"If I was frightened out of my mind, I probably wouldn't be having visions," I returned coolly. "Or at the very least, I wouldn't be able to explain them to you if I did have them."

"Oh, did you have a vision?" came a new voice.

I glanced away from Lucius to see Michael St. John enter the room. He also appeared to have dressed for dinner, although he only wore a black dress shirt and black pants, eschewing a jacket. His dark eyes met mine, and he offered me a malicious smile.

Still holding my gaze, he said, "Lucius, you didn't tell us that our resident psychic has already been delivering."

Lucius' lips pressed together, as if he was annoyed by Michael's remark, but he sounded pleasant enough when he replied, "That's because her vision from last night was...inconclusive." He poured wine into the glass before me and said, "This is a '90 Châteauneuf-du-Pape. I think you'll enjoy it."

"Oh, from Château Rayas?" I asked archly. "Yes, that was a very good year." Then, as his brows lifted slightly, I added, "My father has an extensive wine cellar."

"Of course he does."

Something that might have been a chuckle came from Michael St. John's direction, but when I sent a quick sideways glance at him from under my lashes, his expression was sober enough. A second decanter had been placed midway down the table, nearer to the spot where he evidently planned to sit, and he picked it up and poured himself some wine as well.

I supposed I should be grateful that they were all willing to be drinking fifteen-hundred-dollar bottles of French wine, rather than blood. My mind had conjured that gruesome image as soon as Lucius revealed that it wouldn't be just the two of us dining together, even though I guessed the master vampire would do his best to keep his disciples in check and make sure they didn't do anything too overtly vampire-ish around me.

Speaking of disciples...Leticia and Tristan entered the dining room next, Leticia in a slinky red dress that would have been better suited for clubbing in Hollywood than sitting down to dinner in this faux-gothic mansion. However, I had to admit that her body was spectacular, although I noticed how none of the male vampires in attendance appeared to pay her any particular attention. Familiarity breeding contempt, or did vampires not have sexual feelings for one another? I knew they would stoop to sex with humans if it suited them, but I hadn't even thought to ask Silas whether these beautiful undead creatures had any desire to sleep with each other.

The two latecomers took their seats, and Lucius sat down as well. "Thank you for all coming here to share a meal," he said. "We want to make Serena feel as welcome as possible."

Leticia barely flickered a glance at me, and I could tell Tristan was equally unimpressed by my presence. He picked up the decanter almost as soon as Michael set it down, and poured himself a glass of wine. At the rate they were going, that decanter would be empty fairly soon. In a house like this, though, I guessed that the wine cellar was fairly substantial.

Then Michael St. John gave me a smile I didn't

believe for one second, and said, "Why don't you tell us about your vision, Serena?"

I hesitated. From the corner of my eye, I saw Lucius shake his head almost imperceptibly. So the master vampire didn't want his children to know what I'd seen. Fine. I'd go along with his wishes for now, since it seemed obvious to me that he called the shots around here. "Oh, it was really short. Not much to it. I saw a building on a cloudy day. That's all." I lifted my shoulders in what I hoped was a nonchalant fashion, and added, "Sometimes I don't get much from my visions. It's really out of my control."

For some reason, Lucius smiled at my last comment, a smile I didn't like much at all. There was something knowing about it, as if he hid a secret he planned to spring on me at the worst possible moment. But he only shrugged. "Of course, we're hoping for more than that in the future. We just have to be patient. In the meantime...."

I supposed he'd stopped there because two semi-vives entered the room, each of them pushing a cart of food. The warm aroma of wine-braised meat came to my nostrils.

"Osso buco," Lucius said. "From Antonio's."

Another of Pasadena's more noted restaurants. Actually, it was a place that my parents frequented, and where we used to have a lot of our family evenings out when I was younger, although I hadn't been in a while. Family dinners now took place mainly at the home where I'd grown up, probably because my parents didn't want to take the risk of me having a vision out in public where strangers could see what was happening to me.

But that meant the food was familiar enough—the osso buco and the parmesan risotto and the fire-roasted vegetables. "Sounds great," I replied, then fell silent as one of the semivives plopped a helping of everything onto my plate. The sauce from the osso buco splashed onto the white damask tablecloth, and I thought I saw Lucius frown slightly.

He remained silent, though, as the two semivives continued doling food out to everyone. When they were done, they pushed the carts over next to one of the sideboards, then left the room.

"In the meantime?" said Michael St. John, resuming the thread of the conversation. He still held his wine glass in one hand, and appeared spectacularly uninterested in the food on his plate.

Again I saw that flicker of irritation on Lucius' features. "In the meantime, we should show our guest our very best hospitality."

*Guest.* I wanted to laugh. I was Lucius Montfort's prisoner, no more, no less. But I wouldn't bother to point that out to him. For now, until I was in a better position to plot my escape, I would do my best to appear meek, quiescent. I smiled slightly as I picked up my knife and fork and started to work on my osso buco. Maybe none of the vampires were inclined to partake of the meal, but I was hungry and needed to keep my strength up.

"Oh, absolutely," Michael said, sounding more amused than anything else. It didn't appear as if he was overly intimidated by the vampire who was supposed to be his master, and I couldn't help wondering at their relationship. Had he been "made" earlier than the other two, and so felt it was all right to be somewhat more familiar?

Farther down the table, Leticia tore a piece of garlic bread in two and slowly ate one of the pieces before washing it down with half her glass of wine. Clearly, these vampires weren't repelled by garlic. I tried not to wince at her cavalier treatment of the vintage she'd just consumed. At least my father wasn't there to see such an ignorant display. He'd have a fit — a genteel, well-mannered fit, but still.

"So, Serena," Michael St. John continued, his gaze fixed on me. "How do you like the accommodations so far?"

"They're very nice," I replied, my tone even. I absolutely could not allow him to bait me, because somehow I knew, as I caught the malicious gleam in his dark eyes, that he was bored and looking for a way to amuse himself.

Come to think of it, what the hell did vampires do to keep themselves from going crazy as the years and decades wore on? Somehow I couldn't picture any of the perfect specimens lounging around the table deciding to try scrapbooking or watercolor painting. Silas and I had run into the three of them while they were out clubbing—or slumming, depending on how you wanted to look at it—but did they do that every night? Maybe that was how they found their victims.

"Of course they are...'nice,'" he said, mouth curling.

"Michael," Lucius said. That was all, but the other vampire appeared to subside, and even picked up his knife and fork so he could help himself to some of the osso buco, although he ignored the risotto and vegetables.

I really didn't like the idea of Lucius coming to my rescue. Since I certainly wasn't going to thank him, I instead asked, "So how long have you lived here? I'd imagine moving must be kind of a pain for you...for people like you, I mean. It's not like you can all pile into a U-Haul and hit the road, is it?"

Lucius flicked at an imaginary piece of lint on his sleeve. "No, that's not precisely how such a thing can be accomplished for us, but it's not as difficult as you think. So many services available these days, so many people who cater to unusual requests. But we have been here for a while."

Such a vague reply only meant that he had absolutely no intention of giving me any information I could actually work with. To tell the truth, I honestly didn't know why it mattered for me to know how long they'd been hiding out here in Pasadena's San Rafael district. I certainly didn't have the means to pass that information along to Silas. So I said, my tone noncommittal, "It's a beautiful house."

"I'm glad you like it. After dinner, perhaps we can walk in the gardens. The moon is almost full."

Coming from anyone else, I would have believed such a suggestion was a prelude to a seduction. But that couldn't be Lucius Montfort's motive here. Yes, he'd been with my sister, but only as a means of getting at me. Now he had me, so why bother with a moonlit stroll around the grounds?

No doubt he knew exactly how uncomfortable such a suggestion must have made me, which meant I had to pretend I didn't consider it that big a deal. "Sure," I said. "I've only been able to look at the gardens from my window, so walking around in them would be nice."

*Nice.* What a pablum word. It sounded like I was making plans to go to tea, instead of allowing myself to be alone at night with the vampire who'd murdered my sister not even thirty-six hours earlier.

If he was unimpressed, or possibly amused, by my response, Lucius gave no sign of it. A faint nod as he picked up his wine glass, and he said, "Good."

Conversation after that was limited, to say the least. From time to time, I could feel the eyes of the other three vampires lock on me, as if they were attempting to determine just how juicy my jugular might be, but they didn't try to engage me in conversation. And if they had any vampire-related matters to discuss, such as whether they were below that month's body count and could go out for a little Tuesday-night hunting, well, clearly they weren't going to bring up such subjects in front of me.

At least they did eat and drink a little, although not nearly as much as I did. Eat, that is. They drank plenty, so much so that one of the semivives returned to dump another bottle of Châteauneuf-du-Pape into the decanter the three vampires shared at the other end of the table. In my case, I nursed a single glass of the exquisite wine all through dinner, not wanting to compromise my wits or my reaction times. Maybe they still wouldn't be enough, if Lucius really tried anything funny while we were outside, but it was better than nothing.

Eventually the semivives came back in to clear away the plates, although Michael St. John grabbed the half-full decanter in front of him before they could take it. "I'll keep that," he said. His gaze flicked toward Lucius as he added, "Since it seems it's the best I'm going to do tonight."

"No more until next week," the master vampire said, his tone cold, firm. It didn't take a rocket scientist to figure out that he wasn't talking about wine.

"Yes, I heard you the first time." Michael rose from his chair and strode out without a backward glance.

After a small pause, Tristan and Leticia got up as well, leaving without even a "good night." I saw them lock arms before they disappeared from the doorway to the dining room.

"Are they…?" I stopped there, not sure whether I was brave enough to ask Lucius about the personal lives of the vampires in his strange little family.

However, he seemed to understand exactly what I'd meant to ask. "No, they are not lovers, if that is what you were wondering. Our kind do not form that sort of attachments with one another. More that they are compatriots—they enjoy hunting together, although they know they cannot claim another victim for a while yet. Still, that doesn't prevent them from going out and exploring new territory, deciding where they will strike when the time does come around again."

"Oh." I couldn't let myself think about those future "victims." God willing, I'd get out of here soon enough, and then I could go to Silas and tell him exactly where the vampires were holed up. Would he come back with a *gula* army to smoke out the nest? Yes, he'd told me that his people didn't actively hunt vampires, but surely they'd be compelled to get rid of Lucius and Co. if given the chance.

"I can tell you don't like the sound of that. It is only the truth, however." He pushed his chair back and stood. "Let us go out now."

Since I'd already agreed to this little expedition, I couldn't exactly say no. I nodded, then set my napkin down on the table next to my plate and rose. "All right. It will be good to stretch my legs."

A faint smile played around his mouth, although I couldn't say exactly why. "This way."

I followed him out of the dining room and down the long corridor that seemed to divide the ground floor of the mansion more or less in two, with wings spreading out on either side, each with their own corridors and staircases. Unlike upstairs, where the floors were bare, this hallway had a long Persian runner that covered its entire length. On several of the console tables we passed, I saw vases of fresh flowers, peonies, roses, lilies. It was still too early in the season for the local flowers to really have started blooming, so these must have come from a florist. I thought it strange that creatures whose entire *raison d'être* was to kill humans would care about having flowers around, but I would be the first to admit that I really didn't understand very much about vampires.

Just before we got to the enormous double front door, Lucius paused and opened another door, one which seemed to lead into the coat closet. From within, he extracted a heavy black wool cape. "It will be chilly out, with the sun down," he said. "You may want this."

"Thank you," I replied, an automatic response, and reached out to take it from him.

However, he ignored me, and shifted so he could lay the garment on my shoulders himself. I had to keep myself from shivering as his cold fingers brushed against my hair, but at least he didn't dwell on the procedure, lifting his hands away as soon as the cape was in place.

As he opened the front door, I asked, "You don't need a coat?"

His fingers brushed against the fine wool of his jacket. "I have this. Besides, vampires do not feel the cold, at least not like you would."

I supposed I should have thought of that.

Then it was time to step outside, to wait on the gray stone of the front step as Lucius shut the door behind us. Once again I wanted to shiver, only this time because I realized this was the same scene from my vision—the shallow stone steps, the huge doors flanked by panels of stained glass. True, I stood here on solid ground, rather than looking down from above, and although Lucius' gray eyes were still disconcertingly silver-pale, they didn't seem to bore through me as they had in the vision.

"The rose garden is to the left," he said.

He began to move in that direction, and I went with him, wondering exactly why he'd suggested this outing in the first place. I found it hard to believe this jaunt had been motivated by his desire to allow me a little fresh air, no matter what he might have said earlier.

But it did feel good to breathe, to feel the cool, damp air on my face. Right then I was glad of my borrowed cape, since the knit shirt and cotton skirt I wore wouldn't have done much to ward off the chill. I looked up to see banners of clouds heading west to east, insubstantial and pale as cobwebs.

Even with the clouds moving in, it was impossible to miss the moon, which had just risen above the horizon. Ghostly rainbow colors surrounded the pale orb, although it wasn't perfectly round, instead showing the vestiges of a gibbous hump.

The light it gave off was bright enough that I had no trouble following the pathway of pale gravel. It led us to the rose garden Lucius had mentioned, trimmed and neat. A few of the bushes were just beginning to show buds, although the moonlight bleached away any color they might have had.

He stopped there, so of course I had to stop as well. His pale hair glinted, nearly the same non-color as the moon overhead. Without looking at me, he said, "When the moon is this bright, I can almost pretend it's daytime."

I glanced upward, then back over at him. All I could see was his profile, clean and hard as a marble statue. His expression revealed nothing, and might as well have been carved from stone as well. I cleared my throat and said, "Maybe you should have thought about missing the sun before you allowed yourself to be turned into a vampire."

He didn't move. "It is not a matter of 'allowing,'" he said. "It is a matter of whether you survive the process or not. If a vampire determines that you are a good candidate, then he goes ahead and makes the attempt. And once it is begun, of course you cling to life, hang on to the person who put you in that position in the first place, because the alternative is to fumble in the dark forever."

"Isn't that what you're doing now, though? Fumbling in the dark?"

This time he did turn, and took a step toward me. I held my ground, although I wanted nothing more than to run back to the dubious security of the house. It wasn't exactly a cozy place, but right then it seemed infinitely safer than the spot where I stood.

And...he smiled. A vampire's smile wasn't the most reassuring thing in the world. In fact, I was fairly sure it was pretty far down the list. "I may be 'in the dark,'" he said, and gestured toward the night sky above us, now growing gloomier and more opaque as more clouds began to drift in. "But I most assuredly am not fumbling. No, I'd say instead that you are the one who is fumbling."

"Excuse me?"

"Your visions. You've had them for three years, and yet you have no more control over them now than you did at the beginning. No talent can reach its true potential except through practice, and yet you have done absolutely nothing to train yourself."

What the hell was he talking about? I pulled the cape closer around my body, fighting the chill I'd begun to feel creeping up through the soles of my shoes from the damp ground. "My visions just…come. There isn't anything I can do to control them. This isn't like training for the Olympics, you know."

"Oh, I disagree. Utterly. You've allowed them to control you because you're surrounded by people who fear them, who know nothing about them, about how they work. You should have sought out other psychics—"

Right. That would have gone over really well. I could just imagine trying to explain to my parents why I needed to start hanging out at psychic fairs and going to so-called "spiritual" places like Sedona, Arizona, or Machu Picchu in Peru. If I'd tried anything like that, I probably would still be stuck in an institution somewhere.

I began to shake my head, and Lucius moved toward me again, this time coming so close that he laid a hand on my arm. Yes, his touch was buffered somewhat by the thick wool of the cape I wore, but even so, I had to force myself not to tear away from his grasp. "I can see the objections in your mind. Not," he went on, as my eyes flared in shock, "because I am psychic, but because I know your history, and I can guess what you're thinking. You have kept yourself in a box because it is safe there."

"Of course it's safe," I retorted. "You think I like living like a hermit, having other people drive me everywhere because I don't dare trust myself behind the wheel? As bad as it is, it's still better than wrapping my car around a tree when a vision hits at exactly the wrong time."

"Yes, I can see why you would think that." Those silver eyes studied my face, boring into me. I wanted to look away, and yet…I couldn't. It was like trying to free myself from the gravitational pull of a black hole. His voice softened, became almost pleading. "I can change that for you, Serena. I can help you."

"Help me how?" I asked, my tone a mixture of bitterness and skepticism. For a second I hesitated, not sure I wanted to even put the notion out into the world. But I knew we couldn't dance around it forever. "By making me into a vampire, too?"

"No," he replied. He lifted his hand from my arm, but I couldn't be relieved, because immediately afterward he pressed his cold fingers against my neck, burrowing under my hair in order to do so. And yet, again I found myself unable to pull away. "I cannot turn you into a vampire. Your gift descended on you while you traveled in the worlds beyond consciousness, the same place beyond this plane where we vampires must travel as well, if we wish to return as one of the immortals. The risk is far too great that you would go to that plane and never come back. Or, even if you did return and became a vampire, the gift which makes you so valuable would be left behind in that dark place. Do you understand?"

"I think so." And I did. That place I had gone, the

darkness where I had drifted for days before I managed to come back to the world…it had stayed with me. Not on a conscious level, but sometimes when I dreamed, I would see images of a place where color wasn't exactly color, where up was down and even familiar shapes were distorted into nightmares. Going into that place, that dimension—it was what had awakened my ability to see the visions. Maybe all human beings carried that gift as well, but it slept within them forever unless the necessary combination of circumstances was in play. It seemed the only other way to go there, other than the sort of traumatic injury I'd suffered, was to have the power of a vampire's blood act as a transport device. Even so, there didn't seem to be many who were able to survive the journey.

Lucius' fingers remained where they were, like two rods of cold iron pressing into the tender skin of my throat. I wanted more than anything to move out of reach of his grasp, and yet it seemed his touch forced me to remain where I was, gazing up into his face. "And so you see you have nothing to fear from me."

"I—" I swallowed, felt him finally lift his hand away. Now it seemed I was able to breathe again. I gulped down some cool, damp night air, hoping it would give me the strength I needed. "How can you say that, when I saw you holding my dead sister in your arms?"

"Ah, that."

"Yes, *that*."

His eyes seemed to bore into mine, glinting like pure silver in the moonlight. "I did not kill your sister."

"You—*what?*" Was he really going to be so bold as to try to make me believe he hadn't murdered Vanessa? I'd seen her limp body, seen her blood dripping from his fangs. "I was there. I saw. I saw *you*. And you said—"

"Yes, I know what I said. Theatrics, my dear Serena. You were so focused on me, on the horror before you, that you weren't paying any attention to what my newest slave was doing. You did not have the opportunity to try to fight back."

Well, that much was true. I hadn't seen not-Brian, hadn't even realized that he'd pulled the hypodermic out of his pocket and plunged it into my neck until I felt the sting of the needle in my skin. Trying to fight off the feeling that the earth had just tilted under my feet, I said, "You're lying. You're just trying to make it so I don't hate you for Vanessa's death."

"No, I am trying to make you understand that I myself mean you no harm." He smiled, although I was relieved to see that he remained where he was, didn't try to reach out and touch me again. "Tristan and Leticia killed your sister. As I told you earlier, they like to hunt together. I was...most displeased with them. But done was done, and so I had to make the best of the situation."

I was still reeling. Right then I wished I hadn't

drunk even that one glass of wine with dinner, because my head was swimming, and I wanted nothing more than to stagger over to the cast-iron bench I'd spotted a few yards away so I might collapse on it. A shiver wracked me. "Why didn't you tell me this before?" I demanded. "Why did you make it seem as if you were the one responsible?"

"Because your mind was still unsettled, and you would not have listened to me. Now we have spent a little time together — and, I hope, have begun to understand that all is not always as it seems."

Was that the truth? My body shook. I didn't know what to believe anymore.

"Come," Lucius said. "Let me take you inside."

"I don't want to go inside. Not if they're in the house."

He didn't bother to ask who I meant by "they." "They've gone out. They will not trouble you. I will make sure of that. Come along."

*Like you made sure they didn't "trouble" my sister?* I thought, but I didn't argue as he began to move toward the house and I followed in his wake, my footsteps dragging. Once we were inside, he led me into a room I hadn't seen yet, a small, clubby space where hunting prints hung on the dark-paneled walls. He guided me to a large leather-upholstered Chesterfield couch and had me sit down, then went to a table off to one side, where a crystal decanter and two matching snifters sat. After pouring some of the liquid from the decanter into the snifters, he returned and handed one to me.

"Armagnac," he said. "You look as if you could use it."

Did I dare ask him why he was being so solicitous? No doubt it was just a ploy to get me to trust him, but that wasn't going to happen. Nevertheless, I took the snifter of Armagnac from him and let myself have a very small sip. It warmed my throat the same way cognac might have, but both the flavor and the bouquet were more delicate, not as harsh as cognac.

"Tell me how it happened," I said.

He remained standing, the snifter he held cupped gracefully in one hand. Something about the pose appeared very theatrical to me, but I supposed that was just his style. I couldn't say I knew him well—nor did I wish to—but I'd noticed already his penchant for the dramatic. "Tristan and Leticia met your sister the day after her show. She and I had gone to the Mondrian Hotel to...." Lucius paused there and gave me a smile that I assume he intended to be apologetic, but just made a shudder go through me.

"I can guess why you were there," I said, the words cutting.

"Yes. Well, we went for drinks in the hotel bar, and Tristan and Leticia joined us there. I introduced them as two of my employees, you see, which meant they were slightly acquainted with Vanessa. Your sister said we should all come by her studio on Monday to see the operation firsthand."

"So they had an invitation to her house."

"Yes." Lucius paused there for a moment and swirled the Armagnac in his glass. The liquid glinted with tints of gold and amber. It somehow needed the warmth of a fire to gleam in its depths, but the hearth in this room was cold and bare.

"That doesn't explain why they would go against your wishes and—"

"They didn't know they were going against my wishes. They knew that I planned to bring you here that very day, so they assumed that I had no further need of your sister."

Suspicion woke in me. "And why were you so certain you were going to kidnap me on Sunday?"

"Because I knew that Silas would be gone, and unable to help you."

That revelation made me stare up at the vampire in shock. "You...knew?"

"Of course I did. Serena, your paramour may be one of the Watchers, but just because his people have adopted that name does not mean that those of us who work against them don't perform our own surveillance. I knew Silas Drake had been called to Paris, and so I instructed Brian to act."

"But—" My mind was trying to piece together the timeline and failing miserably. The snifter of Armagnac suddenly felt cold and alien in my hand, and I set it down abruptly on the small table next to the couch. "So when did you make Brian a semivive?"

"Saturday night, when he and Lewis went out to see a movie. Brian went to the restroom, where I was waiting for him. It seemed clear enough to me that I would have need of his services in the near future, so I went ahead and...made him one of mine."

I was going to be sick. Just the mere thought of Lucius Montfort taking Brian, kind, friendly Brian, and coldly turning him into a half-living tool to be used and then discarded when he was no longer needed, made me want to throw up. I pushed myself off the sofa and took a step toward the door, but Lucius caught me by the arm.

"You asked, and so you will stay and listen."

"I don't want to hear it."

"Unfortunate, because you will sit back down and hear the rest of what I have to say."

His fingers bit into my bicep. I could remain defiant, but I knew that would do me no good. There wasn't any way in the world I could prevent Lucius from doing whatever he liked...and of course he knew that as well as I did.

Jaw set, I wrenched my arm from his grasp and went to sit down on the couch. He didn't precisely smile, but I noticed the way the corners of his mouth lifted the tiniest fraction, as if he was all too pleased by my cooperation.

*I'm only cooperating now because I have to. The*

*second you give me an opening, Lucius Montfort, I'll take great pleasure in making sure you lose your "prize."*

"You are angry with me about Brian," he went on. "Understandable, but sometimes we must suffer these small losses for the greater good."

"I find it very hard to believe you did any of this for 'the greater good,'" I retorted. "Your own good, sure. So, fine, you turned one of my best friends into a mindless slave, and your goons killed my sister because they just couldn't control themselves. Do you really think that's going to make me hate you any less?"

"Not now," Lucius said, his voice calm, unruffled. "In the future...perhaps. But I did want you to know the truth. It was not my intention to have your sister killed. I'd intended to cultivate that relationship for a while longer in case it turned out to be useful to me. However, I was forced to act, to take you, because of Silas' departure."

"Oh, so now it's all his fault?"

"I did not say that. However, I am sure his superiors will believe it to be his fault. Such a loss of self-control, you see. He was tasked with being your guardian, not your lover. Not," the vampire added, his gaze seeming to rake me up and down, "that I can particularly fault him for that moment of weakness."

It was as if he'd just thrown a bucket of ice water

over me. No, Lucius Montfort couldn't be looking at me like—like—

*No.*

I wasn't thinking in that moment. Every muscle in my body tensed, and then I was up and off the couch, running for the door. I didn't think I had ever moved that fast, fear and adrenaline turning me into a blur.

But it wasn't enough. I hadn't even reached the doorway before the vampire was in front of me, pale hands reaching out to catch my arms, bringing my precipitous flight to an abrupt halt.

To my surprise, he laughed, showing off his sharp white teeth. "Oh, my dear Serena," he said, amusement clear in his tone. "Did you really think it would be that easy?"

# CHAPTER EIGHT

HE'D STARED AT THE COMPUTER SCREEN FOR SO long, his eyes were dry and aching, begging for him to stop. And yet Silas knew he couldn't stop, would keep going through the records one by one until he found something—anything—that might help him in his quest to find Serena. Hours earlier, he'd had some cold sesame noodles delivered from one of the places over on Flower Street, but even then he hadn't halted his search, had scrolled with one hand while he methodically shoved noodles into his mouth with the other. He hadn't even been particularly hungry, but had eaten because he knew he needed to keep going, couldn't allow himself to become weak or distracted.

And he'd also had to pause when Joseph called to check in. At the moment, Silas didn't have anything particularly useful to report, only that Detective Ortiz was assisting to the best of his capacity. Joseph hadn't replied to the comment at first, signaling to Silas that the senior Watcher wasn't overly thrilled by the idea of an outsider being involved with the case.

"He had a working relationship with Serena," Silas felt compelled to explain, although he knew that, as the Watcher assigned to Serena Quinn, his was the final word when it came to determining how best to handle her case. "He knows her and has a personal interest in her safety. Otherwise, I would never have brought him in."

"That may be, but I'm still not sure it was the wisest thing to do."

"It will be fine. Raoul Ortiz is a good man."

"'Good' doesn't necessarily have anything to do with it," Joseph said. "You know that as well as I do. One slip-up is all it takes."

"I know," Silas replied wearily. He reached up to pinch the bridge of his nose with his free hand, hoping that might help to stave off what promised to be a hell of a headache. *Gula* couldn't become ill the way humans did, but that didn't mean they couldn't be injured—or suffer a stress headache brought on by eye strain, although such ailments were rare. "But it was a calculated risk I was willing to take. I made the call. If it turns out badly, I'll take the responsibility."

"I know you will."

Joseph's words weren't a threat, only an acknowledgment he understood that Silas wouldn't attempt to avoid any repercussions if involving Ortiz turned out to be an issue. Despite what some might have called a lapse in judgment in becoming intimate with Serena, Silas took his responsibilities seriously. He had no choice.

"Anything else?" he asked.

"Senator Quinn is flying out with his wife and children tomorrow. It sounds as if the funeral for Vanessa Quinn will be held on Saturday."

Providing plenty of opportunities for Jackson Quinn to look suitably grief-stricken at his sister's grave. Cynicism at its finest, Silas thought, wanting to shake his head at himself for entertaining such an uncharitable thought. He certainly had no intelligence to suggest that the relationship between Serena's two older siblings was anything but cordial and close. She herself clearly felt isolated from the rest of the family, but Silas couldn't really fault her for that. The trauma she'd suffered, and her family's subsequent inability to handle the changes in her situation, would be enough to make anyone believe they were on their own.

"That seems rather soon," he said. "Will the coroner release Vanessa Quinn's body in time?"

"Our sources say the medical examiner's office should finish the autopsy tomorrow. To them, this all looks fairly straightforward. Lucius Montfort did a good job of covering his tracks."

Of course he did. The crime had been set up to look like a robbery, and the police apparently had swallowed the story without too many questions, especially since the property already had a history of break-ins. That this one had turned violent was tragic, but not all that surprising. The LAPD would have no reason to dig any deeper. In a way, that was good. Silas would prefer to have the Watchers track down the vampire and his cohorts on their own, without having to trip over Homicide officers.

"So they're not going to try to question Lucius Montfort?"

"Actually, they did...last night sometime. He corroborated what was seen on the surveillance video, that he'd met Vanessa Quinn at the Hotel Mondrian for drinks so they could discuss business. The video does show that Montfort and Ms. Quinn were sharing drinks with friends and having a great time."

"'Friends'?" Silas asked, his tone sharpening. "What friends?"

"Dark-haired male around thirty, blonde woman a few years younger. The two of them left fairly early in the evening." Joseph paused. "From the descriptions, my guess is that they must have been two of Montfort's vampires."

"Leticia Carver was definitely the woman. Both Tristan McVey and Michael St. John are dark-haired and appear to be in their late twenties, so it's hard to say which of them it might have been. Do you have any surveillance video?"

"I can get it, if you think it will help."

Would it help? Silas didn't know for sure, except

to pin down an exact time and location when the vampires had been spotted. But it also couldn't hurt. "Go ahead and send it over when you've got it."

"I will. I assume you don't have any further leads on Montfort's lair."

"No. I'm going through parcel records right now, trying to see if I can find something that points to which house might be his. A visual survey of the neighborhood didn't turn up anything."

"Aerial surveillance?"

"That's probably my next step, as much as Detective Ortiz feels it's a bad idea. Apparently, people who pay multiple millions of dollars for their homes don't like helicopters hovering overhead."

"Why does that not surprise me?" Joseph asked dryly. "I'll get on the surveillance camera footage. If they drove to that hotel, then I might be able to track them to their vehicle and get a license plate number. It would be something."

"Thank you, Joseph." Yes, it might be something…or nothing. Silas knew that the likelihood of a vehicle driven by the vampires having stolen plates was extremely high. If they'd even driven to the hotel at all. Getting from Pasadena to West Hollywood without a car was something of a stretch for their vampire abilities, but not impossibly so. When you were grasping at straws, you had to take everything you touched, even the thin stalks that were most likely going to slip through your fingers.

"I'll let you know if I find anything else. Good evening."

"Good evening."

Joseph hung up then, and Silas set his phone off to one side so he could focus once again on the computer, although for a long moment, he stared at the screen without really seeing what was displayed there. The mention of Vanessa Quinn's funeral had awakened a nagging sensation of guilt, one he knew he needed to ignore so he could focus on the task at hand. There would be two other funerals soon, for his fallen comrades. Emanuel and David would be laid to rest in the cemetery next to the Humboldt compound, with all the Watchers not on assignment and their partners there to watch their brothers-in-arms laid to rest. Emanuel had been newly bonded with a woman, too, their first child on the way. Silas could only pray passionately that the baby would be a boy, and of *gula* blood, so he might be able to stay with his mother, rather than sent away to an adoptive family, never knowing anything of his true origins.

That was the underlying fear in all those relation-ships, that a hoped-for child would not be *gula*, and so could not be allowed to live in the compound. And once a couple had a *gula* child, they generally did not try to have any more, simply because the odds were so very high that any additional children would be regular humans. Like so many of his fellow Watchers, Silas was an only child. His companions were other *gula*. No girls to play with, go to school with. Of course there were women at the compound, the mothers of *gula* children. But they were far outnumbered by the men. It wasn't until a *gula* was sent out into the world to do his work that he had any chance of meeting someone to partner with. Even then, he had to be careful…so very careful.

Silas had been careful, until he had seen Serena that first time. She'd been thinner then, drawn and tired from the months of physical therapy she'd endured to get back the full function of her legs and arms. That hadn't mattered to him, however. He'd still thought her the most beautiful woman he had ever seen. And now that he knew her, had kissed her sweet mouth and fallen asleep beside her, he knew she was far more beautiful than he could have ever imagined, mind and soul just as lovely as her face.

The thought of such beauty being held by a creature like Lucius Montfort made Silas want to tear the city apart, block by block, until he found her. However, he knew he couldn't indulge that rage. Instead, he had to channel it.

After rubbing the bridge of his nose once more and attempting to ignore the growing ache in his eye sockets, he sighed and returned to scrolling through parcels on the county assessor's website.

～

Silas had told me of the vampires' strength, but the reality of their inhuman abilities hadn't truly sunk in until Lucius stopped me mid-flight, then held both my wrists together as he gripped them with a single hand. I couldn't keep myself from gasping in pain as the bones ground against one another. He didn't seem to notice, or at least, I thought I could safely say that he didn't care.

And right after he had taken hold of me, we were —well, I couldn't tell exactly what we were doing, only that in the next instant, we moved through the house at such speed that everything moved past me in a crazy, chaotic blur, paintings and doorways and windows flashing past before I could begin to focus on a single element. At last we burst through a doorway, and he flung me down onto a bed.

My bed, I realized a second later, as the room gradually stopped spinning enough for me to recognize where I was. Or at least, the bed I had been using while a prisoner in this house.

I didn't have time to process anything more than that, because Lucius Montfort loomed over me, his already pale face now stark white with fury. He put one hand on my throat and pushed me down into the pillows. His fingers tightened, and I gasped. No, he wasn't actively choking me, but I could feel the threat behind that grasp, knew he would have to do so very little to start cutting off the air I breathed.

"You will listen," he said slowly, the dead calm of

those quiet words somehow far more frightening than shouting would have been. "You are here on my sufferance, Serena Quinn. You are here because I believe you could be of some value. The moment I decide otherwise...." His grip tightened almost infinitesimally, but I still couldn't prevent myself from letting out a small, terrified cough. "When that happens...*if* that happens...the only decision left will be whether to take your life myself, or whether I should hand you over to the others to play with. Do you understand?"

I managed to nod. With that pressure on my throat, I wasn't sure I would be able to get any actual words out.

"I'm glad we understand one another." Suddenly, he let go, and I began to cough in earnest.

All solicitude, he picked up the glass from my bedside table and went into the bathroom. I heard water running, and a moment later he returned and handed me the glass. "Drink."

I didn't dare refuse. I sat up on the bed, then took the water from him and sipped. Slowly, because I knew that to gulp it down, no matter how much I needed it, would only make me cough again.

"Good," Lucius said, after I had drunk about half the contents of the glass. He took it from my shaking fingers and set it down on the nightstand. "Now, are you going to attempt to get away again?"

"No," I whispered. Of course, it was a lie, an

empty assurance to keep him from hurting me. I might have been frightened near to death, but I couldn't allow fear to stop me.

"I am not sure I believe you."

"I—"

"Shh." He laid a finger against my lips, silencing me. His other hand slid down my hair, and I shuddered. "Such a pretty, pretty toy. It would be a shame to break it."

More than anything, I wanted to shout at him not to touch me, to get away. But I only sat there, mute, shivers running all over me. The chill from his fingers seemed to penetrate my entire body, and it was as if I had been frozen in place, unable to do anything at all.

"Good," he said, after a hideous, endless moment. "I think you begin to understand. We will leave it there for now." He lifted his hand from my hair, but I wouldn't allow myself to show any relief. "I would tell you to rest, but I think it better if you attempt to stay up as late as possible. The past two days, I've been accommodating, but now you should do your best to adjust to my schedule. Having you asleep most of the hours I am awake is wasteful, to say the least."

My mind rebelled at the idea that he would want to spend more time with me. I didn't argue, however. All I wanted was for him to go away so I might try to regain some of my composure, however shaky that might be at the moment. "I'll do my best," I said quietly.

His cold, silver gaze rested on me a long while, so piercing that it felt as though his stare could bore right through my skull and see the thoughts roiling inside. At last, though, he nodded to himself and offered me another of those unpleasant smiles. "Yes, I think you will."

He moved away from the bed then, and crossed over to the door and shut it behind him. Immediately afterward came the faint *click* of the key turning in the lock. His footfalls were so light that I couldn't hear him walking away from my bedroom, but a few seconds later I thought it safe to let out the breath I'd been holding, to open my eyes and take in the blessedly empty room.

One hand went to my throat, and I winced. No doubt I'd have bruises there, too.

And then I was shaking all over, body trembling as I began to absorb what had just happened. Never in my life had I been treated in such a way, my body not my own, my physical strength less than useless. Sure, back in college I'd been at a few parties where a guy would get out of hand and go for a drunken grope, but I'd been able to maneuver my way out of those situations without too much trouble, mostly because I was surrounded by friends, and if I'd really needed someone to step in and help me out, they would have been there for me. And the one time a guy at a frat really wouldn't take no for an answer, one of his buddies had intervened, muttering something about "do you know who her father is?", then dragging the offender out of the way before he could do anything besides push me up against a wall and try to stuff his tongue down my throat.

But this....

I reached for the glass of water with one trembling hand and made myself swallow the rest of its contents. Even that simple motion hurt. How much worse would it have been if Lucius hadn't held back, had throttled me with all his unnatural strength?

*A lot worse,* I thought. *You'd be dead, your neck snapped like a twig.*

The hand holding the water shook so badly that I nearly dropped the glass on the floor. Somehow, though, I managed to set it down on the runner that covered most of the nightstand without incident. I was in bad enough shape without having to clean up a bunch of broken glass.

Even though I'd been instructed to stay awake as late as possible, I wanted to crawl into bed and never come out again. The clothes I had on now felt tainted, simply because Lucius Montfort had laid his hands on me while I was wearing them. Mouth grim, I made myself get up and go into the bathroom, where I'd left my night things hanging from a hook on the back of the door. Then I changed as quickly as I could, afraid that the vampire would return when I was at my most vulnerable.

He didn't, however. I was able to get into my

leggings and oversized T-shirt without being inter-rupted, and then to go ahead and wash my face and brush my teeth. My eyes, as I looked into the mirror, were haunted, dark, bruised circles showing in the pale skin beneath them. Already I could see reddish finger marks beginning to form on my throat.

Resolutely, I turned away from the mirror, shut off the overhead light, and went back out into the bedroom proper. *Persuasion* still lay on the small table where I had left it. I decided then that compromise was the best thing—I would get into bed, but I'd take the book with me and read until I couldn't hold my eyes open any longer.

*And if you really wanted me to keep track of the hour, Lucius Montfort, you could have put a damn clock in here or given me a watch. Something. How else am I supposed to know what time it is?*

I supposed I could look out the window and see how far the moon had progressed in its nightly path across the sky, but even that wouldn't tell me very much. I was no astronomer, so I had no idea when the moon was supposed to rise and set, and where it was supposed to be in the heavens at any given hour.

Which meant I didn't even bother. After I'd retrieved my book and set it down on the bed, I went into the bathroom and refilled the glass with water, just in case I needed it later. Then I placed it on the nightstand and crawled into bed.

Even though I was in a vampire's house, I did feel

slightly safer once I'd pulled the covers up around me. Foolish, I knew, because those sheets and that blanket and that duvet cover certainly wouldn't do a damn thing to protect me, should Lucius decide to return and "check" on me.

No, I wouldn't think about that. I opened the book to where I'd laid the little red ribbon to mark my place, and tried to immerse myself in Anne Eliot's trials and tribulations. In a way, I could relate to her all too well—the quiet one who wished to hide herself away, who had little patience for the flashiness of her immediate family. There, however, was where the parallels began to break down, because my father was far too careful with his wealth to ever have to worry about wasting it all, and my siblings likewise were not much like Anne's.

But I did have a Captain Wentworth out there waiting for me...if he could only discover where I was.

Tears burned in my eyes, and I wiped at them angrily. While I probably did have ample reason to weep right then, I wouldn't let myself do it. I'd cried the night before, and it hadn't done a bit of good. What would crying solve? Absolutely nothing. And if Lucius did decide to come back, and saw me sitting in bed with tears rolling down my cheeks....

No. Just...no. I wouldn't let him have that power over me.

All right. Back to the book.

I kept reading until my eyes began to droop closed.

Even then, I didn't give in, but set *Persuasion* down for a moment, and got up and climbed out of bed so I might, in Ms. Austen's parlance, "take a turn about the room." That helped...for a while. Eventually, though, the book slipped over to one side as I fell asleep sitting up, my mind and body so exhausted that I couldn't keep up the fight any longer.

No restful sleep for me, however. Nightmares skirted at the edge of my consciousness, and I knew I moved restlessly while still lost in slumber, just because at some point I shifted, and the book slipped off the edge of the bed and dropped to the floor.

The sound didn't wake me. Instead, I turned over onto my side, even as the edges of the half-nightmare I'd been having—something about standing in line at the DMV and realizing I had no identification with me, and so, in dream-logic, was about to be arrested—began to blur, and the scene grew hazy.

Somewhere inside the dream, I thought, *No.*

Even asleep, I knew what that gauzy quality meant.

I was about to have another vision.

A car. No, *the* car, the Mercedes limo I'd seen in my vision of the day before. The car I'd watched Lucius climb out of. This time, it was pulling up to a house I'd never seen before, a sprawling Mediterranean-style villa surrounded by palm trees, with a circular drive out front. A number of exotic and expensive vehicles—Ferraris, Lamborghinis, a perfectly restored '30s-vintage Rolls Royce Silver Shadow—were already parked in the driveway.

The Mercedes came to a stop, and once again a man wearing one of those dark, high-necked uniforms got out of the driver-side door. He went around to the back of the limo and opened one of the rear doors. A few seconds later, Lucius Montfort emerged, his pale hair gleaming in the bright sunshine.

The sunshine. So my last vision hadn't been a fluke, even though the sky in that scene had been a heavy, cloudy gray.

Lucius blinked once, and reached into the pocket of his dark suit to pull out a pair of sunglasses, which he deposited on his nose. Then he extended one hand into the interior of the vehicle, clearly so he could help whoever was inside get out.

A manicured hand appeared, with blood-red nails. Diamonds glinted on that hand, and on the wrist that followed. A second or two later, the woman who'd been sitting inside the limo emerged. Her eyes were hidden behind dark sunglasses, and her dark brown hair fell in glossy waves past her shoulders. Her lips were painted the same blood red as her nails.

Her features were familiar. As she straightened and smiled at Lucius, I realized exactly who she was.

The woman in the vision was me.

# CHAPTER NINE

THREE PROSPECTS, OUT OF ALL THE ONES HE'D looked at so far. Silas passed a hand through his hair and wondered if his headache was bad enough that it warranted leaving the loft to go in search of analgesics. Normally, he didn't keep any kind of painkillers or other over-the-counter medications in his home; he had no need of them. Now, though….

He glanced at the clock. A little past one. Perhaps it would be best if he simply drank another glass of water and went to bed. Yes, he would need to go look at those three properties, but tomorrow. Prowling around San Rafael in the middle of the night was not a good idea, not if he didn't want to end up explaining to Raoul Ortiz why he'd been arrested for trespassing, or worse. Normally, Silas was skilled enough not to attract any attention, but he also knew that part of his talent for escaping notice was playing by the rules. To skulk around a neighborhood filled with security cameras and patrols and anything else the home-owners there could do to make sure the outside world didn't encroach on their little piece of paradise was to invite trouble. Heading to Pasadena now in an attempt to distract himself was out of the question, no matter how much his brain might be throbbing.

Besides, a walk in the night air might help to clear his head. A few blocks over on Flower Street was a twenty-four-hour convenience store. He could go there, buy a few packets of ibuprofen, and then come home and try to sleep. Then he would be ready to face the morning and go back to San Rafael, only armed this time with actual addresses.

That seemed to decide the issue. Silas retrieved his leather jacket from where he'd slung it over the back of a chair, and headed out. Although a faint misty ring told him the moon was high overhead, the disc itself had been obscured by low-hanging clouds. The air smelled damp from the night breeze that had come in off the ocean, even though the coast lay a good fifteen miles away.

If only he could have taken this walk with Serena at his side. The whole time he'd been working this evening, he'd done everything he could not to think about her, to focus coldly on the task before him rather than dwell on what might be happening to her, wher-ever she was being held. If he allowed worry to over-come him, he knew he wouldn't be effective.

Now, though, her absence seemed far too glaring, especially since the last time he'd walked these streets, she'd been with him, smiling in the rain, her hair taking on a life of its own in the damp air, wavy and soft around her face. He allowed himself to visualize that smile, then tucked it away, a precious memory to sustain him until he could hold her in his arms again.

Would she smile for Lucius Montfort?

No, of course not. The thought was so ridiculous that he refused to entertain it for more than the barest of seconds. She would not smile for the man who had murdered her sister, who had turned her neighbor and friend into a mindless slave.

The neon sign for the convenience store glimmered up ahead. Silas quickened his pace now that the destination was in sight. He had no reason to fear anyone who might be out on the streets at this hour—even though most people would avoid walking alone at night in this neighborhood—but even though the fresh air did seem to be helping, he saw no reason why he shouldn't get his errand over with in a speedy fashion so he might return home and attempt to go to sleep.

No one else appeared to share his desire to shop for sundries at one in the morning. Except for the clerk behind the counter, the place was empty. Good. While Silas had grown used to mingling with people during the years he'd spent living here in Los Angeles, at the moment he didn't want to deal with anything more than the barest of interactions.

"Two ninety-two," the clerk said in bored tones. He was a young Asian man who looked as if he might still be in college. In fact, Silas spied an open textbook of some sort lying nearly out of sight on the counter, along with a small Netbook.

He pushed three dollar bills across the scarred Formica and told the clerk to keep the change, then picked up the small travel-sized bottle of ibuprofen and shoved it into his pocket. Just as he left the pool of bright illumination provided by the security flood-lights mounted to the convenience store's roof, a figure emerged from the shadows.

"Hello, Silas," said Michael St. John.

~

I didn't remember screaming. I didn't want to remember anything. If I remembered, then that scene would flash before me once again—Lucius Montfort reaching out to take my hand…me smiling up at him.

No, that wasn't possible. I couldn't believe these were true visions. They had to be something else, the stuff of nightmares, brought on by being trapped in the vampire master's house.

And then *he* was there, silvery eyes locked on my face, only this time I knew I wasn't dreaming, was hideously, horribly awake. The antique crystal chandelier overhead glinted down at me, making me blink.

The mattress shifted as he sat down on the edge of the bed. "Serena."

I turned my head so I wouldn't have to look at him, glared resolutely at the wall.

"Serena."

Still I didn't move. If I did as he wished, he'd then ask me what I'd seen. He'd known it was a vision, because of the cameras hidden somewhere in my room.

Cold fingers grasped my chin, turning my face toward him. I didn't struggle, partly because I knew there was no point, and partly because I didn't want a set of bruises on my face to match the ones on my neck.

"What was it?" he asked, then let go of my chin. I doubted he'd released me due to mere kindness, more that he knew I'd have a difficult time replying with him holding my jaw.

I'd have to lie. Not because I thought it would do any good, but more because I needed to do whatever I could to delay telling him the truth of what I had just experienced.

"A bad dream. That's all."

His eyes narrowed. Unlike me, he was still fully dressed, in the dark suit and shirt and tie he'd worn at dinner. Well, of course he would be. This was still "daytime" for a vampire, even though I knew it had to be the middle of the night. Even so, I was disconcerted by his put-together appearance, probably because it was far too close to the way he had looked in my vision. All he lacked was the sunglasses.

Still, his voice was mild enough as he said, "It must have been quite a bad dream. You were thrashing about in bed."

I hated that he was able to watch me as I slept. Did he have a little room someplace where he could sit and watch the video feeds? He must, or he wouldn't be able to respond so quickly whenever I did suffer a vision. Since I did recall something of the nightmares that had plagued me earlier in the evening, before the vision visited my sleep, I thought it best to draw on them to help bolster my lie. "Well, you try standing around in the DMV, only to discover you're not wearing any pants."

He chuckled, even though his eyes remained wintry as a Minnesota January. "Luckily, I have never had to visit a motor vehicle office, with or without pants. But I can see how that might be rather traumatic." He paused there, then said, "I am not sure that is everything, however. Your eyes were open. I've seen you sleeping, and I've seen you while you're having a vision. During a vision, you're staring into the darkness, looking at things only you can see."

I knew he was right, only because my mother had described the same behavior. She'd been present for one of my first visions, sitting next to my bed as I clawed my way back from the coma that had held me trapped for three days. At the time, she'd thought I was having a seizure.

Sometimes I wished that was what my visions actually were. You can treat seizures with medications. Visions? Not so much.

"Serena."

God, I hated him right then. Whenever I did have a vision, I generally needed a few minutes to gather myself afterward, to bring myself back to the here and now. The last thing I wanted was for Lucius Montfort to be sitting on my bed, watching me with cold eyes as he waited for me to tell him what I'd seen.

"It was of you again," I said at last. Maybe I could get away with only relating part of the vision. Be as accurate as possible, but leave out the part where he'd been handing me out of the car. "You were getting out of the same Mercedes limo as the one I saw in my first vision. Not at a warehouse, though—it was a mansion, even bigger than most of what you'd see in San Marino. Maybe Bel Air. There were palm trees."

I knew that extra detail wouldn't help too much to narrow down the locale. Palm trees were even more ubiquitous in Southern California than out-of-work actors.

Lucius seemed to agree, because the pale skin of his forehead puckered slightly as he frowned. "What else?"

"I saw a lot of expensive cars—Italian sports cars, mostly. Ferraris and such."

"That's hardly enough to have sent you screaming the way you did."

Well, I couldn't really argue with that observation. However, having determined not to give him any more information, I thought it best to lift my shoulders, to play dumb. "It's all I saw. Your driver helped you out of the car, and the vision ended. I have no idea why it upset me so much."

A long pause as he sat there and stared down into my face. "I think you do."

I remained silent, hoping he would let it alone. A vain hope, of course.

"Serena."

Only my name, but it served as warning enough. As I tried not to writhe under that silver-bright gaze, I thanked God right then that I slept in such modest clothing, that I wasn't the type to go to bed in filmy lingerie, or worse, naked. Otherwise, his proximity would have been even more alarming.

Even so, I pressed my lips together and tore my eyes away from his, focusing on the dresser of carved oak on the other side of the room, the odd little dancing lights that glittered from the chandelier. He couldn't force me to talk...could he?

His hand descended on my wrist. It only lay there on top of my arm and didn't move, but I got the message. If I didn't tell him what he wanted to hear, he would take hold of me. I had no doubt that he could snap the fragile bones without even blinking.

"Serena."

Escaping would be even more difficult with a broken wrist. Did he have anyone who could set it, or would I be left to suffer on my own, the bones knitting together awkwardly or not at all?

Besides, I had no idea what he could even do with the information I was trying so hard to withhold. It would be mortifying to relate those details to him, but in the end, I didn't know if they would prove to be all that useful.

"I—I saw you reach into the car." I paused then, knowing I must continue and yet dreading what was about to come next.

"And?"

"And someone stepped out. That person was me."

"Ah." From the way he shifted his weight ever so slightly, I got the impression he hadn't been expecting that particular detail. "So you were in the car with me?"

"It looked that way."

His mouth twitched. "I can see why you were upset. At least, I assume that in the vision you were cooperating, weren't struggling."

Blood rushed to my cheeks, even as I tried to tell myself that my reaction was ridiculous. After all, I had absolutely no control over what occurred in my visions. They merely scrolled past, were like watching movies projected on the inside of my eyelids. "No, I wasn't. It was a bright day, so the diamonds I was wearing sparkled in the sun. I remember that clearly."

"Daytime again."

"It looked that way. Although you did put on a pair of sunglasses as soon as you got out of the car, as if the sun bothered your eyes."

He didn't respond. His gaze shifted away from me, moving to the window, although of course all was still dark outside, with many hours until dawn. But maybe he was imagining what it would be like to stand in the sun and not need any more protection than a pair of Ray-Bans.

Good. I wanted him to focus on that particular detail, and not on the far more troubling fact of my being with him willingly, of being his companion at… whatever event we'd been about to attend. At least, I assumed it must be some sort of special event, with so many cars parked in the long, curved driveway of that Mediterranean mansion.

But then he returned his focus to me, eyes fixing on my face once again. "What were you wearing?"

What kind of a question was that? I began to shrug, but decided it was better to answer honestly. "I —I can't recall for sure. I think my arms were bare… maybe a black dress. Something plain. A sheath, I think. And black pumps with high heels. I didn't see anything else, because the vision ended just as I was starting to step out of the car."

"But you remember the diamonds."

"Yes, because my hand was the first thing I saw of me."

"Reaching out to take my hand."

"I suppose so."

He went silent then for a few moments, clearly pondering everything I had just related. I still didn't know what any of it meant, especially when placed in conjunction with the first vision I'd had, the one at the warehouse. Somewhere along the same timeline, because the car was the same, as well as the uniform worn by the man driving it. But I hadn't been present in the warehouse vision, except as my usual disembodied spectator.

Then he moved his fingers so they no longer lay on my wrist, but drifted across the back of my hand. The touch was almost a caress, and I had to will myself not to shudder.

"What would you do if I gave you diamonds, Serena?"

All I could do was lift my shoulders. In truth, I wasn't much of a diamond girl. I'd seen them glittering on my mother's fingers and on the fingers and ears of her friends throughout my entire youth, and now that I knew how much suffering went into mining those stones, the way the market was manipulated to artificially increase their value, I found I didn't have much use for them. I liked handcrafted pieces in silver and semiprecious gems, jewelry where I could see the individual effort—and love—

put into it by the craftspeople who had made the items.

But even if I'd wanted to drown myself in diamonds, I certainly wouldn't have wished to receive them as gifts from someone like Lucius Montfort.

"No diamonds?" he asked a moment later, appearing to interpret the reason for my silence. "What about emeralds? They would bring out the green in those hazel eyes of yours."

I couldn't answer. I only shook my head and looked away from him, hoping he would take the hint.

Probably he did, but that wasn't enough to stop him. "Your visions showed us together. Together in the sunlight. That is a marvelous thing, is it not?"

Well, I supposed you could call it "marvelous" in the old-fashioned sense, in that our being together would be something to marvel at, i.e., something so strange —and horrible—that it should never happen at all.

He leaned forward, even as I shrank back against the pillows. His eyes were so close that they were all I could see, gray seas I knew I would drown in…if I let myself.

"And your visions always come true, don't they?"

Somehow I managed to stammer, "I-I don't know. Mostly. But 'always' is a stretch."

"I think I'm willing to go with those odds. 'Mostly' is far better than 'sometimes,' isn't it?"

"Lucius, I don't—"

I'd intended to say, *I don't know what to tell you,* but he never gave me the chance. His mouth descended on mine, body moving so it was pressed against me, heavy, implacable.

Shouldn't a vampire's kiss have tasted of death, of all the souls he had taken? But Lucius Montfort didn't taste like that at all. Instead, something on his lips was warm and almost spicy. Traces of the Armagnac we'd shared earlier? Possibly, although I wondered if he'd drunk more after he'd left me here in my room.

Then my body rebelled, as if it had just realized who—*what*—was kissing me, forcing his tongue into my mouth. I gagged, and pushed against him, turning my head to one side so the kiss was broken.

"You didn't like that?" he asked, sitting up as a smirk stole across his lips...the lips that had just been pressed against mine a few seconds earlier.

"How could I like it?" I shot back. "You're—you're a monster!"

He only laughed then, even as—to my great relief —he pushed himself up off the bed entirely. That was much better, although I didn't like the way he loomed over me. "A monster? Well, I suppose some people might think that. I would say rather that I am merely a man trying to make his way in the world, playing the cards he was dealt."

"Oh, yes, you're quite the victim." Maybe it was reaction that made me so bold—or rather, gave me the strength to confront him in such a way. If we sparred verbally, then there was less chance that he would try to kiss me again.

Or worse.

"Now, I never said that. There might have been a 'woe is me' period several centuries ago, but I'm well over that now." He smiled, a smile that made me want to go take a bath. "I can see from the expression on your face that you're somewhat resistant to further dialogue at the moment, so perhaps we should let this go for now. I'll let you rest...and will see you again tomorrow night. Then we can discuss this situation like rational adults." As he spoke, he moved toward the door. He paused there for a moment, adding, "But remember, Serena—if you saw it, then it will happen. You only need to reconcile yourself to the notion. Good night."

He went out then, once again locking the door behind him. I lay in bed for a long while, mind churning, body shuddering at the memory of his touch, of his tongue invading my mouth.

It was too much. I pushed myself out from under the covers, then went into the bathroom and brushed my teeth, and rinsed my mouth several times with mouthwash.

Maybe if I did that enough times, I'd be able to remove the sensation of his lips on mine, the taste of him on my tongue.

~

"What do you want, St. John?"

The vampire lounged against the wall of a shuttered electronics store, wearing the sort of smile that Silas would have dearly liked to knock off his face. "To talk. Thought you might want an update on your lady love."

"Serena?" Silas demanded. "How is she? Where is she?"

"Sorry, I can't tell you where." Michael St. John made a "lips zipped" gesture, thumb and forefinger pressed together in front of his mouth, dark eyes glinting with amusement. "You know that as well as I."

"I could make you tell me."

"You could try. But actual vampires are a lot faster than semivives. I'd be gone before you even started to transform."

Which, as much as Silas hated to admit it, was only the truth. Strength for strength, a vampire was no match for a *gula*. But first that *gula* needed to lay hands on the vampire, which was a far trickier proposition. And if the vampire in question had no personal honor—which of course none of them did—then he or she would have no problem with turning tail and fleeing the scene before risking unnatural life and limb.

"Very well," he gritted. "Tell me about Serena. You have seen her?"

"She had dinner with us earlier. It was very cozy."

Silas shot a narrow-eyed look at St. John,

attempting to determine whether he was actually telling the truth, or whether he had merely invented a story that had the maximum probability of annoying his audience. The vampire's expression was now quite bland, with no trace of the amused smile he'd worn only a moment earlier.

Actually, Michael St. John was something of an enigma. The Watchers' records seemed to indicate that he was a fairly young vampire, and had probably been "made" in the last decade, after Lucius Montfort had already moved into the greater Los Angeles area. Vampires did not age, and so St. John would always appear to be perpetually in his late twenties, no matter how old he grew to be. The other two vampires in Montfort's household had been with him since at least the turn of the last century, possibly even earlier, although the master vampire had seemed to be on his own when he lived in London. So Tristan McVey and Leticia Carver were also probably American, if from an America now gone for more than a hundred years.

Silas doubted that either McVey or Carver would have approached him like this. No doubt Lucius Montfort would be quite angry if he were ever to find out that Michael St. John had decided it would be a good diversion to torment one of their *gula* watchdogs with tidbits of information about the woman he loved.

"Cozy, was it?" Silas asked, deciding the best strategy was to be as neutral as possible in his responses.

"Yes. Lucius has rather a tough time keeping a cook, as you might imagine, so we had takeout. Not bad, although obviously it wasn't the exact thing we all wanted."

Rising to that bait would only reward the vampire, so Silas merely offered a nod, rather than allowing the surge of anger and disgust that he experienced after hearing St. John's words to affect what he said next. "Serena is well?"

"Oh, she's fine. You really don't have to worry about Lucius hurting a hair on her little head. But…."

"But what?" The words had come out sharper than he'd intended, but there was nothing Silas could do about that now.

St. John's smile returned. "But it does seem she's getting kind of close to Lucius. I would have said it was a little soon for Stockholm syndrome to be clicking in, but what do I know?"

Damn it. Silas wanted to believe that everything the vampire had just said was an outright lie. He needed to believe it was a lie. And yet…what he'd shared with Serena was so very new and fragile. Perhaps too fragile. Alone, feeling abandoned…she might very well have begun to succumb to Lucius Montfort's charms, especially if he had appealed to her delicate self-worth, had told her that her visions were valuable and made her unique in the world. After the way her family had tried to pretend those visions didn't exist, had viewed her as less than because of her "impairment," Serena might let down her guard in the face of such approval.

No, it wasn't possible. She had said she loved him, and Silas believed her. No matter that their love had just begun to blossom. It was still strong. He had to hold that truth close, no matter what Michael St. John might say.

"Yes, what *do* you know, St. John?"

The vampire's dark eyes flashed, a glint of blood red entering them before it disappeared again. "Well, I know that she took a moonlit stroll with Lucius right after dinner. Not exactly captor and prisoner behavior, as far as I can tell. But...again, I didn't see what happened between them while they were out in the rose garden. I had a date with a '90 Châteauneuf-du-Pape, since I couldn't get anything better."

A horrific vision of Lucius Montfort's pale head bent toward Serena's dark one flitted through Silas' mind. Moonlight bathing them as the vampire moved to sink his fangs into her neck....

His fists clenched. "And does your master intend to add another member to your little family?"

"Oh, I don't think so. At least, not yet. Once that option is gone, he doesn't have much to hold over her, does he?" Michael St. John stood and tugged on the hem of the dark jacket he wore, adjusting the fall of the garment. "But I should probably be going before he misses me. Tristan and Leticia are out on one of their interminable pre-hunts, but I don't operate that way. When the way is open, I go for the kill immedi-ately. Have a good night, *gula*."

Before Silas could respond, Michael St. John had disappeared in a dark blur, gone so quickly that it would have taken a camera equipped with high-speed film to capture his movements. It was the vampire way, but Silas couldn't keep himself from grimacing.

Once…just once…he'd like to catch one of the bastards.

## CHAPTER TEN

BECAUSE OF ALL THE DISTURBANCES THE NIGHT before—and, quite frankly, because it was easier to sleep than be awake and face the nightmare my world had become—I didn't get out of bed until almost noon. By then, filtered daylight slipped in past the heavy curtains, although I could tell that the clouds of the night before had lingered, and the sun might not make an appearance at all.

The gray day seemed to fit my mood. I contemplated trying to go back to sleep, but then realized that I would only be giving up the few precious hours of daytime I had left before the sun went down and Lucius prowled the house once more. So I showered and dressed and did all the things required to get ready for the day. As I was giving my hair one last brush, someone knocked at the door.

I tensed, even though I knew that couldn't possibly

be Lucius. About five hours of daylight were left before I had to deal with him again. So I opened the door to see a semivive I didn't recognize, a man who might have been a few years older than I. Did semivives age? Or were they like the vampires, forever trapped at the age they'd been when their transformation occurred?

No point in asking, probably. The semivive held a tray with a sandwich and a bowl of cut-up fruit— melon and pineapple and strawberries. Clearly, I'd slept right through breakfast and wouldn't be allowed to make up for my missing meal.

Which was fine. I knew I'd have a hard enough time choking that sandwich down, but I'd make myself do it. The last thing I wanted was to be weak from hunger when Lucius woke up and came looking for me.

Just as I had yesterday, I instructed the semivive to put the lunch tray on the dresser. He did as I asked and then left. Before I could lose my nerve, I went over to the plate with its sandwich and made myself take a bite. It was good—ham and Swiss cheese and Dijon mustard on sourdough bread. I had to wonder who planned these trays. Lucius himself, trying to employ another means of buttering me up?

I shivered. All the hot showers and toothbrushing in the world couldn't erase the sensation of his lips on mine, the taste of his mouth. And let's not forget about the way he'd lain half on top of me, using his weight to push me down into the pillows. If he'd wanted to press matters further than that, he could have. He was far too strong for me to effectively fight back. So he could have….

My brain skidded to a halt there, even as the last bite of sandwich I'd taken seemed to lodge itself in my throat. Somehow I managed to choke it down, though, even as I set down the sandwich and hurried into the bathroom to get myself some water. My reflection looked almost as wan and tragic as it had the night before, although the makeup I'd put on did help to mask somewhat how pale I really was.

What would happen when Lucius awoke this evening? Would he pretend nothing had happened? Or would he try to pick up where he'd left off?

Oh, God.

I forced down another swallow of water, then another. I couldn't lose it now. I had to try to think of some way to get out of here before the vampire and the rest of his household were awake. No, I couldn't do anything about the semivives, but from what I'd been able to tell, the ones Lucius had working here weren't exactly candidates for a doctoral program. Maybe they were assigned duties on his property after they'd been enslaved long enough that they could no longer function in the real world, could no longer fool their friends and loved ones that they hadn't changed forever.

Anyway, if I could just manage to evade them

somehow, then I would have a real chance of escaping. While I believed with all my heart that Silas was doing his very best to track me down and get me out of here, I couldn't wait for that rescue to happen. Not when Lucius Montfort's interest in me had taken such a sinister turn.

As I had several times before, I went to the window and looked outside. I couldn't see any of the semivives right then, but that didn't mean they weren't out and about, patrolling the grounds. I'd have to do a better job of keeping track of their movements so I could see if there was any obvious pattern to them.

However, my biggest problem was the security cameras in the bedroom. I still hadn't been able to determine exactly where they were located, and I didn't see how I could poke around and look for them without whoever was watching the feed on the other end figuring out exactly what I was up to. My best guess was that at least one of the cameras had been hidden in the chandelier somewhere. I supposed I could get my most voluminous skirt from the collection of garments that had been brought here for me, and throw that over the chandelier, but I'd have to be ready to run quickly afterward, since that kind of ploy would immediately signal that I was trying to make a break for it.

The window itself presented another problem. As I pushed the curtains aside and pretended to look out at the sky, I shot a surreptitious glance down at the window frame. To my dismay, I saw for the first time how dozens of small nails had been driven into the wood, effectively making it impossible to open the window.

Breaking the glass was an option, but it would be noisy enough that the semivive guards would be sure to hear it, even if they weren't loitering in the immediate vicinity. And that sort of escape took for granted my possessing adequate climbing abilities so I'd be able to scramble out onto the ledge outside the window, find some way to get down from there, and bolt across the property before one or more of the semivives caught up with me.

You know, the movies made this sort of thing look so much easier. However, that didn't mean I still wouldn't try it—if I could only figure out some way get out of the house.

As I stood there, hands planted on my hips in frustration, my gaze shifted to the open doorway into the bathroom. As Lucius had already pointed out, it didn't have a window, but maybe I could find something in there I could use. Even a toilet paper holder might be helpful in prying up the nails around the window.

Since I didn't have many other options available to me, I headed into the bathroom to inspect it a little more closely. At first glance, I didn't see much, except that toilet paper holder—which, luckily, was metal, not plastic. Apparently, the dark lord's decorator hadn't skimped on the finer details.

But as I looked upward, past the bronze and glass fixture above the mirror, up to the ceiling itself, I realized that I could see the thin outlines of what had to be some sort of an access panel. Why it was located in the bathroom, and not in the hallway, which was generally the norm for those sorts of things, I had no idea. The house was clearly old, though, and so it didn't seem terribly strange to me that some aspects of its architecture might be nonstandard.

If I stood on the toilet, I might just be able to reach the panel and push it up and out of the way.

What was on the other side of the panel? Probably the attic; my room was clearly located on the second story of the house. I pictured a large, dimly lit space filled with whatever bits and pieces of furniture hadn't been deemed appropriate for use in the rest of the house. Not exactly the most inviting scene, but frankly, I would rather have crawled through the most frightening attic conjured by Hollywood horror producers than stay here and wait for Lucius Montfort to reappear once the sun went down.

All right. I'd put on flats and jeans and a long-sleeved T-shirt, so I wouldn't have to change my clothes to embark on this particular expedition. I shut the bathroom door and locked it, then turned on the faucet to make it sound as if I was brushing my teeth or washing my hands. Then I got up on the toilet and reached for the access panel.

My fingers scrabbled against the edge and slipped

off. If I'd been just a few inches taller, I would have been able to reach it without any trouble, but as it was, I couldn't get a good grip on the thing. Fighting back a curse, I looked around the bathroom to see if there was anything I could use to extend my reach and push up against the panel. The towel rack caught my eye first, but it was heavy antiqued bronze, screwed directly into the wall. I could try to yank it loose, but doing so would only make a racket that was sure to bring the semivives running.

Damn. I got down from my perch on the toilet and opened the doors to the vanity. At first all I saw in the under-sink storage area was an extra package of toilet paper and a container of liquid toilet bowl cleaner. As I squinted into the dark space, though, I realized there was a plunger shoved up almost against the wall. Perfect.

I reached in and grabbed it, and got back up on the toilet. Using the wide rubber cup on one end of the plunger, I pushed up against the access panel. To my relief, it lifted out of the way immediately, revealing a dark rectangle. I couldn't see what was up there, but I could only hope it would lead to freedom.

After tossing the plunger up into the attic, I hesitated for a moment. Because my fingers could barely reach the edge of the opening, I knew I would have to jump upward to grab onto it, then pull myself through. I'd only have the one chance, because if I fell, I might break the toilet seat if I hit it directly—or break a few bones. At the very least I'd make such a commotion that every semivive in the house would probably come running.

Was I strong enough? I had to pray that I was. Yes, I did yoga almost every day, and I had one of those pull-up bars installed in the garage at my condo, but although I knew I could lift my weight, I couldn't be sure that I'd be able to raise it all the way into the opening to the attic.

Better to take a chance, though. I knew what would come at the end of the day if I went meekly back into my room and resumed my reading. Lucius Montfort, probably all too eager to pick up where he'd left off the night before.

Well, that decided things.

I took a deep breath, and used every ounce of power in my legs to propel myself up toward the attic opening.

My fingers caught the edge, the wood biting into my flesh. Good thing this house was old, with solid construction; if the ceiling had been modern-day wall-board, it probably would have broken under my weight.

But it didn't break. I hung there for a moment, then pulled in another breath and hauled myself upward, muscles screaming at the strain. An inch, and then another. And another. Somehow I was able to get one elbow placed on the floor of the attic, and that gave me enough leverage to swing my legs up and through the opening.

Right then, I felt like an Olympic gymnast who had just nailed her landing. I lay there for a second, panting, every muscle in my arms screaming at me. But that was all right. They'd served their purpose.

The attic wasn't quite as pitch-dark as I'd feared. Faint light came from somewhere over to my right, and I looked past canvas-shrouded shapes that must be furniture to see a window built into the wall.

Perfect. I picked up the access panel and dropped it back in place. With any luck, it would look to the semivives as if I'd vanished into thin air. No doubt Lucius Montfort would be able to put two and two together once he came on the scene, but I still had several hours before I had to worry about him being up and about. If all went well, I'd be long gone by then.

I hurried through the crowded confines of the attic, dodging furniture and trunks of clothing and lord knows what else, too driven by my need to escape to allow myself any feelings of triumph at managing to access the attic. Judging by the motley collection, Lucius must have bought the house furnished, then had his minions dump anything up here that he didn't want downstairs in the main part of the house. Before my accident, I'd loved to go to the Rose Bowl swap meet and the flea market at Pasadena City College, looking for antique jewelry or that perfect vintage sweater to wear with skinny jeans and flats. Lord knows what kind of buried treasure this attic contained, but I certainly didn't have time to stop and take a look now.

When I got to the window, I paused and took a cautious peek downward. The glass was grimy—obviously, whatever cleaning staff the vampire utilized never made it up here—but I could still see the nearly bare trees, the gravel-paved walkways of the garden. I even caught a glint of sunlight on water and realized that must have been from the pond. Its faint shimmer was enough to make me yearn that much more for freedom, for escape.

I'd only been in the gardens the one time, but I recalled enough to remember that the pond was some distance from the rose garden, around a corner of the house. That meant the spot where I stood overlooked the rear of the property and must be closer to the road. The orientation still felt strange to me, with the front door facing toward the arroyo, and therefore inconveniently far from the garage and the driveway, but I supposed the original builder had wanted to take advantage of the views. Not that I'd seen those million-dollar views; the one time I'd been outside, it had been nighttime, and although my room looked east, the trees on the grounds prevented me from seeing the canyon, or the city beyond.

Right now, though, I just needed to focus on my current location, on my need to get away from here as quickly as possible. I didn't see any semivives as I stared out the dirty octagonal window, but that didn't mean much. Their circuit of the grounds could have taken them to another part of the property, but that didn't mean they wouldn't be back soon.

The window had a brass latch on one side. With shaking fingers, I fumbled with it. To my relief, the latch came free after a single tug. I ran my fingers around the opening, looking for any wires or signs that it might be connected to the house's security system, but I didn't find anything. It seemed obvious enough to me that Lucius Montfort had never considered this one flaw in his plan, this one escape route he'd left untended.

Well, better luck next time.

The window opening was small, but I thought I should be able to squeeze through it as long as I was careful. I looked down and saw a ledge immediately under the window, a ledge maybe ten inches wide, if even that. The footing it offered would be precarious at best, but it was better than nothing. Because of the way the house had been built, I couldn't see much beyond that. Still, I thought there must be a place where I should be able to drop down onto the roof of a porch or some other section of the structure that jutted out from the rest. Failing that, I'd have to look for a friendly tree branch. Right then, I really didn't care which method I ended up using, as long as it got me away from here.

I made myself take a breath, then another. No, I'd never really had a fear of heights, but I was still a long way up. A fall might not kill me, but it would definitely break a few bones. And I'd had enough broken bones to last me a lifetime.

If I waited any longer, I might lose my nerve. So I put my hands on the sill of the oddly shaped window, and pulled myself through.

It was a tight fit, tighter than I'd thought it would be. Good thing I wasn't a fan of big belt buckles, or I could have gotten hung up on the sill as I squeezed past. Once my hips cleared, though, I knew I'd managed it, and the rest of me followed easily enough. Without looking down, I planted both my feet on the ledge and began to inch along to my right, away from the front of the property.

The air was colder than I'd expected, biting through the thin shirt I wore. I risked a quick glance upward and saw that clouds had gathered again. All I could do was pray any rain would hold off until I was down from this ledge, because it was hard enough to negotiate without being slippery into the bargain.

One sideways step, then another. I sent a silent "thank you" winging upward for the gymnastics classes my parents had forced me to take when I was younger. I might not have been Olympic material, but those four years had definitely helped with my balance and agility.

Another few feet, and then several more. The stone

of the house was cold against my back, reminding me of the iciness of Lucius Montfort's touch. No, I couldn't think about that right now. I couldn't think about anything except the immediate world around me, the slender ledge beneath my feet, the rough stones beneath my groping fingers.

I moved around a corner, and let out a relieved breath when I saw what I'd been hoping for, either a covered porch or merely a section of the house that jutted out from the main three-story section. Either way, a flat roof only a dozen feet down beckoned. If I sat on the ledge, then maneuvered myself so I hung by my fingertips, I'd have a drop of a mere seven feet at the most, which felt a lot less intimidating than twelve. Because I couldn't see what was directly below me, whether any windows overlooked that flat roof, I didn't know how big a risk I was taking by dropping down there. All I could do was hope that if there were any windows, Lucius Montfort's semivives wouldn't be passing by at exactly the wrong time, or that there wasn't anyone occupying the room below the flat roof.

My arms still ached slightly from hauling myself up into the attic, but I made myself ignore the pain as I gingerly sat down, then leaned to one side and grasped the stone ledge with my fingers. My feet dangled in the air, and I closed my eyes and let myself drop onto the roof I'd spotted.

The solid surface hit the soles of my feet with a distinct jarring sensation, and I clenched my jaw to keep myself from letting out a curse. Bad enough that someone might have heard the thud. I wasn't about to start swearing and really alert them to my presence.

However, I didn't hear anyone shout at me to get off the roof, and neither was there any other kind of response. Everything remained deadly still. I didn't even hear birds singing in the trees. Then again, maybe my presence had frightened them off.

I tiptoed to the edge of the roof and looked down. Another twelve feet or so to the ground—the *real* ground, one of the garden paths winding close enough to the structure that I thought I'd probably land right on it. After that, I'd still have to manage getting past the fence, but I'd worry about that when the time came. I'd come this far, which was miraculous enough in and of itself.

Because of the cloud cover, I had a harder time determining the time of day. Still mid-afternoon, though, with several hours to go before Lucius and the rest of his dysfunctional family awoke. I crouched there for a moment, letting my gaze sweep the grounds as best it could. From this spot, I was able to spy the pond but not the rose garden. The pathways appeared deserted.

Far off in the distance, I heard the sound of a leaf blower. It didn't seem to be coming from the actual grounds of the house itself, but from the street beyond. Even though I'd always hated those damn things, right then I just wanted to run out and hug whoever was out there blowing leaves. Because that meant there was someone nearby, a regular person cleaning up a yard, not a vampire or one of the half-living slaves they controlled. All I had to do was get past the gate, and then I could run and get help.

Another quick glance around, just to make sure none of the semivives had chosen that moment to stroll past. But the path remained empty. It was now or never.

I dropped to a crouch, then once again grasped the edge of the roof and swung my legs over and dangled there by my fingertips. My arms protested this further abuse, but I ignored them and let myself land on the path.

Solid ground. I honestly couldn't believe I'd made it this far, but I knew I had to keep moving. Any hesitation might cost me the freedom I so desperately sought.

I hurried down the path, looking over my shoulder and then all around. Still no sign of anyone. Did the semivives have a mid-afternoon coffee break or something? Whatever the reason for their current absence, I wouldn't question it.

Away from the house, half-running on the gravel walkway. My flats made very little noise, but I still tried to move as quietly as I could. The sound of the blower grew louder, drawing me toward the street, toward the promise of freedom.

The trees opened up enough that I finally was able

to spot the fence itself, gleaming black iron. Those pointed fleur-de-lis on the top would probably give me some trouble, but right then I didn't care how sliced up and bruised I might get during my escape. I'd have plenty of time to heal afterward.

A low border of boxwood edged the fence, providing yet another barrier. Damn it. For a second I paused, wondering if I should follow the fence down to the gate. It had to open up there, obviously, but maybe Lucius had camera surveillance at the entry to the property. I know I would have, if our situations were reversed.

I decided I'd better not risk it. Since I'd had the foresight to wear jeans, I decided I should be able to get around the hedge with minimal damage. I began to move forward again, then froze at the sound of feet running in my direction. Lots of feet.

Shit.

My paralysis departed as swiftly as it had come, and in the next second I was bolting toward the fence, scrambling over the hedge while I ignored the sharp bite of leaves and branches scratching at my palms. Then I was clear of the hedge, and reaching to grasp the crossbar immediately below the fleur-de-lis ornaments that topped the gates. My fingers curled around it, and I began to haul myself upward.

Crunching sounds told me that the semivives must be plowing their way through the hedge, oblivious to the damage they were causing. Terror flooded through me, and a burst of adrenaline gave me the strength I needed to swing one leg up to land on the crossbar, positioning myself so I could get up and over that final barrier.

Rough hands grabbed the leg that still dangled, and I kicked out blindly, my heart hammering in my chest. My foot connected with someone, but the semivive I'd struck didn't make a sound. Instead, more hands grabbed me, and in the next second I was falling, my desperately clutching fingers torn away from their grip on the cold metal fence.

I didn't even hit the ground. The semivive who'd dislodged me grabbed me around the waist and flung me over his shoulder. Cursing, I beat against his back with my fists, but he showed the same reaction as the semivives I'd battled back in Little Tokyo only a few days earlier—that is, he didn't react at all, only dragged me back to the path as his companions, four in all, surrounded him while he carried me back to the mansion.

Tears of impotent rage spilled from my eyes. Not that Lucius Montfort's minions could see them, with the way my loose hair fell all around my face. All that effort, and for nothing. I was now a prisoner more than ever.

And I really, really didn't want to think about how the vampire would react when he learned of my escape attempt....

## CHAPTER ELEVEN

THREE PROPERTIES. SILAS STOOD IN FRONT OF THE first one, a handsome chateau-style home, and realized he could scratch it off the list he'd sent to his phone. For one thing, unlike many of the other houses in the neighborhood, it was protected only by a waist-high hedge of carefully clipped arborvitae, with no gate and certainly no tall iron fence. Also, while trees had been planted around the structure, there weren't enough to match the description Serena had provided.

Silas slipped his phone back into a jacket pocket and headed toward his rented car. Not the Mercedes today, but an unobtrusive silver Camry that he'd rented from the Enterprise office downtown. He'd decided the Mercedes wasn't necessary, since he had no plans to cruise around San Rafael, but only to visit the three properties he'd thought the most promising. This first house had seemed like the most likely suspect, based purely on the location of its lot, but it was clear enough that it bore only the most superficial of resemblances to the mansion of Serena's vision.

The next place was also located off San Rafael Avenue, only a few blocks from where he stood. Silas got into the Camry and drove away slowly, making sure he wasn't doing anything to attract attention. Just as he had when he last visited Raoul Ortiz at the police station, he'd pulled his hair back into a ponytail, made sure he was clean-shaven and had on one of his good shirts. He hadn't wanted to put on an actual disguise, because that would have seemed even more suspicious. At the same time, though, he thought he shouldn't invite too much notice.

After driving those couple of blocks, he parked again. Normally, he would have walked such a short distance, but he figured it was better to keep the car close in case he needed to make a fast getaway. This second property appeared slightly more promising at first, just because it was set back from the road and nearly hidden by trees, with only the protrusions of its chimneys telling an onlooker that there was a house back there at all. Also, the fence which surrounded the lot appeared to be black iron, although those weren't fleur-de-lis at the top of each rod, but arrowhead shapes. Still, they were close enough that he paused on the sidewalk for a long moment, eyes narrowed, as he tried to determine whether Serena might have mistaken arrowheads for fleur-de-lis. Did she sometimes make a mistake when it came to minor details like that?

A dark green Range Rover came down the street, then slowed so it could turn into the driveway of the very house he'd just been inspecting. The driver-side window of the SUV rolled down, and an attractive blonde woman, probably in her late forties, peered out. She didn't appear worried or even irritated that a complete stranger was standing on the sidewalk in front of her house, but instead offered Silas a pleasant smile. "Can I help you?" she asked.

"Sorry," he replied. "I was looking for a house on this street, but I must have gotten the number wrong." He pulled out his phone and opened the notepad document he'd used to jot down the addresses of the properties he'd come to inspect. However, he knew better than to give her one of the actual street numbers he was looking for, and instead substituted one of the digits, just to be safe. "This isn't 242, is it?"

"No," she said, still smiling. "That'll be another block down, on the left. The Morrisons, right?"

Obviously, Silas didn't know the Morrisons from a hole in the ground, but he only nodded. "Right. Thanks so much."

"No problem." The woman rolled her window back up and continued on to her driveway, which curved enough that he couldn't see much of the garage which must be her destination.

Silas didn't linger. He returned to the Camry and

drove down to the block in question, bypassing number 242 altogether, and coming to a stop a little past 248, which was his true destination.

Only...this couldn't be the house he was looking for. The street address, which matched parcel number 111987, was correct. However, instead of the Norman-style home that was supposed to have been built on this lot, Silas found himself staring at a large house vaguely Mediterranean in design, with white stucco walls and a red tile roof, and somewhat improbable towers at either end of its expansive façade. Yes, it had a gate, and an iron fence, but the design was all wrong, the poles topped with smooth spheres rather than the fleur-de-lis Serena had seen in her vision.

Frowning, he got out his phone and flipped over to the web browser so he could look again at the notes from the county assessor's page. Yes, the property was supposed to be occupied by a stone house built in 1922, but that sure as hell wasn't anything close to what he stared at now.

The only rational explanation seemed to be that the original house had been torn down and this mansion erected in its place. He'd heard of people leaving one wall intact on these sorts of remodels so the homeowner could retain their Proposition 13 tax status. Maybe the same thing had happened here, and the assessor information on the property had never been updated because, technically, it was the same house.

All right, that made some sort of logical sense, but....

*But it means I'm back to square one,* he thought, doing his best to shove back the worry that rose in him all over again. *I was so sure Lucius had to be hiding in one of these houses. Now I don't have a goddamn clue where he might be.*

Or what he might be doing to Serena. That was the most frightening thing of all, the one worry Silas did his best to ignore but which still wanted to overwhelm him. Time kept slipping away, and, unlike a vampire, he knew he didn't have forever.

They took me to a room I'd never seen before. Large, formal. The living room, I supposed, although in a house like this, "salon" seemed to describe the enormous space a little better. Dark wood overhead and halfway up the walls. A huge reddish marble fireplace at one end, and more of those heavy antiques, the ones that looked as if they'd been shipped directly over from some impoverished English lord's estate.

I had plenty of time to inspect the space, because the semivives took me to a large throne-like chair near the fireplace, then proceeded to bind my wrists and ankles to the armrests and legs of the chair. During this entire procedure, they didn't say one word to me. Afterward, they went out and closed the door behind them, leaving me to stew in my thoughts.

Every muscle in my body ached, and the pin in my leg was singing, too. My mouth was dry, partly from all the exertion, but mostly, I realized, from abject terror. Lucius Montfort was not the type to show anything close to mercy. This escape attempt would make him very, very angry.

Angry enough to hurt me? I couldn't begin to guess, but I wouldn't put it past him. After all, he'd already made the threat, had already told me he wouldn't scruple to cause me physical harm…just not too much. Not so much that I wouldn't be able to have visions for him. Only enough to remind me who was in charge around here.

As if I had any doubts on that subject.

With excruciating slowness, the room got darker. And darker. The semivives hadn't bothered to turn on any lights, but the curtains had been pulled halfway open, enough to let me watch as afternoon slid into dusk, and dusk became night.

And then his voice, coming from directly behind the chair where I was bound. "You disappoint me, Serena. I thought we were becoming friends."

I startled, even as I mentally cursed myself. Because of course he'd made that sort of entrance just so he could frighten me, throw me off balance.

"'Friends'?" I repeated, hoping I sounded scornful

rather than scared out of my wits. "I think you must have a different idea of friendship than I do."

Although I couldn't see him, I just barely sensed him moving past my chair, over toward the fireplace. A soft *whush,* and the hearth came to life, flames licking at the logs there. Clearly some sort of gas setup, although I couldn't tell where the key was located. Even with the fire going, details didn't immediately leap to the eye.

I did see Lucius, a tall, slim shadow standing next to the hearth. For a long moment, he remained where he was, hands stretched out to the flames, as if he wanted to coax some of their warmth into his cold fingers. Then he turned away from the fire and walked over to me, stopping directly in front of the chair where I'd been tied up for all those hours.

"I will admit your escape was rather resourceful," he said. His tone was so neutral, I had a hard time deciding whether he was angry, or merely somewhat amused by my pitiful efforts. "I did not even think of the attic access. You must be very…limber…to have gotten out that way."

Well, I was, simply because if I didn't do my yoga routines regularly, I got stiff enough for someone three times my age. However, I didn't like the insinuation behind his choice of words. "I suppose so." Not exactly the most coherent rejoinder, but right then, I was just glad that my voice didn't shake.

"But," he went on, "I would like to get to the

bottom of your little escape attempt. What could be worth risking life and limb in such a way?"

"My freedom," I gritted. My hands clenched into half-fists; I couldn't close them any tighter than that, not with the way my wrists were bound to the chair.

"Spare me the *Braveheart* theatrics," Lucius said. Still, he didn't sound angry, but wore a half-smile on his thin lips.

That smile scared me far more than any threats would have.

He moved away from the firelight, disappearing into the darkness that filled the rest of the room. Obviously, vampires didn't have any problem with seeing in the dark. A clink of glass, and then he returned, a crystal highball glass half filled with amber liquid in one hand.

"Drink," he said, holding it up to my lips.

"I'm not thirsty," I lied. I certainly didn't want anything he might be offering. From the strong fumes that rose to my nostrils, I guessed it must be brandy in the glass, or maybe cognac.

"After all that exertion? I think you must be."

"Then get me some water."

"Later. You will drink this first." Lucius pressed the glass up against my lips and tilted it so the liquid inside would run into my mouth. Or rather, that was clearly his plan, but I kept my lips firmly pressed together, so the brandy or cognac or whatever it was ran over my chin and down my neck. He made a sound of annoyance, and reached up with his free hand to pull the black silk pocket square out of his jacket pocket. "Wasteful," he chided me as he wiped the liquor off my chin and throat. "Not a good use of thirty-year-old brandy. Drink it this time, Serena, or I shall become angry with you."

Once again he pushed the glass to my lips. This time, I let some of it spill into my mouth, enough that I hoped it would satisfy him. The alcohol burned my tongue and throat, and I tried not to cough. It didn't matter how good the brandy was; I'd always hated the stuff.

"Better," he said, this time raising the glass to his own mouth so he might drink some of it as well. "Now, shall we talk about this like civilized people?"

"Very civilized, to keep me tied up like this for hours."

A lift of his shoulders beneath the dark suit jacket. "You must forgive my servants. They only did what they thought was best. After all, they knew they couldn't put you back in the room you'd escaped from, and because I was...asleep...they could not ask me for advice. This seemed the safest route to take. I apologize for the discomfort."

"Then untie me," I said, glaring up at him.

"Eventually," he replied. "For now, though, I think it safer to keep you where you are. At least until you have answered a few questions."

"Questions about what?" I asked warily.

"For one thing, why you felt the need to run away. What was different about today?"

Oh, he knew exactly what was different. I could see it in the gleam of those quicksilver eyes. And I was damned if I would tell him that I'd tried to run away because of the way he'd assaulted me the night before, because of that horrible vision where I'd seen the two of us together.

It was impossible. I would never....

I looked away from him, made sure my gaze was fixed firmly on the floor, on the faded but still priceless Aubusson rug that covered the oak parquetry.

"Ah," Lucius said at last. He swallowed the rest of the brandy in the glass, and went and set it down on the mantel. For a moment he lingered there, again spreading his long-fingered hands in front of the fire. Then he closed up the space between us, pausing immediately in front of the chair where I was bound. Again he waited a moment before he reached out and cupped my face in his hands. This time, though, they weren't cold, had been given a false impression of life because of the heat of the fire. Even so, I shivered. "This frightens you, doesn't it? To have me touch you?"

"It disgusts me."

The corners of his mouth lifted, but I wouldn't have called the expression he wore a smile. He took his hands away, but otherwise remained where he stood. "Truthful. And yet in your last vision, you didn't appear to be disgusted by me, did you?"

"That was a vision," I retorted. "It wasn't real."

"Ah, but your visions tend to become reality, don't they? Perhaps you need to have another, so you can see what happens next."

"My visions don't come on command," I said, although this time my voice shook. What the hell was he playing at?

"But what if they could? I have pondered this, Serena. You recall our conversation of the other night, when I told you that you had done your gift a disservice by doing nothing to train it?"

"Yes. So?"

"And how I believe your visions, your talent, come from the same place we vampires must venture to throw off the shackles of mortality?"

"Yes," I replied. This time I couldn't suppress the tremor in my voice. I'd already guessed where he might be headed with all this, and I wanted nothing to do with it.

Not that Lucius Montfort intended to give me any choice.

"So I will take you there, and then...." He let the words die away, instead offering me another of those malignant smiles.

And again his hands were touching my face, cradling it, index and middle fingers pressed against my temples. I writhed in my bonds, but the semivives had done a good job of restraining me; I couldn't move enough to get away from him.

Any warmth from the fire had long since left those hands. Cold, so cold, feeling as if icy water was seeping in through my skin, working its way into my veins so that they, too, became cold, my circulatory system now like rivers and tributaries of ice.

The haze descended.

*No.*

But I couldn't fight it. I didn't know how.

The same Mediterranean mansion, all bright, sunny Southern California splendor. An attendant in a white jacket opened the door for us, and Lucius and I strode inward, his arm around my waist. As we made our way through the foyer and then down a long hallway that led to the back of the house, we passed people I thought I recognized—celebrities, local and national politicians, those who wielded their power from behind the scenes but who I knew because of my family's connections.

They smiled and called out their hellos, and Lucius responded by nodding or, in the case of a favored few, greeting them by name. At his side, I did much the same thing, exchanging pleasantries with false enthusiasm. Or at least, it felt false to me, in this strange position I currently inhabited, both observer and participant.

A waiter came up to us and offered champagne, and Lucius and I both thanked him and took a flute, tall, engraved...Waterford, I thought. In my vision, I tasted the exquisite fizziness of Cristal, smiled up at my vampire escort as he allowed himself a sip of champagne as well.

Did all these glittering, perfect people around us know he was a vampire? Could I even still call him such a thing, when he was clearly able to go out and about during the daytime?

"Lucius, Serena."

My brother's voice. The crowds parted to reveal Jackson and his wife Bethany standing over by the window, both of them looking perfectly coiffed and groomed as usual, Bethany's blonde hair catching sparks of gold from the sunlight coming through the plate glass. The senator Jackson had been speaking with excused himself and moved away so Lucius and I could approach, but not before I heard him say, "Thank you, Mr. President."

So...whatever I was seeing, it was far enough in the future that Jackson had been elected. The bright sunshine and the preponderance of sleeveless dresses made me think this scene had to be taking place in the late spring or summer, which meant I was looking at something at least a year out from now, possibly more.

Jackson smiled at me, at my companion. His hazel eyes, so like mine, glowed with welcome. A few gray hairs had just begun to show at his temples, but they looked good on him, would probably help with the detractors who might have thought he was too young to be President of the United States. "I was worried you wouldn't make it."

"Oh, you know we wouldn't miss one of your California visits, Mr. President," Lucius said.

"We're among friends here. Let's forget about the 'Mr. President' stuff when we're not in public."

"Of course." Lucius sipped some champagne. "A very good turnout today."

"Well, everyone wants a chance to press the flesh, so to speak. How are things at the facility?"

Facility? What was Jackson talking about? I studied his expression, the expression of my sister-in-law, but they were both smiling and pleasant, not revealing much of anything. What I'd come to think of as their "public" faces, the ones they plastered on whenever they had to make an appearance somewhere. The ones that didn't give anything away.

"Excellent," Lucius replied. His hand still rested on my waist. Even though I normally didn't get any sensations of hot or cold from a vision, somehow I could tell that this vision-Lucius' fingers were warm, his touch no different from any other human's. "We're processing almost at capacity."

"Good." Jackson paused there, his gaze traveling around the room as he seemed to survey all the rich and beautiful—or merely rich and powerful—people in attendance. "Demand is much higher than I would have anticipated. Everyone wants a chance to be immortal, after all."

Although I was merely observing this conversation, not participating in it, I couldn't help starting at that comment. Immortal? What the hell were they talking about?

"Luckily, not everyone can afford it, or we'd be overrun soon enough."

All of us—Jackson and Bethany and Lucius and the vision version of me—chuckled, as if Lucius' comment was a very funny joke. "No, the price does make it exclusive," Jackson said. "Which only works to my advantage, of course."

"Of course," Lucius echoed. "Do you mind if Serena and I circulate a bit?"

"Not at all," Jackson replied, with a slight wave of the hand that held his champagne flute. "There's a pavilion out back, too, if you want to go outside."

Lucius didn't look too thrilled by my brother's suggestion, but he only nodded and said we'd have to swing by at some point. Then the two of us moved away from Jackson and Bethany, our places next to my brother and his wife almost immediately taken over by several more partygoers.

"The sun is very bright today," Lucius murmured into my ear. "I think I need another dose."

My vision-self nodded. "Let's go find a bathroom."

I flagged down one of the waiters and asked where the nearest bathroom was located. He pointed down the hallway and said it was the second door on the left. Since everyone seemed to be congregating in the large adjoining rooms at the back of the house, the hall was nearly empty, and Lucius and I were able to slip into the bathroom without anyone appearing to notice us.

As soon as I closed the door and locked it, he took off his suit jacket, then unfastened the cufflink on his left sleeve, rolling it up after he'd set the cufflink down on top of the onyx-topped vanity. His skin was very pale, with blue veins that stood out clearly, especially around the elbow.

I opened my purse and took out a syringe, one pre-filled with some sort of clear liquid. In a brisk, businesslike fashion, as if I'd done this sort of thing countless times before, I tapped my index and middle finger against Lucius' arm to find a suitable vein, then pushed the needle into his skin.

Almost at once, he let out a sigh of relief, as if he was a heroin addict who'd just been given his latest hit. "Better?" I asked.

"Oh, yes," Lucius replied. He didn't immediately refasten the button of his cuff, but instead reached over and ran a caressing hand along my cheek.

My eyes closed, as if I savored that touch. He took my hand and pulled me close, his mouth finding mine. We kissed passionately, so passionately that one of his hands moved down my back, over my ass, and then begin to slip upward between my legs.

The me in the vision let out a little gasp, then shook her head and backed away. "Not here, Lucius."

He sent me a lazy smile. "Sorry, darling—you know how those shots make me feel."

"I know. But...."

"But hundreds of L.A.'s movers and shakers are just outside the door, and you're embarrassed."

"Well...."

"It's all right." He rolled down the cuff of his shirt, and picked up the cufflink and reinserted it. After he was finished with that procedure, he retrieved his jacket and shrugged back into it. "You're worth waiting for." A pause, and he added with a lascivious smile, "Just don't make me wait too long."

"I won't. We just need to put in a little more face time, and then we can go home. You know how I hate these things."

"Yes, you do, my little introvert." He bent down and kissed me again, a kiss that was so long and so lingering, I laughed afterward and dug a tube of lipstick out of my bag so I might repair the damage. Then he opened the door, and we both left the bathroom and went back to the party.

And the world shimmered, and I realized I was still in Lucius' mansion, still bound to that damned chair. He stood a few feet away, watching me like a cat at a mouse hole.

A shiver went over my body, and cold sweat dripped down my back. I could feel the way my heart was pounding, racing away inside my ribcage as though I'd just run a marathon.

"Well?" Lucius said.

I couldn't tell him what I'd just seen. I wouldn't. Of all the horrors my visions had shown me, this had to be the worst. Lucius and I—and the vampire and my brother obviously collaborating on something, although I couldn't quite figure out what. Immortality. And Lucius walking in the daylight, Lucius mingling with the cream of L.A. society.

Lucius kissing me in a bathroom, and clearly wanting more. And me being just as eager for his touch. *God....*

"I saw this house again," I told him, saying the first thing that popped into my head. Anything but the truth. "Rain...something moving in the gardens. I don't know what it was."

His brows drew together. "What else?"

"That's all."

"You're lying."

Well, of course I was, but how the hell could he know that? "I'm not lying. That's what I saw."

"You were in the vision a long time. Far more time than necessary to see what you've just described."

"Time isn't the same in my visions as it is in the real world," I countered. Another lie, but a plausible one. Lucius had never had a vision, so how would he know?

He moved closer, then bent down and pulled my hair away from my neck. Moved closer so I could feel the brush of his lips against my throat. His words were barely a whisper. "Remember our discussion earlier?"

I nodded.

"Your skin is so beautiful. I would hate to break it." Something touched me, sharp.

The threat of those teeth was obvious enough. My voice trembled slightly, but that didn't prevent me from saying, "I won't see the visions if you turn me into a vampire. Isn't that what you told me?"

He withdrew—only a little, but enough so he wasn't touching me any longer. "Not in so many words."

"It was implied. Anyway, I'm sorry I didn't see more, but, as I keep trying to tell you, I can't control these things."

"But apparently I can. For it seems obvious enough to me that I was able to bring on your latest vision, when you told me you couldn't summon them at will."

I couldn't argue with that particular point. Always before the visions had come from nowhere, interrupting my life when they chose. If I could somehow figure out how Lucius had managed to make the vision come when he wished, it would make my life so much easier.

Assuming that I'd ever get out of here, of course.

"Yes, you managed to make it happen, but that doesn't mean you were able to control what I saw. And I'm telling you that all I saw was this house, and something moving in the garden. Intruder, stray cat—Silas coming to rescue me—who knows?"

The mention of Silas made Lucius' eyes narrow. It seemed obvious enough to me that he had very little use for my lover and protector. "Silas will never come here," he said coolly, although an edge of anger ran underneath those words. "He will never be able to locate this house, or you."

I wanted to believe Lucius' comment was only bravado, that underneath his apparent unconcern, he actually was worried that Silas would eventually track me down. But then, I'd been here for almost three days. I wouldn't allow myself to give up hope, but... where the hell *was* he?

"I suppose we'll just have to see what happens," I replied. "But for someone who likes to keep his lair secret, you might have made a very big mistake. Silas will never stop looking for me, which means that sooner or later, he'll find me. Which means he'll find your house. And then you'll have to find a new place to live—assuming you survive the encounter, that is."

If I'd been expecting my words to anger him, I would have been very disappointed. When I was finished with that salvo, he only shrugged. "We shall see."

He came toward me, and I flinched. But it seemed he'd only approached so he could pull a small silver penknife from his pocket and cut through the ropes that bound me to the chair. As soon as my arms were free, I began flexing my fingers, trying to get the circulation back. While I would have loved to lunge at the vampire, attempt to overpower him so I could try once again to get away, I knew such a ploy would be useless. I'd already seen how fast he was. I wouldn't stand a chance.

After he was done cutting the ropes around my ankles, he straightened and extended a hand to me. The last thing I wanted to do was take it, but I had to choose my battles. Besides, after being confined in one place for so many hours, I didn't trust my balance.

He helped me up to a standing position, my legs pins and needles now that they'd been freed. At once I tried to let go of Lucius' hand, but his fingers tightened around mine. "Do you want to tell me the truth now?"

"I did tell you the truth."

"Serena." He shook his head. "So much defiance, for so little reason. What can Silas give you that I cannot?"

The word slipped out before I could stop it. "Love."

Lucius' mouth curled slightly. "You may find that the love of a *gula* is not precisely what a woman should dream of. But if you wish to cling to your illusions, be my guest."

I didn't know what he'd meant by that remark. Part of me really didn't want to know, either. I told myself that I should disregard everything he said, because if nothing else, Lucius was certainly a master of deception. I couldn't believe anything that came out of his mouth.

Instead, I gazed at him steadily and said, "Can I have that glass of water now?"

The smirk he wore didn't fade. "Of course, my dear. And after that...I will show you to your new quarters."

New quarters? It made sense that he wouldn't put me back where I'd been staying, not after I'd proved how easy it was for me to get out, but....

From the unpleasant smile he wore, I had a feeling I wouldn't enjoy my new home one bit.

## CHAPTER TWELVE

BACK AT THE LOFT. SILAS HATED COMING HOME, because to do so was only to admit defeat. After he'd struck out in Pasadena, though, he had little choice. Where else could he go? Any research he needed to undertake could best be done here. Besides, Detective Ortiz had made it abundantly clear that he wouldn't appreciate any more drop-in visits. Silas would have to wait for the detective to contact him.

If he even bothered. The man had his hands full, and while of course he was concerned for Serena's safety, he probably wouldn't go out of his way to pursue the case, not when other people in his department were already working on it.

They wouldn't succeed, though. They didn't know what they were looking for.

Not that Silas was particularly certain of such a thing, either. He'd snapped some pictures of that last house, the one which should have been a largish Norman *faux* chateau, and instead was a sprawling Mediterranean villa. If nothing else, he could try to compare the footprint of the current house with what the assessor's site claimed should be there. But then, if his theory about the entire place being remodeled from the ground up turned out to be true, then the floor plans wouldn't match anyway.

He poured himself some water from the fridge, then returned to his laptop, which he'd hooked up to his phone so he could download the images he'd taken earlier that day. Just as he was beginning to scroll through them, the phone buzzed.

Joseph. If the senior watcher from Humboldt was calling, that meant he'd encountered some new wrinkle in the case. Better not to get his hopes up, though; the news probably wasn't good.

Silas pulled the connector from his phone and held it to his ear. In the background, the laptop complained about the phone not being disconnected properly, but he ignored it.

"Silas here."

"Some news. The LAPD has decided to postpone releasing Vanessa Quinn's body to the family. According to the medical examiner, there are some anomalies that bear closer inspection."

"Anomalies?" *Besides having her throat torn out by a vampire?*

"Apparently, the blood at the scene doesn't account

for the overall amount of blood she lost. They're going to perform more tests."

One would have thought it was a given that a vampire's victim would be missing an enormous amount of blood. However, Silas knew—as did Joseph—that vampires did not have to drain their prey entirely, but only take enough to replenish the vampiric antibodies in their bloodstreams. Lucius Montfort was a very old, very careful vampire. He wouldn't have made such an amateurish mistake. Which meant...what? That Montfort wasn't Vanessa's murderer after all?

"Will they find anything?"

"Probably not," Joseph said. "My best guess is that Lucius Montfort's fledglings—McVey and Carver—are the actual killers. It makes the most sense, since they were in Vanessa Quinn's company two nights before she was murdered."

Silas had been so focused on trying to locate the house where Serena was being held that he'd nearly forgotten about that thread of the story. "Right. Have you had any success in tracking them down?"

"Not really. I did find the video footage of them leaving the hotel, but they went out by the front door. Another camera tracked them walking away, but nothing after that. I don't think they drove at all."

Which was what Silas had worried about, although he'd still held on to the hope that they'd taken a car to the hotel. A hope that now had been dashed, apparently. That was the trouble with observing vampires; they could so easily drop off the radar. "Why don't you think Michael St. John was involved?"

"Just a hunch," Joseph replied. "He seems to hunt alone, while Leticia Carver and Tristan McVey tend to work together."

"I talked to him last night."

That remark appeared to startle Joseph out of his usual phlegm. "You what?"

"I went out for a walk to clear my head." Silas decided not to mention the headache, as it might come across as a sign of weakness. In general, even though they were as mortal as the humans they appeared to be, the *gula* did not suffer the same ailments as mankind. "He approached me as I was returning home."

"What did he want?"

"I'm not sure. He did tell me that Serena Quinn was safe, but when I pressed him for more details, he disappeared, as vampires do."

"Interesting. Why would he care whether you knew she was safe?"

"Again, I'm not sure. St. John is the youngest of Lucius Montfort's fledglings, and the least predictable. He could merely have been amusing himself."

"True enough." Joseph paused there, then said, "You do know we're working on this from our end as well."

That was about the closest Joseph would ever get

to offering actual comfort or sympathy, but right then, Silas was willing to take what he could get. "Yes, I know. Has the delay from the coroner affected Jackson Quinn's travel plans?"

"Not that I'm aware of. He's still scheduled to fly in late Thursday night."

"All right. Are we going to have a detail assigned to him?"

A pause. Then Joseph responded, his tone dry as a Santa Ana wind, "You do realize that he'll be accompanied by Secret Service agents."

"Yes, but…."

"I think he'll be adequately protected. We're spread thin enough now as it is, now that David and Emanuel…." Joseph's words trailed off there. He didn't need to say anything else. The loss of one *gula* was bad enough, but for two of them to have been murdered in such a short space of time was an unspeakable tragedy.

"You're right, of course. Just let me know if you hear anything else."

"I will."

Joseph hung up then, and Silas took his phone and plugged it back into his laptop. What this new information meant, he couldn't be sure. He just knew it probably wasn't anything good.

❧

I stared at the room where Lucius had brought me and attempted to hold back a wave of dismay. Oh, it wasn't that it had turned out to be less luxurious, or small and cramped, or a space that had been neglected during the previous remodel, the one that had clearly involved updating the bathrooms. No, the real problem was that it adjoined the master vampire's suite, and even had a door connecting the two rooms.

"I will keep it locked, naturally," Lucius said. "It wouldn't do to have you wander in on me while I am sleeping. But I thought it best if I should have direct access to you."

My mouth was dry. The water I'd asked for still hadn't materialized, but I had far bigger things to worry about at the moment. "I won't try to run away again."

"No, of course you won't. One of my semivives will stay outside the door at all times, and there is also a camera installed directly outside the window. Even if I am…at rest…you won't be able to get very far. Oh, and there is definitely no attic access in the bathroom. So that avenue of escape is also denied you."

I wanted to scream. Absolutely no way out, and now I would be trapped right next to the vampire who held me captive. At least in my previous bedroom, I could count on some space between us, a little bit of mental distance where I could try to keep myself from completely losing it. But now?

"You appear distressed, Serena." Lucius had been

standing a little distance away, but he came toward me then, the smugness of his expression almost unbearable. "But it is your own fault, after all. I chose your former room because I thought you might find the decor soothing. Clearly, I should not have been as gracious."

"'Gracious'?" I repeated. "That's not exactly the word I would use for making someone your prisoner."

"Ah, but you see, you have made yourself the prisoner. If you would only work with me, tell me the truth of what you saw, I might be more inclined to trust you."

"I did tell you the truth." That was a lie I knew I would repeat for as long as necessary. I couldn't possibly bring myself to tell him what I had seen. I didn't even want to admit it to myself.

His brows drew together, but the half-smile he wore remained in place. "Perhaps if you tell yourself that enough times, you might come to believe it. I, on the other hand, am old enough to recognize a lie when I see one…or hear one. At any rate, you might as well make yourself comfortable here. I have some business to attend to, so I will leave you for now. But you will join me for dinner at nine. In the meantime, I would advise you to consider whether it is useful—or wise—to continue withholding information from me."

After delivering that parting shot, he turned and left my new cell, and locked the door behind him. From out in the hall came the faintest creak of floorboards, signaling that one of the semivives had taken up his position guarding the bedroom.

Jesus. Since I really didn't know what to do, I went over to the window and peered out. Night had fallen, and immediately outside was a large fir tree, so I couldn't see very much. However, when I looked up, it was impossible to miss the pale gleam of the camera mounted directly above the window. Lucius hadn't been making idle threats about the surveillance, apparently.

I made a disgusted sound and closed the drapes, making sure they overlapped so the camera couldn't possibly capture what was going on inside my room. Those drapes were a deep, dark crimson, to match the covering on the bed. As in my former chamber, the walls here had dark mahogany wainscoting. The ceiling wasn't as intricate, though, just plain dark beams, and the walls above the wainscoting had some kind of faux finish, a warm parchment-y sort of vibe. However, I didn't find anything all that warm about the room, since no pictures had been hung to liven up the space. Just the bed and the tables on either side of it, and a large Victorian monstrosity of a marble-topped dresser opposite the four-poster bed. No chairs at all; if I wanted to sit down, I'd have to sit on the bed.

Likewise, the bathroom wasn't as large as the one that had been attached to my previous accommodations. Clean and up to date, with rosy granite on top of the vanity, but that was about it. My toiletries had already been put away in the medicine cabinet and under the sink, and when I went back out to the main room and peeked in the closet, I saw my clothes hanging there as well. Say what you wanted for them, but Lucius Montfort's semivives were very efficient.

On the wall opposite the window was a door. I didn't bother to test it, since I already knew it led to the suite Lucius called his own. I really didn't want to know whether it was locked, or whether he had left it open as a sort of challenge to me, despite what he had said about it being kept locked at all times.

Right then, all I really wanted to do was sink to my knees and sob. My situation had seemed hopeless before, and now....

*And now you'll have to come up with a Plan B,* I told myself. *Whatever that is.*

At the moment, though, no plans offered themselves. I seemed to be well and truly trapped, outmaneuvered once again by the master vampire. Really, how was I supposed to prevail against him? He held all the cards, and had hundreds of years of experience when it came to making things go his way.

Someone knocked at the door, and I stiffened, worried that Lucius had already completed his "business"—whatever that might be—and had returned to torment me some more. As I began to move in that direction, however, the door opened, and a semivive I hadn't seen before, an Asian man who looked to be somewhere in his thirties, entered the room, a pitcher of water and a glass in his hands.

"The master said to bring these to you," he told me, and set the pitcher and glass down on the dresser. "He also said to change for dinner."

"Oh, really?" I retorted. "I don't think I brought any cocktail dresses with me."

The semivive appeared puzzled by that remark. As I'd observed earlier, the ones on duty here at the mansion seemed to be used mainly for muscle and for fetching and carrying, and didn't have a lot of processing power. "You will change for dinner. He will come for you in two hours." And then he let himself out and locked the door after him.

Two hours. Well, at least I had that measure to guide me, although it would be difficult to really keep track when I didn't have my phone or a watch or a clock.

As for the rest….

First things first. My throat was parched, since one swallow of brandy hadn't exactly quenched my thirst. I went to the dresser and poured myself a glass of water from the pitcher, and drank it all down, then poured some more and drank that, too. The hydration made me feel marginally better, although once I wasn't so thirsty, I could begin to take stock of how banged up I felt, how the muscles in my arms and legs ached, how my right bicep particularly throbbed where that semivive had grabbed me. My face was sticky from the spilled brandy.

However, I hadn't been dealt any permanent damage, and I knew the rest of my aches and pains would go away eventually. As I looked down at myself, I could see why Lucius had requested that I change for dinner—my jeans were streaked with dirt, and I'd somehow caught the hem of my shirt and torn out some of the stitching. Yes, I would change, and take a shower, but not to please the vampire. I just didn't want to eat dinner in those dirty and bedraggled clothes, while I stank of fear sweat.

No cocktail dress, though. I actually did have the black one Vanessa had loaned me, but no way was I going to give Lucius Montfort an opportunity to stare at the amount of leg that dress revealed. However, I did stop for a moment and touch the fabric of the gown, feeling the heavy silk challis flow under my fingertips. Tears burned in my eyes, and I suddenly wondered what my parents were doing right then. Still reeling from the shock of their daughter's death, of course. Was Jackson already here in California? When would they hold the funeral? I knew Vanessa would be buried at Forest Lawn in Glendale, just as my grandparents were. Nothing but the best for the Quinns, after all.

Did my parents think I was dead, too? Were they preparing a second plot, one next to my sister's?

Right then, it was all too much. Grief overwhelmed

me like a punch to the gut, cramping my already abused muscles. I sank down onto the hard wooden floor of the closet and sobbed, rocking back and forth in misery, wanting Silas, wanting him to hold me and tell me that everything was going to be all right.

Only I knew better. It most definitely was not going to be all right. Not now, and maybe not ever.

~

Silas hadn't been expecting the text, since he figured Raoul Ortiz wouldn't bother to be in touch unless he had some additional information to impart. He'd been trying to summon some enthusiasm for takeout sushi, since he knew he should eat something, but at the moment his appetite was just as MIA as Serena herself.

But then his phone buzzed at a little after seven.

*Let's talk. Casa Bianco, Eagle Rock. 8 o'clock.*

He didn't even have to stop and think, only grabbed the phone and texted back. *See you then.*

Silas hadn't heard of the place, but that didn't mean much. It wasn't as if he'd had much reason to frequent Eagle Rock and its environs, even though it was just over the hill from Pasadena. If he hadn't been downtown at his loft or someplace nearby, he'd been keeping watch in the area around Serena's condo, or in the extremely upscale neighborhood where her parents' house was located.

The drive would probably take most of the time remaining between now and eight, just because rush hour in Los Angeles extended far past six o'clock, and he'd be on the road with everyone else who was trying to get out of downtown and out to their more affordable homes in the suburbs. He got his jacket from the hall closet, slid his phone into his jacket pocket, and made sure the retractable blades he always carried were secured in the front pockets of his jeans.

Not that he expected to meet with much trouble at an Italian restaurant in Eagle Rock, but you just never knew.

As he fought his way up the 5 Freeway, Silas tapped his fingers on the steering wheel, trying to push back his impatience. Right then, Humboldt was beginning to beckon to him, with its redwood forests and foggy mornings, and a serene atmosphere that was a welcome respite from the hectic day-to-day world. He'd spent too many years fighting traffic, being jostled by millions of other people. His first year in Los Angeles had been complete culture shock, and although he'd grown accustomed to it, he knew he'd never love the city.

Question was, would Serena love the country?

He knew he was getting ahead of himself. First he would have to find her, and even getting her safely away from Lucius Montfort didn't necessarily mean that they would spend their lives together. He'd witnessed firsthand far too many relationships falling apart because the women involved couldn't live with the aftermath of giving away a much-wanted child for adoption, or because they simply couldn't reconcile themselves to a life spent isolated from the world, away from everything they'd known and loved. He'd never faulted those women, or thought them weak. Life among the *gula* was hard for human women.

At the same time, he'd prayed his case might be different, that he would find the one woman who could be his partner through all the phases of life, no matter how difficult. He thought he'd found that woman in Serena Quinn. But now....

*Now you will find her,* he thought fiercely. *And then you will drive one of your silver blades through Lucius Montfort's black heart so he can trouble her no more.*

Wishful thinking? He hoped not.

After turning onto yet another freeway, he got off at Colorado Boulevard and headed northeast. Street parking around the restaurant was practically nonexistent, so he turned down a small side road and left the truck in a slightly shabby residential neighborhood. When he got to the restaurant, which at least was easy to find because of the enormous "Pizza Pie" spelled out in neon letters on the side of the building, he found Detective Ortiz already waiting inside, in a tiny area packed with other people trying to get a table.

Silas glanced at his watch. Two minutes after eight. "I hope I didn't leave you waiting too long."

Ortiz grinned. "Not at all. There's always a wait here, which is why I came early and got my name in."

The food must be good, then. Silas couldn't imagine why else such a modest-looking establishment would be so busy on a Wednesday night.

"Ortiz?" the girl at the hostess stand called out.

The detective got up from the bench where he'd been sitting. "Right here."

She smiled, the expression growing a bit warmer as her gaze traveled toward Silas. "This way, please."

They were seated at a booth toward the back of the restaurant. Good, because the place was quite noisy, and a booth would offer far more privacy than one of the tables set out in the middle of the floor.

The hostess told them their waitress would be along shortly, and left. Silas lifted an eyebrow at the detective. "So…?"

"So we'll talk about it after we order," Ortiz said. "Less chance of being interrupted that way."

"Of course."

They decided on pasta, despite the blazing neon enticement to order pizza on the outside of the building—lasagna for the detective, linguini carbonara for Silas. No alcohol, though; when Ortiz asked for iced tea, Silas requested water. Just as well, since he needed to stay sharp.

But then the waitress had come and gone, leaving their drinks behind. Raoul Ortiz picked up his iced tea and sipped at it. When he set the glass down, he said,

"The Quinns have hired a private detective agency to look for Serena."

There was a vote of confidence for the Pasadena P.D. Silas lifted his shoulders. "It won't do any good."

"Well, you know that, and I know that, but in the meantime the Quinns will be spending a lot of money to get nowhere."

The Quinns had money to burn. That wasn't the point. "What do they think having private investigators will do? You already have a team on the case."

"They don't think we're moving fast enough. Kosky tried to tell them that the private detectives wouldn't have access to any more information than the police department—less, really—but they didn't want to discuss it." Ortiz drank some more iced tea and tapped his fingers against the glass once he'd set it back down. The lighting in the restaurant wasn't very good, but Silas thought he detected additional shadows under the older man's eyes, stress lines that looked more pronounced than they had a few days earlier. "And the Quinns really aren't the sort of people you argue with. But I wanted to tell you that if you had any ideas about going back to snoop around Serena's condo, don't. It's being watched twenty-four/seven."

Silas had toyed with the idea, even though he knew it would be risky because of the compromised nature of her next-door neighbor. What he'd thought he would find, he wasn't sure, but at least it would have felt as if he was doing something. "All right," he said. "You do need to avoid saying anything around her neighbor Brian. Lucius Montfort got to him."

"'Got to him'?" Ortiz repeated, raising an eyebrow.

"Made him a semivive. A slave to his will. He's basically a spy for Montfort now. I'm sure he was the one who gave out my description, hinted that I might have had something to do with Serena's disappearance."

That particular piece of information made the detective settle against the back of his seat, disbelief and concern warring in his expression. "A what?"

"Semivive. Half living. Or half dead, I suppose, depending on how you look at it. Anyway, I'm fairly certain he's the one who actually kidnapped Serena. It makes sense. She was being careful. She wouldn't have let anyone in that she didn't know and trust. Which I'm sure is why Lucius went after Brian in the first place."

Ortiz's mouth went grim. Clearly, his misgivings on the subject of vampires were gone now, maybe because he'd realized that a world which contained psychics could also include vampires. "Son of a bitch. Should I bring the neighbor in for questioning?"

"It won't do any good. He'll tell the lies that Lucius Montfort has told him to tell. And his own will is so subsumed that you could give him a lie detector test and he'd pass, simply because he truly believes all of Montfort's fabrications."

Right then, the detective looked as if he wished there was something stronger than iced tea in his glass. "Do you have any good news?"

"Not really." Silas was about to mention his failed attempt to locate the vampires' lair, but the waitress arrived then with their food. She deposited their plates on the table, asked if there was anything else they needed, and then headed back toward the front of the restaurant once they'd reassured her that everything looked fine. The food looked good and smelled even better, but once again Silas found he was forcing himself to eat because he knew he should, and not because he really wanted to.

Both of them were silent for a few minutes as they dug into their meals—Ortiz with far more gusto than Silas. After they'd both made a respectable dent in their food, though, Silas said, "I thought I'd narrowed down possible locations for Montfort's house, but when I went out to San Rafael, I couldn't find a damn thing. The most promising prospect turned out to be nothing like what the assessor's website said it should be. So now I suppose I need to start digging around in the databases to see if I can find any construction permits for a remodel."

Ortiz frowned, then pushed a forkful of lasagna around on his plate. "Do you think Serena might have been wrong? About what the place looked like, that is."

It was a possibility that had floated around in Silas'

mind on more than one occasion, although he hadn't wanted to admit it. Because if it turned out that this was one of those rare cases where her vision had betrayed her, led her astray for some reason, then they'd be back to square one. Was Lucius Montfort's power of concealment so great that he'd somehow been able to obscure the true nature of his lair even in Serena's vision?

Damn it.

"I don't know," Silas replied after a long pause that must have been only too obvious to the other man. "At this point, anything is possible. I know she's usually very accurate. Has she ever steered you wrong?"

"Not a single time," Ortiz said. "In the beginning, she'd always preface her descriptions of her visions by saying that she hoped they were right, but she couldn't guarantee anything. After the fourth or fifth time, I told her she needed to stop saying that, because it was obvious enough to me that she knew her stuff. Wherever she was getting these visions from, they were always right. So I have no reason to believe she would have gotten this wrong."

"Where does that leave us, though? Is there any chance that there might be a property somewhere in San Rafael that was never mentioned in the assessor's records?"

"Maybe," Ortiz replied, although his tone was dubious. "I don't think that's very likely, though, especially when you're talking about such expensive pieces of land. Then again, it's possible that Lucius could have paid someone to make sure his property 'disappeared,' for lack of a better word, even though I've never heard of something like that happening before."

So many possibilities, and no real facts. Nothing that would help them to locate Serena. And in the meantime, she was completely at Lucius Montfort's mercy. Silas wouldn't allow himself to ponder all the ramifications of her current situation, because a mind paralyzed with fear and worry was an utterly ineffective one. Even so, he realized he didn't have any appetite for the food remaining on his plate, and he pushed it away.

Ortiz's shrewd dark eyes didn't miss the gesture, but he refrained from comment. After breaking off a piece of garlic bread, he said, "What if it's not that Serena saw the wrong house, but merely the correct house at the wrong time? Maybe, for whatever reason, her vision showed her the mansion before it was remodeled."

"That's possible, I suppose," Silas replied, turning over the idea in his head. From what he'd been able to tell, sometimes she saw things that were still out somewhere in the future, and sometimes the visions revealed events as they were happening—like the girl in El Monte she'd helped to save only a few days ago. "But she never talked about any visions of events in the past, only the present and the future. Besides, she says she saw Lucius Montfort in a chateau-style mansion, not the Mediterranean place I drove past earlier today."

"Time can be tricky. I'm certainly no expert when it comes to visions, but...." The detective tapped his fingers on the dark wood of the tabletop. "How long did you say Montfort had been here in Southern California?"

"Best guess is about ten years, maybe a little more. So, what...you're saying Serena might have seen him in the house as it originally existed, and not as it is now?"

"Maybe. It's a theory. If nothing else, it might merit taking a closer look."

"I've got the property records right here." Silas had taken off his jacket when they sat down at the table. Now he leaned over and rummaged around so he could retrieve his cell phone from the jacket's pocket. He entered his passcode, then went back to the web browser page he had cached on the phone. "According to this, the house last changed hands eighteen years ago, which doesn't match up with Lucius Montfort's timeline. We—I know for a fact that he was in Long Island at that time. But it also seems to indicate that Montfort was somehow able to fudge the title transfer."

"Then I don't know what to say. Maybe Serena really did get it wrong."

It was beginning to sound more and more as if she had, but Silas didn't want to admit defeat just yet. "I don't know. I feel like there's something missing, something that's right under our noses. We just can't see it."

"Possibly. I'm not saying we should give up. But I did want you to know what was happening on my end."

Which wasn't very much. Silas wouldn't give the detective grief over the slow progress of the case; it wasn't the Pasadena P.D.'s fault that they were up against an ancient, wily vampire who had centuries of evading the authorities under his belt. "I'll keep digging. There's got to be a clue somewhere. We just have to find it."

Ortiz nodded. His phone buzzed right then, and he unclipped it from his belt and took a look at the screen. "I need to go."

"Trouble?"

A wry grin. "You could call it that. My wife Manuela was down in San Diego visiting her sister and just got back. Now she's wondering where the hell I am, since she knows I only work until six-thirty on Wednesdays unless there's an emergency. So…time to go home."

"Wouldn't want to get you in trouble with your wife."

"That you wouldn't." Rather than appearing chastened, though, Ortiz just looked amused, as if he was glad that his wife wanted to keep tabs on him. He got out his wallet and removed two twenties. "For dinner."

"You don't need to cover the whole thing."

"This was my idea. Anyway, it's not like I invited you out to Spago." The detective pushed himself out of the booth and stood. "If you find anything, text me."

"I will."

"And I'm telling you again to stay far away from the police department offices or Serena's condo. The private investigators hired by the Quinns have your description, and no doubt they'd love to talk to you."

"No doubt," Silas replied dryly. "I'll make myself scarce."

"Good."

Then Ortiz was off, threading his way through the crowded restaurant before disappearing into the waiting area. Silas eyed his uneaten food and wondered if he should have it boxed up to take home. Then he realized he really didn't want to waste his time on such a thing. It was nighttime, and he didn't know what, if anything, he would see, but he wanted to drive past the Mediterranean mansion again. Just to satisfy his curiosity.

He didn't want to admit to himself that such a drive was probably a fool's errand.

# CHAPTER THIRTEEN

A SEMIVIVE, THE BROWN-HAIRED, GOOD-LOOKING one, came to get me. Evidence of Lucius Montfort's displeasure?

In a way, I was glad. Not that I enjoyed the company of the vampire master's brainwashed semivives, but at least I had a few extra minutes to steel myself for the confrontation ahead, center myself with some yoga breathing, and try to reassure myself that Lucius wouldn't do anything too dreadful. After all, he still wanted to ferret out the secrets I'd been hiding from him.

This time, the semivive led me to the large dining room. Unlike the previous evening, when Lucius had invited the entire crew to dine with us, only two place settings had been laid out on the enormous shining mahogany table. The vampire sat at the far end, candlelight catching in his cobweb-pale hair, but he stood as soon as I entered.

"Ah, Serena. You look much improved."

I glanced down at myself, even as the semivive quietly let himself out of the room and closed the double doors behind him. The black cocktail dress still hung in the closet of my new prison cell, but I'd put on one of my long skirts, this one with an intricate paisley pattern in shades of black and gray and teal, and a black ballet-neck top. It was one of my favorite outfits, and I'd hoped it might give me a little courage. As for the rest of me, well, I'd covered up the worst of the damage my crying spell had caused by using good deal of concealer, and put on makeup. I didn't give a damn what my captor thought of my looks, but the last thing I wanted was for him to figure out that I'd spent the previous two hours weeping in a closet.

"Thanks," I said carelessly. I didn't move, though, but remained standing by the door.

Lucius' mouth thinned. "Come and sit down. Dinner will be served soon."

I could have argued, but I didn't see the point in wasting my energy on a useless battle of wills this early in the evening. Instead, I shrugged, and went ahead and took my seat in the place to his left. I noticed that he didn't offer to help me with the heavy chair. My mother most definitely would have disapproved.

The thought was so incongruous that, despite

myself, my mouth curved in a half-smile. I could just hear her. *Well, Serena, he obviously has a good deal of money, but I don't approve of long hair on men. And really, I think he might be a little old for you....*

"Something amuses you?" Lucius asked as he sat down as well.

"Not exactly. I was just thinking of something."

For a moment, it looked as if he was going to probe further. But then his shoulders lifted in the faintest of shrugs, and he reached over and picked up the carafe of wine that sat off to his right. "We're having tapas, so I thought a good Rioja would do well."

"For someone who's supposed to live off other liquids, you do seem to like your wine," I remarked. Before coming downstairs, I'd resolved to do everything in my power to remain unruffled, detached, maybe more than a little sarcastic. Maintaining that kind of mental distance seemed to be the best tactic for remaining sane.

His lips quirked. "In a life as long as mine, it helps to have a varied diet. There is no reason not to amuse myself with other...diversions."

There he went again. As he'd spoken, his gaze had flickered down to my mouth and moved lower. Just for a second, certainly not long enough for that particular glance to be mistaken for outright ogling. Besides, my shirt wasn't low-cut enough to show off much of anything. And yet I'd known he was only trying to put me on edge, to make me wonder if he was going to try a repeat of the previous night, when he'd pushed me down onto my bed and forced his kisses on me.

"I suppose so," I said, my tone brittle. I lifted my wine glass and allowed myself a sip. It really was very good, strong fruit underlaid with a trace of earth, making me think of warm hillsides and vines ripening in the sun. "I was actually wondering about that just yesterday. What do you all do to keep from getting bored? It's not like you can volunteer at the local animal shelter or something to pass the time."

The faint smile he wore didn't budge, although I thought I detected a brief flicker of irritation in his silvery eyes. "Whatever we must. Some, like Tristan and Leticia, like to spend their nights hunting, even if they know they must hold off on the actual kill to escape detection. Michael is quite a musician, actually, even though he doesn't have much opportunity to play in public, for obvious reasons. And I?" He shrugged again. "I do enjoy my wines. And reading. I walk in the garden, once it is dark enough to do so. When the star jasmine blooms, it is quite pleasant."

Those activities all sounded so innocuous. What he'd left out, of course, was that in between playing at the modern-day country gentleman, he went out and killed people so he could drink their blood. And let's not forget his plans for world domination by the vampires, and making sure that anyone who got in his way ended up dead or enslaved to his will. Yes, he was quite the poor misunderstood creature of the night.

The double doors opened, and the same semivive who'd brought me down to dinner entered, pushing a serving cart laden with a number of small plates, each covered with one of the ubiquitous silver domes. He began to set everything out on the table with such a quick economy of movement that I wondered whether he'd been a waiter before Lucius had enslaved him.

The vampire hadn't been joking about tapas. When the semivive took the domes off all those plates, I saw an enormous variety of items—mushrooms in olive oil with peppers, skewers of grilled chicken, plates with an assortment of Spanish cheese, bacon-wrapped dates, some kind of potato dish I couldn't quite identify.

"This is all for us?" I said after the semivive had left, taking the serving cart with him.

"Of course. I thought you might be hungry, after the day you had."

Was that a note of concern I detected in his voice? If it was, it was just as false as his need to eat any of the morsels spread out on the table before us. He really didn't think I would be so weak, so stupid as to fall for that sort of ploy, did he?

"I could eat," I said, my tone neutral in the extreme.

No response then, except for him to offer the plate

of dates outstretched on one hand. "Perhaps you can start with one of these."

Despite what I'd just said, I was actually starving. Apparently, climbing on roofs and being forced to have hideous visions could really work up an appetite. I picked up one of the dates and bit it in half, tasting the combination of sweet and savory, although I did my best to not show any reaction to what I'd just eaten. It wasn't that I was enjoying myself, more that, no matter how bad things might be, food did help.

Lucius chose a date as well, and chewed it slowly as he set down the plate he was holding. After that, he put a little bit of everything on both our plates, even though I certainly hadn't asked him to do such a thing.

"Do you want to tell me now?" he said then.

"Tell you what?" I asked, purposely obtuse. Of course I knew exactly what he wanted me to tell him.

"Serena."

I stared straight at him, expression guileless. "Lucius."

For the first time, a faint frown pulled at his brow. "Don't try my patience."

"That wasn't my intention. I'm sorry, I suppose I'm just tired from everything I've gone through today."

"Which was your own doing."

"All of it?"

He didn't blink. "Yes, all of it. I wouldn't have had to force that vision on you if you hadn't been so stubborn. But you may want to remember that if I did such a thing once, I can most certainly do it again."

I set down the piece of bread and cheese I'd just picked up, my appetite deciding it was no match for Lucius Montfort's threats. Instead, I sipped some wine, hoping the alcohol would give me the courage I needed to continue sparring with him. "I'm not sure that's such a good idea. After all, the vision you forced me to have wasn't of much use, was it?"

"Oh, I think it was. But I will know for certain very soon now."

What the hell was he talking about? I would never, ever tell him what I had seen in that vision. It was absolutely hideous, on a number of levels.

The room blurred. A shudder went through me, and I hurriedly set down my wine glass, afraid that I was about to have yet another vision. And yet, this blurriness wasn't quite like the haze I experienced when a vision descended on me, more that I couldn't seem to focus on any one thing with any clarity. The floor seemed to tilt under me, and I grasped the edge of the table in a desperate attempt to keep myself upright.

"What…?"

"I am sorry it had to come to this." Lucius got up from his seat and bent toward me, one arm slipping around my waist. I pushed at him, but feebly, as though I had no more strength than a baby. "It was in the wine, my dear. If you had not been so intractable, then I would not have resorted to such methods. As it is...."

His words stopped there, as though he knew he didn't have to waste any more effort on trying to explain himself to me. His other arm slid under my knees, and in the next moment he had lifted me from my chair and was carrying me toward the door. I made an incoherent sound of protest, but he ignored me and opened the door, then took me out of the dining room and down the hall. His destination became clear enough as he mounted the stairs, heading toward the upstairs hall.

For one horrible moment I thought he was going to take me to his bedroom, but even in my daze I realized that the room where he set me down on the bed was actually the one I'd been moved to only a few hours earlier. I stared up at him, willing my body to do something, anything, but all my limbs felt as if they'd been fitted with lead weights.

Since this room didn't have any chairs, Lucius sat down on the bed next to me. I let out a cough of disgust and tried to move away from him. All I accomplished was to make an odd little wriggling motion, and he chuckled.

"No, Serena, don't bother. Your body isn't your own right now. But I do want you to speak." He leaned toward me and touched a finger to my mouth. "I want you to tell me what you really saw in your vision."

I shook my head—or rather, I moved it a fraction of an inch. Not exactly a very impressive protest. At the same time, I could actually feel the words piling up within me somewhere, wanting to get out.

What the hell had been in that wine? Some kind of truth serum? Did such a thing even exist outside of film and television and books?

Lucius moved closer, so close that his lips brushed against my cheek. "Tell me, Serena. Tell me all of it."

"We—" No, I would not. I would not tell him a goddamn thing. I pressed my mouth closed, even though as I did so, a horrible queasiness roiled within me, as though I would be sick if I didn't let go of the secret I held, as if it was some sort of terrible malignant child I had to birth.

"We what?" he persisted, his breath cool against my skin. "You saw the two of us again?"

To my horror, I nodded.

"At the same place?"

I nodded again, grimacing the whole time, my soul rebelling against what my body was doing.

"What were we doing?"

"I—we—"

And then it was as if a dam burst. My feeble limbs couldn't move, but my traitor mouth went a mile a minute, describing the scene at the party, the way we had talked with Jackson, that comment about selling immortality. Even, to my shame, the way he had kissed me after I'd given him his shot, the way I'd let him touch me.

Through it all, he wore a steadily broadening grin, as though what I had told him pleased him very much. "So," he said at last, his voice almost a murmur, the words more for his ears than my own, "it will work. It is going to work."

"W-what?" I croaked, my voice spent now that I had given him what he wanted. "What is going to work?"

"You'll see, my dear." To my relief, he got up from the bed. However, that relief was short-lived, because he bent and kissed me, mouth lingering on mine, as I lay there and had to submit to the caress, my body still not my own. "Oh, yes, you'll see."

Then he went out through the door that adjoined our two rooms, and closed it behind him.

That was something. It would have been far worse if he'd left that door open.

I wanted more than anything to reach up and wipe his kiss from my mouth, but my arm wouldn't obey the commands my brain was so desperately sending it. All I could do was remain as he'd left me, head cradled on the pillows, legs straight out in front of me, arms at my side.

And then…the haze. Not the blurry vision Lucius' drug had brought on, but the familiar shimmers of a vision coming once again. *No,* my brain begged. *No.*

It was all too much. They were coming too fast.

Was this more of Lucius' doing? Could he somehow make my visions appear even when he wasn't even in the room with me?

The same limo. The two of us getting in the back, separated from the driver by a thick barrier of dark Plexiglas. No sooner had the car pulled away from the curb than Lucius drew me to him, his mouth on mine, demanding, smearing the lipstick I'd reapplied in my earlier vision. In this new vision, I didn't struggle. No, I willingly opened my mouth to him, tasted the tang of champagne on his tongue. His hands moved over me, moved downward, slipped up between my legs, pushed past my underwear so his finger could slip into me.

I—that other Serena—moaned and writhed against him, let him bring me to a climax. When I was done, I fell against him, murmured, "I love you, Lucius."

Oh, God, no. Maybe it was the drug wearing off, or maybe my outrage had finally overcome the narcotic's effects on my system, but I pushed myself upright and sat there for a long moment, breath coming in harsh gasps as I tried to push away the horrors I'd just seen.

But what was worse...so much worse...was that I could feel the echoes of that vision in my own traitorous body. For just a second or two, before I willed it away, I throbbed with desire. I wanted him. *Needed* him. Wanted him to—

Bile rose in my throat. On wobbling legs, I staggered off the bed and hurried to the bathroom, making it to the toilet just in time to throw up the meager amount I'd eaten at that interrupted dinner. Vomited and vomited, until in the end I was only dry-heaving. Then I wearily leaned my head against the side of the toilet, feeling the porcelain cool against my cheek as I waited to see if there was anything more that wanted to come up.

Apparently not. I grasped the vanity's marble top and hauled myself to my feet, then ran cold water and splashed it on my face, drank a cupful and another, once I was sure I wouldn't throw it right back up again. And after that I brushed my teeth to get the foul taste of the vomit out of my mouth.

Cautiously, I opened the bathroom door and looked out, halfway afraid that Lucius might have returned and sat there through the whole episode, listening as I tried to expel the dregs of that horrible vision from my body. But the room was empty.

I went back over to the bed, kicked off my flats, and lay down. My heart kept hammering in my chest, pounding as though I'd just made another rooftop escape attempt.

Deep breaths. I made myself breathe in and breathe out, listened as my heartbeat gradually slowed, as the last of the nausea dissipated.

What the hell was all that? Why did my gift—my curse—seem so hell-bent on tormenting me with these visions of Lucius and me together? I would rather die than be with him, so why was my future apparently intertwined with his?

*Be rational,* I told myself. *Think it through. Pick it apart.*

All right. I'd focus on the details that didn't involve Lucius, just so I wouldn't lose it all over again. Clearly, the vision had been of the future. How far in the future, I didn't know. Jackson and Bethany had looked more or less the same as they did now, except for that bit of silver in Jackson's hair. The same for the celebrities and local officials whose faces I recognized. But with that comment about immortality, for all I knew, I could have been looking at a scene ten, fifteen, even twenty years from now.

Immortality. Vampires were immortal. And yet Lucius had been acting like a normal human—well, except for the part where I shot him up with something in the bathroom. Some kind of serum to allow him to move in the daylight, act like a regular man. I didn't understand the dynamic, not really, but I was beginning to think that I must have glimpsed a future where vampires had possibly traded the secret to their own immortality in exchange for the science necessary to make—if not an actual cure—then at least some kind of treatment to give vampires a semblance of humanity.

A fair trade, at least according to the actors involved—Lucius and my brother and God knows how many other people. And the warehouse from my first vision…maybe it wasn't an actual warehouse, but some kind of facility that produced whatever was used to allow vampires their artificial normality. Were those people donating blood…or something far worse?

No, I absolutely could not believe that my brother would allow American citizens to be hurt on his watch. Not even for the gift of immortality. Sometimes Jackson's drive and unwavering need to be a larger part of history had bothered me, as if he'd sacrificed his connection to individual people in his quest to give back to his country. But I didn't think he would so utterly abandon his morals to give the vampires what they wanted, and damn the cost.

I stared up at the ceiling, at the warmly tinted plaster and the dark beams which crossed it. They appeared blurry, only this time I knew that was simply because of the tears which filled my eyes, not because another vision was about to occur.

In that horrible future, had Lucius made Jackson a semivive? It would explain why he was in bed with the vampires. However, despite how jarring the scene had been, with me acting as if it was the most natural thing in the world to be at Lucius Montfort's side, I hadn't noticed anything particularly strange about the way Jackson behaved. He seemed like himself, as far as I could tell. Silas had told me that the longer semivives were enslaved, the less of their old selves remained, which explained the near-brain-dead creatures working here at the vampires' mansion. So how could Jackson not have given signs of such a loss of self, if I truly had been looking at a future far enough off that the sort of biotech necessary to give people immortality and allow vampires to walk in the sunlight even existed?

I couldn't answer that. The visions were only that —pictures in my head that might or might not come true at some point. It was up to me...or the people I told about the visions...to interpret them, to attempt to divine what they might actually mean.

Right then I wished I had the notebook where I'd written down descriptions of my visions, or the sketchpad I'd used to help bring them to life. Maybe if I went back and looked at some of those earlier accounts, I could begin to piece the whole story together, could find clues to the visions that plagued me now. There had been several which made no sense at the time, and which I'd dismissed as misfires of a sort, images that had nothing to do with either my present or my future. However, it was entirely possible that I would finally see a pattern, a series of signposts to a future I really didn't want to accept.

The door to Lucius' room opened then, and he entered. He'd taken off his suit jacket, and his pale hair, usually pulled severely back into a ponytail, now lay loose on his shoulders.

What his unusually casual appearance meant, I didn't know. I didn't want to know. Just the sight of him was enough to send the nausea churning in my stomach again. I ignored it, however, and pushed myself up to a sitting position.

"What do you want?" I snapped.

"I should think that is clear enough," he replied. That faint smirk was back, the one that made me wish I had the power to reach out and smack it right off his face. When I stayed quiet, refusing to rise to the bait, he went on, "I wanted to check on you, make sure you were well. The drug I gave you is usually harmless enough, but occasionally it can have some negative side effects."

*Like making me puke like a freshman on a bender in Baja?* I thought caustically, but I didn't say anything. After all, it might not have been the drug that had made me vomit so much, but just the after-math of that last horrible vision. About the only good thing I could say about it was at least it hadn't showed the two of us actually fucking.

But I couldn't allow Lucius to see how shaken I was. Feigning unconcern, I shrugged. "I'm fine."

"Are you sure? You sounded…not well."

Did this room have surveillance everywhere, including the bathroom? Maybe the walls were thin… or maybe vampires simply had very good hearing. "I'm fine," I repeated. Which was true enough. At the moment, I didn't think I was in too much danger of getting sick again, despite my uneasy stomach. Lying down had helped more than I thought.

"If you say so." He crossed over to the side of the bed and stood there, gazing down at me.

*Please God don't let him sit on the bed again....*

But he didn't. His expression was almost blank, as though he didn't quite know what he should say or do. When he spoke, his tone was musing. "I must say that I've never had as much difficulty with a woman as I have had with you, Serena."

"Oh, really?" I replied. "What, do they usually drop into your hand like so much ripe fruit?"

"Yes, something like that."

What a conceited son of a bitch. "Sorry, Lucius— even if I were able to overlook the fact that you're a killer a thousand times over, I'm not the sort of person who would want her sister's sloppy seconds."

My remark actually made him chuckle. "How forthright of you. But, in the interest of honesty, I should tell you that I did not sleep with your sister."

More lies. "You wouldn't know honesty if it bit you in the ass. So I'm sorry if I have to say that I don't believe you for one minute."

"It's the simple truth." He rubbed his chin, as if trying to decide exactly what he wanted to tell me. "Yes, I did meet your sister for drinks—at the Hotel Mondrian, to be exact. Her intentions were clear enough, because of her choice of venue. But when she invited me up to her room, I declined. I told her that I didn't think it would be ethical for us to have an intimate relationship if we were also going to be business partners."

"'Ethical'?" I repeated, and shot him a disbelieving stare. "That's pretty rich, coming from you."

"I can see you don't believe me. That is your prerogative. But I know what happened between your sister and me—which was nothing."

I couldn't believe him. And yet...my sister had been royally pissed off when I talked to her the Saturday after the fashion show. At the time, I'd chalked up her annoyance to being irritated about my fabricated story of Lucius hitting on me at the reception, but...what if she'd been that angry because he'd turned her down, and hearing that he'd been interested in me instead was the last straw?

It made sense. However, what Lucius might or might not have done with my sister wasn't the issue here. My comment about "sloppy seconds" had been a diversionary tactic, nothing more. No inducement existed that would make me want to be with him. Everything about him repelled me to my very core. Even if I hadn't already been in love with Silas, I still would want nothing to do with Lucius Montfort.

And yet, those goddamn visions would seem to indicate otherwise.

"Fine," I said. "So you didn't sleep with her. Great news. Now can you leave me alone?"

"If you wish. For now," he added, before I could

get my hopes up very far. "You have had a trying day. Perhaps tomorrow you will listen to reason."

*Not if it means agreeing to anything you want from me,* I thought, but I only shrugged again. "Maybe. Good night, Lucius."

His lips twitched. "Good night, my sweet Serena."

I wanted to tell him I wasn't his sweet anything, but that would have only given him a reason to stay there and argue with me. Instead, I rolled over on my side so I wouldn't have to see him. A few seconds later, I heard the door open, then shut again. No sound of a key in the lock this time, though; it was pretty clear that he wanted me to know he could come back in at any time.

Well, two could play at that game. I would sleep, and in the morning I'd get up while he was in his daytime vampire coma, and then I would...what? Drive a stake through his heart? Looking around the bedroom, I could tell that sharpened stakes were in pretty short supply. But there had to be something I could do. In the meantime, though, I was exhausted. I needed to get some rest, or I wouldn't be good for anything.

One way or another, I intended to keep on resisting, no matter what.

# CHAPTER FOURTEEN

SILAS SLOWLY DROVE DOWN THE STREET IN SAN Rafael—but not so slowly as to rouse suspicion. He honestly didn't know what he would find here, and no doubt would discover that this little side trip had been a complete waste of time. Still, he found himself overcome by the need to be doing something, and going home and sifting through contractor's records didn't seem like a very good use of his time. His instincts told him he wouldn't find anything that might help him locate Serena.

The streetlights here were widely spaced, providing just enough illumination to keep the narrow road from being in utter darkness. Most of the houses had their lights on, although with the way they were set back from the road, or had high hedges around them, he couldn't make out much of what was going on inside. Which of course was the whole point.

He slowed as he came up on number 248. Two landscape lights had been placed at the entrance to the driveway, presumably to make it easier for anyone coming home at night to see where they needed to turn. From what he could tell, more of those low-slung lights followed the driveway as it curved around to the garage. In the house itself, several of the windows on the lower floor appeared to be gauzily lit by lamps behind drawn curtains. The entire upper floor was dark, but that wasn't so strange. By that point it was only a little past nine, still somewhat early for most people to be retiring for the evening.

Other than the lights on the ground floor, he couldn't detect any signs of life. But why should he? This was a weekday night, not the sort of evening when people would be entertaining, or have cars coming and going from the property. The weather had been on the cool side, not really suited for dining al fresco or lingering on a patio or in a swimming pool.

Although Silas didn't want to admit it to himself, he knew he had come here because he had hoped against hope that this truly was the lair of the vampires, and that he would see, if not Lucius Mont-fort himself, then one of his vampire fledglings coming or going from the property. Such a sighting would prove that this mansion really was their home, no matter whether or not it matched the description Serena had provided.

All remained calm and quiet, however, and Silas

knew he would have to keep going. Yes, he could turn around and double back, take another look, but that was the sort of suspicious activity guaranteed to draw notice. And what would such a maneuver gain him? Nothing at all, based on what he had seen so far.

He didn't turn around. His study of the maps of the area told him that he could continue on San Rafael Avenue and jog onto San Pasqual where it passed into Highland Park, and from there get on the 110 Freeway, which would take him straight back to downtown Los Angeles and his loft. As he drove, he could feel his fingers clenching tighter and tighter on the truck's steering wheel. While the life of a Watcher could often be one of frustrations, of countless days of observation with very little to show for it, never before had he been filled with such an overwhelming sensation of impotence. It seemed that no matter what he did, he only continued to batter his head against an impregnable brick wall.

Traffic going in this direction was light. Barely twenty minutes had passed before he found himself turning off onto Flower Street. A short while later, he was back at his loft complex, parking his truck in its allotted space. As he headed toward the gate that opened from the parking lot to the complex itself, a dark shadow emerged from behind one of the dumpsters.

Michael St. John.

Silas ground to a halt, frowning. Technically, the

vampire could be here on the complex property, because the strictures that kept vampires from a place they hadn't been invited only applied to individual homes, and not public areas such as this. Even so, it was disconcerting to see one of the undead creatures so close to where he lived.

"Hello, Silas," said the vampire.

"What are you doing here, St. John?"

Michael St. John didn't reply at first. His gaze swept the area, but they were alone here. The hour wasn't so late that people might not still be coming and going in the parking lot; for the moment, however, it appeared that everyone was safely inside for the evening. After that pause, however, he said, "You look annoyed."

"Of course I'm annoyed. I just found a vampire loitering near my house."

The vampire grinned. His teeth weren't quite so pointed as Lucius Montfort's, nothing that would invite comment. Not for the first time, something about St. John's appearance nagged at Silas, as if there was a particular feature in the creature's face that should be familiar, but somehow wasn't. "Oh, I suppose that's part of it. But I have a feeling the source of your irritation is your continuing failure to locate your lady love."

"I'll find her." The words sounded almost confident. Silas didn't believe them, but he certainly didn't want Michael St. John to know that.

"Maybe. I think Lucius might have finally pulled one over on you, though."

Silas' hand, the one that wasn't holding his house keys, slipped down toward his jeans pocket. There was no way in the world he'd be able to transform in time before the vampire pulled one of his kind's disappearing tricks, but maybe—just maybe—he would be able to retrieve the silver knife from his pocket and ram it through St. John's heart. Killing him wouldn't help find Serena, but it would make Silas feel much better.

"You're entitled to your opinion," he said easily. He didn't move, though. They would finish this discussion where they stood. The creature was already far too close to home for comfort.

"Hey," Michael St. John said, raising his hands as if in mock defeat. "Such hostility. I'm here to help."

"You're what?" If the vampire had said he was on his way to the local blood bank to make a donation, his words wouldn't have been any more fantastic. "Help how? Are you going to tell me where Montfort is holding Serena?"

"I can't do that," St. John replied. "He made me, so I'm stuck with being loyal to him, and that extends to keeping his secrets. I just wanted to let you know that I don't really agree with what he's doing."

Silas' eyes narrowed. The vampire's expression was open, almost pleading, but Silas didn't believe him for a second. One of the fundamental rules about vampires was that they—to pardon the mixed metaphor—ran in packs. No dissent, no disagreement with the master who had made them. Loyalty was hardwired into their natures. A vampire could no more go up against his master than he could walk in daylight. "I hope you won't be offended if I tell you that I don't believe a word you're saying."

"Fair enough. I probably wouldn't believe me, either." St. John paused then, his brow furrowing, as though he wrestled inwardly with what he was allowed to say versus what he wanted to say. "But I think Lucius is going too far with this whole thing. He—"

"He hasn't hurt her, has he?" Silas growled, and stepped forward.

"No," the vampire replied. To his credit, he didn't flinch...but then, he probably knew he could be well away from Silas' reach before the *gula* had a chance to blink. "That is, not exactly."

The mere notion that any harm might have come to the woman he loved made Silas want to reach over and shake the truth out of Michael St. John. "What do you mean, 'not exactly'?"

"I mean he—" St. John broke off there, running a nervous hand through his hair.

That gesture in itself only increased Silas' worry tenfold. Vampires by definition were not nervous types, their self-assurance almost guaranteed because of the powers their undead natures granted them. What the hell was going on here? "He what?"

"He's making plans...based on her visions. He says it's all going to change very soon. But it's more than that. I think he wants her."

"Wants her blood?"

"No. He wants *her*. Like a mortal man wants a woman. I haven't seen him act like this before. Granted, I haven't been with him as long as Tristan and Leticia have, but—"

All of Silas' anger and worry erupted into a volcano of rage. He didn't even stop to think as one hand shot out and caught Michael St. John by the throat. The vampire let out a startled gasp, as if shocked that a *gula* had been able to get the drop on him. "Tell me where," Silas rasped. "*Tell me.*"

"I—I can't," St. John choked out. "You know I can't. But...." He paused, then said, "Just know all is not as it seems. Look with something besides your eyes."

"What the hell is that supposed to mean?"

"That's all I can say."

The vampire twisted in Silas' grasp, slithering away as if he had been made of the same quicksilver compound the *gula* used to dispatch his kind. At once he was just a shadow, gone before Silas could even attempt to grab him again.

Damn it.

He remained there, staring at the spot where Michael St. John had stood only a moment earlier.

*Look with something besides your eyes.*

Scowling, Silas turned away and unlocked the gate.

∽

I slept in fits and starts, terrified that Lucius would return at any moment, would slide into bed with me, do as he willed. He didn't, though. The house remained silent and still around me, until at last I opened my eyes and saw faint traces of sunlight slipping in past the heavy crimson velvet curtains.

I'd survived the night.

Even though I knew the sun was up, and therefore the vampire had been rendered impotent until night fell once again, I couldn't relax. I pushed myself out of bed, and went into the bathroom and showered as quickly as I could, not bothering to wash my hair. In less than twenty minutes, I was cleaned up and dressed, and not as worried about a semivive barging in with my breakfast. If Lucius even intended to feed me. It was entirely possible that he'd decided it would be better to withhold my meals for a while, to see if he could use hunger to control me.

Well, that wasn't going to happen. My stomach ached from emptiness, but I vowed to ignore it.

I went over to the door that separated our two

rooms and stood there for a long moment, not sure I had the courage to turn the knob, thinking that even if I did, the door must surely be locked. At last, however, I put my hand on the doorknob of chased brass—obviously another antique—and gingerly moved it to the right.

No resistance. The door creaked open a few inches, revealing utter blackness.

My breath seemed to halt in my chest, but I made myself push the door open enough that I could slip through, even as I fumbled with my free hand to find a light switch. There it was, cool under my fingertips.

I flicked it on.

The crystal and brass chandelier overhead flared into life. I saw a room much larger than mine, with an enormous Persian carpet covering the entire floor. Heavy velvet curtains hid the windows, but since absolutely no light came through, I guessed that underneath the drapes, the windows must have blackout blinds, or simply be boarded up. Despite the illumination from the chandelier, large sections of the room remained in shadow, the light not sufficient to cover such a huge area.

Across the room was a large canopy bed, hung with more black velvet. Lying on top of that bed was Lucius Montfort.

He wore a black silk dressing gown, the kind of thing Victorian gentlemen might have favored back in the day. His near-white hair was spread out across the pillowcase, nearly indistinguishable from the pale cotton fabric, and his hands were folded on top of his chest. I didn't seem them rise and fall, so I didn't know if he breathed. Actually, it had always been difficult for me to tell whether any of the vampires needed to breathe, or whether they only let out a huff or gasp or something similar at those times when they wanted to appear human.

I approached the bed and stared down at him. His sharply etched, pale features might as well have been carved from marble, except for the heavy dark brows and the dark lashes that now lay closed against his cheeks.

If I wrapped my fingers around his throat, would he suffocate and die? Or did I need Silas' quicksilver compound, or possibly a handy stake? Maybe one of the legs from the little marble-topped table I spied over against the window....

"No closer," came a deep voice, and I startled and stepped back.

From the shadows on the other side of the bed emerged a semivive I had never seen before, a hulk of a man who had to be at least six and a half feet tall. His flat, dark eyes met mine. "You will come no closer."

"Okay," I said, raising my hands to show they were empty, that I didn't mean any harm. Well, truthfully, I'd meant all kinds of harm. I just didn't have the tools to make that threat a reality. "I—I just wanted to see him."

The semivive watched me narrowly. I realized that he must be Lucius' bodyguard, his only task to watch over his master while he slept away the daylight hours. That was probably why I hadn't seen the half-dead man patrolling the grounds. He had a much more important duty to carry out here.

"You have seen him," the semivive said. "Now go back to your room."

"But—"

One step toward me, the menace clear in his stance. "Go back."

"All right, all right."

I beat an ignominious retreat, feeling the eyes of the semivive on my back the entire time. As I closed the door behind me, I realized why the door had been left unlocked. Lucius might come and go as he pleased, but he certainly had nothing to fear from me. Not with that hulk guarding his bedside.

Since I didn't have anything better to do, I went over to the window and looked outside. The day was bright and sunny, not a cloud to be seen. My stomach grumbled, but I ignored it. In a minute, I'd get some water to appease my increasing hunger, but for now I only wanted to watch the sunlit world outside, to remind myself that I was still part of that world, no matter what Lucius Montfort had tried to do to me. I might be trapped in this mausoleum of a house, but I was still alive. That had to count for something.

Of course, being alive only got me so far. This room had been locked down tight as a drum. I didn't have any way of escaping. At least, none presented themselves at the moment.

A semivive walked past, under the window. A few seconds later, he came right back, following the same path. Obviously, someone had been assigned guard duty. Even if I was crazy enough to try breaking the window with a lamp and then jumping out, all I would do was land in the waiting arms of one of Lucius Montfort's minions.

The house creaked slightly, the only sound I could hear. It was going to be a very long day.

I got up and went to the door that led into the hallway, touched the knob. Of course it wouldn't budge. I'd known it wouldn't, but I had to try. Because I literally had nothing else to do, I walked over to the closet and flicked on the light switch. This closet wasn't quite as large as the one in my former room, but it was still a walk-in style, with drawers built into one end and a variety of shelves above the clothing racks, probably to hold purses and such. My meager assortment of clothing looked very sparse indeed in that space.

As I glanced upward, though, the overhead light gleamed on gold lettering from one of those shelves. I frowned, not sure what I was looking at. Then I realized the lettering was stamped onto the spines of a set of books—the copy of *Persuasion* I had been reading, and the rest of the Austen oeuvre.

Tears almost started to my eyes. Yes, things were just about as bad as they possibly could be, but if I had those books to keep me company, then maybe I'd be able to survive the day.

I took down *Persuasion* and went back out into the bedroom. After I laid it down on the bed, I picked up my water glass and filled it from the bathroom faucet, then climbed onto the bed. Reading would let me escape for a while at least. I couldn't quite prevent my mind from churning away, wondering what Lucius Montfort planned to do next, trying to think of what might be happening in the world outside. Surely by now Jackson and his family would be here to share in my parents' grief. And Silas must be going crazy, trying to find me, using all the power of the Watchers to track me down.

Problem was, I didn't know if it would be enough. The vampire master seemed to be at least two steps ahead no matter what I—or anyone else—did.

Through it all, the utter wrongness of the future I'd glimpsed made me wonder how we all could have gone down that path—my brother, myself, the world in general. Never had I questioned Jackson's principles, but I couldn't help questioning them now. How could he have handed over the safety of his people to help a monster like Lucius Montfort?

The visions weren't giving me the whole picture,

but then, they never really did. All they had ever provided was quick-moving snapshots, images I was left to interpret. But I couldn't connect the dots this time. I couldn't get from where I was now...hating Lucius with every ounce of my being...to being his willing accomplice and lover.

Maybe that didn't matter. Maybe it was important that I now knew what was supposed to happen. If I had seen the future, that must mean I had some way of changing it. After all, I had changed the futures of the people whose lives I had saved.

Maybe this time it was all about saving my own.

# CHAPTER FIFTEEN

ANYTIME ONE OF THE WATCHERS HAD AN encounter with a vampire, they were required to log a report, although Silas hadn't done so formally after his last meeting with Michael St. John, knowing that Joseph would handle the reporting for him. Once he'd triple-checked the locks on his door and the security system—a futile maneuver, really, since no vampire could come where he wasn't invited—Silas poured himself a glass of water and took his phone into the living room. For a moment, he wondered if he should turn on the fireplace, try to cheer himself up by watching the flickering blue flames. But no. The last time he'd had a fire here was when Serena had stayed the night. It would be far too much of a reminder of those few precious hours they'd spent in one another's arms. He wouldn't torture himself like that.

Instead, he stared out the window with stony eyes,

looking at the glittering nightscape of Los Angeles without really seeing it. He pushed the entry on his contacts list to connect with headquarters in Humboldt. At this hour, he wasn't sure if Joseph would still be on duty, or whether he might have already been relieved by Felix, who usually kept watch during the overnight hours. Felix was only a year older than Silas; they'd shared several classes in the small school for *gula* children on the Humboldt compound. In general, he tended to be in a better mood than Joseph most of the time, but at the moment, Silas thought he would have preferred Joseph's jaundiced view of the world.

But it was Felix who answered the call. "What news, Silas?"

"A run-in with Michael St. John. He was... behaving oddly."

"Oddly how?"

"I'm not entirely sure. It was almost as though he wanted to help me, which isn't exactly in character."

Felix chuckled. "I'd say that was decidedly out of character. Did he provide any information?"

"Not in so many words. I could sense that he wanted to tell me more than he did, but was unable to because of his loyalty to Lucius."

"Sounds like a grudging loyalty at best."

"True. It certainly isn't a loyalty that's given by choice."

A short pause, and then Felix said, "We're fairly

certain that Michael was made after Lucius came to California, correct?"

"As far as we've been able to tell. There was no evidence of an association between them back in New York."

"Well, sometimes the younger fledglings can act out, especially if they were made against their will. After a few decades they settle down, but if St. John really didn't become a vampire until after Lucius Montfort settled in the Pasadena area, then it's understandable that he may still be somewhat rebellious. My guess is that his behavior had a lot less to do with helping you than annoying his master."

That did seem to be the most likely explanation. Even so, St. John's words haunted Silas. Vampires generally didn't desire anything except blood and power. But Lucius wanted Serena. Michael St. John had sounded fairly emphatic about that point, even if he hadn't provided much else in the way of useful information.

Back at the reception, Silas himself had noted an odd gleam in the master vampire's eyes as he looked at Serena. At the time, that strange flicker of unnatural interest had seemed more like a desire to possess the psychic for himself. But what if her powers were only part of her attraction for the vampire?

She was very beautiful. Silas had understood that truth from the first second he had laid eyes upon her. Lucius Montfort, however, shouldn't have cared about such superficial physical qualities in a human being. When vampire masters made their fledglings, they did tend to choose, for lack of a better term, pretty people, simply because they didn't want to spend decades or even centuries with those they didn't find aesthetically pleasing. But to desire a human because of their beauty…no, this development made very little sense at all.

And that worried Silas the most. Because if he couldn't understand Lucius Montfort's reasoning, then he would have an even more difficult time coming up with a way to thwart the vampire's plans.

He didn't want to admit such things to Felix. No doubt the story of Silas' involvement with Serena had already gone around the Humboldt compound, but to speak of it openly was only to invite comment. Felix had no partner, had once declared he preferred to direct his energies toward making sure that their little community continued to run smoothly. It was difficult, after all, to go out into the human world and attempt to find a woman who might be open to becoming one with a *gula*. It was even more difficult when one considered the odds of such relationships failing. Oftentimes, a woman would rather give up her *gula* partner than her human child, and so would leave, taking the baby with her. Even for couples who were blessed with *gula* offspring, the way was not easy. Their love had to be very strong for a woman to live in such isolation, to never speak of who she was with or that she had borne a child. The Watchers had to remain utterly secret, or their long history of guarding humanity and protecting it as best they could would be in jeopardy.

"From what I've seen of him, St. John appears to be something of a trickster," Silas said at last. "So it is possible that he was only toying with me. The only thing he said that appeared to be of any value was that everything was not as it seemed, that I should try to see with something other than my eyes."

"That still sounds rather cryptic, and not very helpful."

"True. Probably just more of his mind games. Anyway, I wanted to report our meeting. He spoke with me in the parking lot at my complex, which means the vampires must know where I live."

"You suspected that anyway."

Which he did. Just as the Watchers kept track of the vampires, the vampires did their best to keep tabs on where their enemies might have established bases. Occupational hazard, and one Silas had been warned about when he first settled into the loft. The only upside was that, few as the *gula* might be, they still far outnumbered their vampire prey. The undead tended to be intensely territorial, and so Silas knew there wasn't another coven within a radius of several hundred miles. One in Las Vegas for sure, where the nocturnal habits of the vampires would be of little note, and others in San Francisco, Seattle, and Portland, but that was it for the western part of the country. In general, they did not like the heat and hard, bright skies of the desert Southwest, and so no covens had been established in Arizona or New Mexico or Texas.

"Still, it was...unsettling. Anyhow, that's my report. Anything new come up that I should know about?"

"Not very much. Serena Quinn's brother and her family got in at LAX earlier today and are now at their home in Claremont. Standard Secret Service detail, which means the vampires will probably leave them alone."

Yes, the last thing Lucius Montfort would want was a confrontation with federal agents. Jackson Quinn's involvement in all this remained a mystery to Silas; more and more it appeared that the master vampire's true focus was Serena, but then why would she have had a vision of her brother on the campaign trail? True, not all of her visions were related, but....

"That's good," Silas replied. He knew he sounded distracted—how could he not be, after hearing what Michael St. John had to say about Lucius and Serena?

*He wants her.*

The only good part about St. John's remark was that it seemed as though nothing had yet happened between the Serena and Lucius. For whatever reason, the master vampire appeared to be holding back...for now. Silas couldn't count on that particular state of affairs to last indefinitely, which lent even more urgency to his search for Serena.

"And the medical examiner went ahead and released Vanessa Quinn's body to the family. Whatever additional information they were looking for, it doesn't sound as if they found it. So the funeral is still scheduled for Saturday."

"Where?" Silas asked. He didn't know for sure what he might do with that particular piece of information, but better to file it away, just in case.

"Forest Lawn—Glendale. Four o'clock. Then a reception at the Quinn house in San Marino." Felix paused there for a moment. "You planning on crashing it or something?"

"No." *Not unless I have to....*

"Good. Since the Pasadena P.D. has been circulating a description of you in conjunction with Serena Quinn's disappearance, better to lie low."

Thanks to Raoul Ortiz, Silas already knew all about that. He decided not to mention his connection to the detective, however. Even if Joseph had filled Felix in on that particular detail, Silas didn't see any point in bringing it up, just in case.

"That was my plan. I'm still working on one lead, though it's nothing that involves the Quinns directly."

"Still trying to track down the lair?"

"Yes. There's something I want to double-check tomorrow, when it's light."

Another pause. Then Felix said, "Remember to call for support before you do anything drastic."

"I'm not planning on doing anything drastic."

"Still. You know the rules. And with David and Emanuel gone, your closest *gula* backup is Malachi. He's currently in San Francisco."

Which wasn't very close at all, even though San Francisco was only a short hop by air to Los Angeles. It was all right. He'd just begun to have the vaguest beginnings of a hunch, nothing that merited pulling Malachi away from his current post in the northern part of the state. If Silas decided to take direct action, he'd make sure to ask for backup first.

"I will. That's all for now."

"Thanks for the report. Stay vigilant."

"Stay vigilant," Silas responded, and ended the call.

He set down his phone on the coffee table and stared out the window. A magnificent full moon was just beginning to rise over the hills to the east. With the skies so clear, that moon would do a good job of illuminating the city.

Unfortunately, the brightness of a full moon wasn't enough to prevent vampires from going on the hunt.

I actually fell asleep toward the end of the afternoon. Maybe it was hunger, or boredom, or simply overwhelming, soul-sucking weariness, but at one point my head dropped forward, and *Northanger Abbey*—I'd finished *Persuasion* around three o'clock—slid off my lap and onto the bed.

"Serena."

The voice was pitched low, almost tentative. For one brief, glorious moment, I thought maybe it was Silas come to wake me, that this whole episode of being trapped in Lucius Montfort's home was only a terrible dream brought on by a bad combination of beer and sake and sushi.

No such luck, though. I opened my eyes to see the master vampire standing next to my bed, one hand stretched partway toward me, as if he'd begun to reach out and grasp my shoulder to shake me awake.

Thank God I'd woken up enough to realize where I was...and to draw away, putting a little more space between us. He hadn't been able to touch me.

"What do you want?"

One eyebrow lifted slightly, but his tone was mild enough as he replied, "There's no need to be rude. I thought you might want something to eat."

"Yes, I thought that same thing seven or eight hours ago," I retorted. Since it didn't seem like a very good idea to remain lying on the bed, not with him looming over me like that, I moved over to the edge opposite from where he stood and pushed myself to a standing position.

"An oversight. Or rather, I forgot to inform my

semivives that they should bring you your meals here. It was not done out of malice, I assure you."

As far as I was concerned, just about everything Lucius Montfort did was out of malice. I wouldn't bother to point that out, though. An argument might have been morally satisfying, but right then I was more concerned about getting something into my desperately empty stomach. I was so hungry, I could barely think straight.

"If you say so," I replied.

"Then come with me." His hand was still halfway outstretched, as if he expected me to take it.

Not in a million years. I ignored the gesture, and went to the door and waited there. After a brief pause, during which his silvery eyes narrowed, he seemed to shrug and came to meet me by the door. He pulled a key out of the pocket of his black trousers, and inserted it into the lock.

"This way."

I followed him down the hall and to the staircase. Different hallway, same stairs, since my new cell was in the other wing of the house. Quite possibly there were more than two wings. The place seemed enormous, and I hadn't been able to see enough of it during my abortive escape attempt to know for sure how much ground it really covered.

The downstairs seemed the same, though. We bypassed the dining room and went into the small game room where I'd shared my first meal with

Lucius. Was that a good or a bad thing? True, the last time I'd been in the large dining room, he'd drugged me just so he could get me to spill all my secrets about the vision I'd had of him and me together. So maybe it was better that he'd brought me here, although in some ways I would have preferred the more impersonal nature of the bigger room.

The round game table in the corner had a tablecloth laid over it, and two places set. In between the two place settings was a plate with neat stacks of sourdough bread, and a little bowl with pats of butter next to it.

My stomach growled, and Lucius smiled. "Help yourself. The rest of the food will be in momentarily."

Ravenous hunger had very little of scruples about it. I hurried over to the table and picked up a piece of bread, then took the knife from the nearest place setting and spread some butter on top. Nothing had ever tasted as good as that simple piece of bread and butter — or so it seemed right then.

Still smiling, Lucius came over to the table as well and lifted the bottle of wine that had been sitting off to one side. "Still sealed," he said, as he retrieved the corkscrew that had been placed next to it, and used the small knife attachment to cut off the foil before he started in on the cork itself. "I didn't want you to think there would be a repeat of last night."

"How gracious of you," I replied, picking up another piece of bread. This time I ate a little more slowly, but I could tell it was going to take more than bread to fill my stomach.

"It seemed the least I could do." The cork came out with a slight *pop,* and he leaned over so he could pour some wine into the glass nearest my place setting.

Even though I'd seen him open the bottle myself, I still sent the glass a dubious look—partly because I still wasn't sure I could trust the wine inside, and partly because I knew that having any alcohol without something more substantial than bread to soak it up would be a recipe for disaster. However, in the next moment, the door opened, and a semivive with a serving cart came in and set down a large green-glazed bowl in the center of the table. A peek inside told me it contained spaghetti and meatballs.

"Something simple and hearty," Lucius said. He nodded at the semivive, who deposited a second bowl on the table, this one with salad inside, before he took the serving cart and went back out. "Will that work for you?"

Of course it would. I wondered if he'd gotten this food from Antonio's again, or someplace else. Not that there was any shortage of Italian restaurants in Pasadena where he could have gotten the takeout. "It's fine," I said, and pulled out my chair so I could sit down.

Lucius followed suit. He still wore a slight smile on his lips, which seemed to indicate that my shortness amused him more than anything else. After settling his napkin on his lap, he dished up some salad and spaghetti for me, and then some for himself.

I had to admit that it was going to be rather intriguing to watch a vampire try to eat spaghetti. Would he twirl it around his fork, or cut it up so he wouldn't have to worry about the long strands of noodles splattering sauce on his face?

The former, it appeared—with casual ease, he twisted a decent amount of pasta around his fork, and put it in his mouth. I decided I'd better do the same. The meat sauce was thick and rich, almost enough on its own, even without the meatballs. Of course, I'd eat those, too. Right then, I was so hungry I probably would have eaten spaghetti served by Satan himself.

Then again, when it came to Lucius Montfort, one might argue that he and the devil were one and the same.

After I'd had a few mouthfuls, I allowed myself a sip of the wine. Chianti. I had to hope that fava beans weren't on the menu.

"Better?" the vampire asked.

"A little," I said cautiously.

"Any more visions today?"

"No." Well, technically that was true. The second vision—the one of him pleasuring me in the back seat of the limo—had come the night before.

"I was informed that you paid me a visit."

Damn. I supposed I'd been hoping that the hulking semivive who served as his bodyguard during the daylight hours wouldn't be inclined to tell tales. So much for that notion. "I was curious."

A tilt of the dark brows, so striking in contrast to his pale hair. "Curious?"

"I wanted to see if the reality was like the movies. If you didn't want me coming in there, you should have locked the door."

He lifted his wine glass and sipped at the Chianti. "True. Perhaps I was inviting you in. What did you think? Disappointed there wasn't a coffin?"

"No," I said. "Silas told me that real vampires don't sleep in coffins. So I was expecting that part."

"Silas," Lucius repeated. The glint of amusement disappeared from his eyes, and he sent me a considering glance. "I would prefer we not speak of him."

Some imp goaded me to ask, "Jealous?"

I'd expected the vampire to say I was being foolish, or to tilt an ironic eyebrow in my direction. To my surprise—and discomfort—he returned, "What would you say if I told you that I am?"

A chill inched its way down my spine. "I'd say you were messing with me."

"Oh, no. I am not messing with you." He put down the wine glass he held. "May I ask you a serious question?"

"Are you implying your last question wasn't serious?"

A corner of his mouth twitched. "Touché. No, it was serious as well. But something has been preying on my mind, and so I must ask. Tell me, Serena—would you be so vehemently opposed to me if you had never met Silas? If you hadn't—however foolishly—given your heart to him?"

"There's nothing foolish about it," I protested. All right, on the surface, there were probably about fifty reasons why my budding relationship with Silas would seem crazy to anyone who didn't know him. He wasn't even human...we'd known each other for only a little more than a week...any woman entering into a romance with one of his kind was setting herself up for a really good chance at heartbreak. And yet, none of that seemed to matter to me, because I'd seen into his soul. He was honorable and strong and loving—everything Lucius Montfort was not.

"You say that, Serena, but I wonder." Lucius retrieved a piece of bread but did not butter it, instead tearing it in two and then two again, so he might put one of those smaller pieces in his mouth. After chewing thoughtfully, he went on, "What does he have to offer you? At best, a life away from everyone you know and love, a life lived in secret. The very real possibility of having to give up a beloved child. Is Silas Drake worth all that?"

I didn't even hesitate. "Yes."

Lucius chuckled. "You put on a very brave front. But I must ask you again—if there were no Silas, would you be so violently opposed to me?"

"I don't know," I said. "Why don't you tell me how

many people you've killed over the years, and I'll think about it."

He went still then, although I noticed the way his fingers, currently resting on the base of his wine glass, curled up, as if in anger. "I did what I must to survive."

I glanced around the room. "It looks like you're doing a little bit better than merely 'surviving.' And besides, from what Silas told me, you don't even need to hunt anymore. Not really. You could just set yourself up with regular deliveries from the local blood bank and call it a day."

His lip curled. "That is true…up to a point. Unfortunately, back when I was made, there were no such things as blood banks. Even now, asking that a vampire take his nourishment solely from such a source is like asking you to spend the rest of your life consuming baby food. It might keep you alive, but there is certainly nothing in it to satisfy the soul."

"Well, there's your answer," I said. "Because I couldn't possibly be with someone who thought of taking human life as something to be justified, merely because blood tastes better that way. Besides," I went on, trying to ignore Lucius' increasing frown, "I'm trying to figure out where this strange attraction of yours comes from. I'm human, aren't I? To you, shouldn't I be just another meal?"

"No," he replied at once. "That is the strangest thing, isn't it? I should be looking at you that way…

and yet I cannot. Perhaps it is your gift, which makes you far more than an ordinary woman. Perhaps it is your beauty, or perhaps it is a combination of the two."

His silvery eyes bored into mine, and I found myself looking down at the neglected food on my plate. There had been something almost naked, pleading, about his expression. In that moment, he looked more human than I had ever seen him.

Again, a little shiver went over me, only this time I couldn't really identify the emotion behind it. Fear? Worry? An odd echo of the attraction I'd felt in the vision I'd had of him?

No, it couldn't be that. Anything but that.

"Let's say we're being academic here," I said. I did my best to make sure my tone was cool, detached, but I honestly didn't know if I was at all successful. My mind churned. I hated even the possibility that some horrible, hidden part of my soul might feel attracted to the vampire. I forced myself to go on. "Let's say there is no Silas, or let's say that a *gula* doesn't have much to offer a woman. What would you have to offer me?"

Lucius smiled then, a real smile, instead of a smirk or that ironic lift at the corners of his mouth which annoyed me so. "I could give you everything, Serena. *Everything.* That is what your vision has told me. There have been theories, notes scribbled and handed down over the centuries. A way to keep the best of being a vampire, and discard all the petty inconveniences of such an existence. Foolish dreams, one might have thought, but now I know they are not dreams at all. They are hope."

"What theories?" I asked, horrified and yet somehow intrigued by what he had just said. "What are you talking about?"

"You saw me walking in the daylight. You saw me selling immortality to those humans who could afford it. The theories said that there are certain elements in vampire blood which could be used to give humans long life, rather than turning them into vampires...or into semivives. Just a different distillation of the same compounds. Likewise, it has long been thought that there must be a way to take certain factors in human blood and use them to make a vampire's existence more tolerable. But because we must live in hiding, must keep ourselves away from anyone with the expertise to help us, these theories have only remained theories." With his free hand, he reached over and took mine. I wanted to pull away from those cold fingers, but I made myself stay where I was. He needed to keep talking so I could learn more of his plan.

"And now...?" I prompted.

"Now you have shown me what needs to happen. Your brother will be President, Serena. As such, he will be able to give us access to all the scientists and laboratories we need. Of course he will help, because who would pass up such a chance for immortality?

Such power would make him not only the leader of this country, but of the entire world."

No, Jackson would never do such a thing. And yet...I'd seen it. In my vision, I'd seen him, secure in his power, surrounded by those who were all too willing to curry favor in exchange for the priceless gift of immortality—or at least, very long life.

But because I'd seen the vision, and now knew what Lucius' plans might entail, I also had a better idea of why he needed to be stopped. How was an entirely different matter, unfortunately. By talking to Jackson, stopping this entire crazy train before it could even leave the station. That seemed simple enough, except for the minor detail of my being Lucius' prisoner.

*Then you have to stop being his prisoner,* I thought then. *And there's only one way to do that. You know what you have to do. You have to make him think you're going along with all this.*

Although it killed me to do so, I tightened my fingers around his, and did my best to smile. "That sounds intriguing."

Again he was still, his eyes searching mine. Thank God that Lucius, for all his vampiric powers, wasn't able to read minds. Very slowly, he took my hand, lifted it to his lips. I couldn't help shuddering slightly, but I had to pray he thought it was only a shiver of arousal, or anticipation.

Then he got up from his chair, his hand remaining

on mine, so I had to stand up as well. We were very close. If I'd been standing that close to a normal man —or Silas—I should have felt something of his body heat. Now there was nothing, except maybe the faintest gust of breath as he let out a sigh.

He pulled me close, lowered his head so his lips touched mine. At least now I knew that his kiss wouldn't be utterly repulsive, would taste only of the wine he'd just consumed, and not the blood of all those people he'd killed.

The kiss lasted a long time, endless seconds during which I made myself think of Silas, pretending it was him kissing me, and not Lucius Montfort. I had to submit to that kiss, because I knew now that my best chance at saving myself, at saving the world, was to make him think he'd won me over. I had to hope he would stop with a kiss; despite my best efforts, my mind went back to that vision of us in the back of the limo, of the way he'd so easily been able to bring me to orgasm.

I sort of doubted I'd respond that way if he took me upstairs now.

Finally he released me, stepped back a little so he could gaze down into my face. I stared up at him as guilelessly as I could, praying that I looked flushed and aroused, like any woman would who'd just been given a lingering kiss from the man she wanted.

Long, pale fingers brushed a strand of hair back

from my forehead. "Oh, Serena," he said. "I can't wait to give you the world."

# CHAPTER SIXTEEN

HE'D WOKEN BEFORE DAWN, HIS SLEEP FITFUL. BUT Silas knew there was no point in going back to San Rafael before nine o'clock at the earliest; before then, there would be too many people leaving for work, too many chances for someone to see what he was up to.

A slim chance. The slimmest. And yet he knew he had to try. If this didn't work, well, he supposed he could attempt to convince Raoul Ortiz one more time that having a helicopter fly over the neighborhood wouldn't be all that disruptive, that it was the only way to find the elusive lair of the vampires.

In the meantime, Silas showered, made a bigger breakfast than he wanted to eat, perused the day's headlines on his laptop. Nothing wonderful about the news, but nothing earth-shatteringly bad, either. The coverage of Vanessa Quinn's death had already disappeared, along with the commentary on Serena's disappearance. Maybe there would be something else tomorrow, when the actual funeral took place. He could only imagine that the papers and the local news would want to cover Senator Quinn attending the services for his sister. Probably the tabloid sites, too—they loved it when tragedy struck the famous. More clicks, more ad revenue.

*Ghouls,* Silas thought, even though he knew it was just part of their job. When someone as prominent as Jackson Quinn was associated with any kind of a tragedy—or a crime, or both, as was the case here—then the press, both reputable and disreputable, was bound to cover the story.

At last nine-thirty rolled around. Silas exited his loft and sent a suspicious glance around the grounds of the complex, even though he knew there was no chance of seeing Michael St. John or any of his cronies at this hour of the morning. True, the vampires could have sent a semivive to tail him, but he didn't think they'd be that transparent. They knew as well as he that a semivive could easily be outsmarted, left behind to wonder where his quarry had disappeared.

The parking lot was empty as Silas climbed into his truck. Overhead, the sky was a half-hearted blue-gray, the sun partially obscured by a thick marine layer. No real rain, but still enough to make the world seem dismal, robbed of its color.

But traffic was light as he headed out of downtown and drove up toward Pasadena. Even so, he tapped his fingers impatiently on the steering wheel, wishing the narrow, winding freeway allowed him to go faster than a cautious sixty-five miles an hour. Soon enough, though, he spotted the sign for Marisol Avenue, the exit that would let him to come up into the San Rafael area from underneath, taking a route he usually didn't follow. Here, too, he didn't see many cars, most of the residents of these neighborhoods already safely at work.

The houses grew larger, their grounds more well-kept. He turned off onto San Rafael Avenue and intentionally overshot his destination, parking three houses down from the big Mediterranean mansion that had begun to obsess him. As he walked toward the property, he heard the sound of a leaf blower.

It wasn't coming from the place where he was headed, but rather the house next door, a large Colonial-style structure set well back from the street, with extensive lawns to help maintain that distance. Standing on the sidewalk and blowing leaves and other debris into the gutter was a young Hispanic man —not much more than a boy, really, probably at least ten years younger than Silas himself. He wore protective headphones and clearly was focused on his work.

For a moment, Silas considered passing him by. After all, one of the strictures he lived by was not to attract attention, and to engage with the public as little as possible. However, the gardener clearly worked for the people who lived next door to what might be the vampires' lair, which meant the young man might have some useful information.

Silas stopped a few feet away from the gardener and pointed at his headphones. At once he turned off the blower and removed the headphones, his expression curious but not particularly wary.

"Yeah?"

"Sorry," Silas said. "I just wanted to ask you something. Have you worked here for a while?"

"About a year. I had to take over for my dad when his back went out."

Perfect English. Good. Silas' Spanish was pretty rusty, and you just never knew until you opened a dialogue whether you were talking with a third-generation Angeleno or someone who'd arrived in the country only a few months earlier. He glanced over at the Mediterranean monstrosity next door. "You know the neighbors?"

The young man chuckled. "Nah, man, they don't talk to anyone. I've seen a couple of cars coming and going—they have a big black Range Rover and an Audi SUV. A dark gray Mercedes, and a red Porsche."

"Do you ever see who's driving?"

"A couple of different guys. They don't look related." The gardener shot a sideways look at the house in question. "I've wondered whether that house is owned by a cult or something."

"Really?" Silas asked, his pulse beginning to speed up slightly, although he told himself it was far too early to get excited. The house could simply be owned by a group of eccentrics. "What makes you say that?"

"Couple of times, I seen them come out to get the mail. Their eyes are...weird." A lift of the young man's thin shoulders. The blower dangled, neglected, from one hand. "If my *abuela* was able to see them, she'd probably make the sign of the cross and tell me to stay away, that they're possessed. I don't know about that, but something ain't right over there."

Possessed. Semivives who had been in the service of their vampire masters for years or even decades began to look that way, their eyes dead, seeing nothing but what their masters wished for them to see in order to carry out their duties. "You ever see anyone else?"

"One time I did. I was working late, later than I usually would, because the alternator in my truck died and I had to wait for my cousin to come over with a replacement so he could help me fix it. So anyway, it was almost dark by the time I was finishing up over here, doing my last sweep, getting ready to throw bags of trash in the back of the truck. Out from the driveway came the Mercedes—one of those big ones, expensive. The Porsche was following it." The young man stopped there, something almost frightened in his expression. "I couldn't see inside, because the windows were so tinted. Illegal kind of tinted, if you know what I mean. Me and my bros, if any of us had tinting like that, you know we'd get pulled over and be lucky to just get a fix-it ticket. But

I doubt any of the people around here have to worry about that."

No, they probably didn't. Silas gave what he hoped was a sympathetic nod. "Did you see which way the cars went?"

"They turned left, so I guess that meant they were headed toward L.A. or something. I didn't want to look as if I was paying too much attention. I was glad they were gone, though."

"Why?"

Another shrug. This time, the gardener looked over his shoulder at the house where he was supposed to be working, as if making sure that no one would come out and ask him why he stood there talking to a stranger rather than finishing up his job. "Just a bad feeling. My *abuela* would say I felt someone walking on my grave. The guys who came out to get the mail were bad enough, but...." The young man trailed off and then shot Silas a deprecating grin, as though trying to disclaim what he was about to say. "Whatever was in that car...it was evil."

What could he say to that? If Lucius Montfort and the other vampires truly did live next door, then what the gardener had sensed as their cars drove past really was evil, plain and simple. Probably not a direct threat, because vampires weren't stupid enough to foul their own nests. They'd hunt miles away from wherever they were holed up.

"Thanks," Silas told the young man. "I won't keep you any longer."

"You a cop or something? That why you're asking about them?"

"No. I'm...trying to help a friend."

A shrug. "Well...good luck, I guess." He put the headphones back on and started up the blower again, effectively preventing any further conversation.

Which was fine. Silas had heard everything he needed to hear. Time to do something about it.

He turned and began to head toward the property next door. When he reached its boundary, he stopped, thinking that perhaps it would be better to attempt his experiment here, where he wasn't in direct line of sight of the house. In this location, he had the advantage of being partially hidden by a tasteful grouping of pine and fir trees.

Even though he'd resolved to do this, he stood there for a moment, taking in a breath and steeling himself for what might come next. Michael St. John's words echoed in his ears.

*Look with something besides your eyes.*

Silas planned to do that very thing.

He studied the fence before him. Tall, but not so tall that he couldn't reach the top if he needed to. The lower three feet were made up of ornamental stacked stone, very attractive. The top portion of the fence was black wrought iron, each rectangular pole topped by a sphere of metal.

Another breath, and he shut his eyes. Reached out and wrapped his hands around two of the fence poles. They felt exactly as they should—cool metal, the edges of each pole hard against his palms. Eyes still shut, he hauled himself upward so he stood on the lower stone portion of the fence. Now he would be able to grasp the tops of the poles, which should be smooth, rounded.

His fingers inched upward, closed on something sharp, pointed. Pulse accelerating, he moved one of his hands over the top of the pole it held. A hard point at the top, and two curved pieces underneath. Not the sphere his eyes had told him should be there, but something very different.

A fleur-de-lis.

Lucius had been hiding in plain sight all along.

How he had managed it, Silas didn't know. But the master vampire was very old, and had only grown in strength and cunning while he accumulated years as surely as he accumulated victims. Vampires had always been able to use darkness as a shield, to work in tricks and illusions. Silas had never heard of an illusion this elaborate, but now it made perfect sense. This was the correct plot of land, the only one where Lucius' lair could have been located. The vampire had simply made sure that anyone walking or driving by would see what he wanted them to see. Eyes could be deceived. A sense of touch…apparently not.

Silas murmured a silent thank-you to Michael St.

John for his cryptic piece of advice. What the younger vampire intended by helping one of his mortal enemies, Silas didn't know, but he'd save those questions for later.

Right now, he had to save Serena. Yes, he'd told Felix he would wait, would call for backup, but the urgency that had driven him back here continued to drive him now. The thought of waiting hours for Malachi to fly down from San Francisco and assist him was absolutely unbearable. Besides, it was daytime. Silas would have semivives to confront, true, but his odds were infinitely better during the hours the vampires were asleep.

Still holding the decorative tops of the poles, he swung himself up and over to the other side. An observer might have been astonished by this display of acrobatic prowess, but Silas barely thought about it, just as he'd long ago accepted all the abilities his *gula* blood had given him. He might look human, but he could accomplish physical feats usually reserved for Olympic gymnasts.

Or runners. Once he'd dropped down onto the ground on the other side of the fence, he quickly surveyed his surroundings. The trees here sheltered him, and there were more past this small planting, the gardens thick with them. Well, Serena had said that a number of trees clustered around the house in her vision, protecting the inhabitants of the mansion from prying eyes. Now they would do the same for him.

He sprinted from the cover of the nearest trees, moving as fast as he could. Still slow compared to a vampire, but much, much faster than a human, or a semivive.

That sprint sent him approximately fifty yards closer to the house. He could see it now, see it as it truly was—the faux Norman chateau of Serena's vision, with its walls of gray stone and multiple chimneys sprouting from the steeply pitched, slate-covered roof. In size it was close to the Mediterranean mansion it had pretended to be, only its true aspect was far more formidable. It did look exactly like the sort of place where a vampire coven would take shelter. No wonder Lucius had chosen the house as his hideaway here in Southern California.

By that point, the sun was almost directly overhead, a pallid orb barely visible through the thin cloud cover. No worries about running into any of the vampires now, and not for another six hours or so, until sundown came and freed them from their unnatural sleep. But Silas knew that semivives must patrol these grounds. How many, and how often, though—that was the real question.

Almost as if in response to his thoughts, footsteps crunched on the gravel of a pathway only a few yards from where he stood, hidden behind an enormous pine tree at least sixty years old, or more. Silas held his breath, staying absolutely still. Another of his people's talents, the ability to make oneself nearly undetectable, unless one's pursuer knew exactly where to look.

In this case, that didn't seem to be a problem. The footsteps didn't falter, and continued following the path until the sound of crunching gravel slowly faded away.

Silas allowed himself to peer around the trunk of the tree where he stood. His immediate surroundings seemed absolutely unoccupied, except for the chirping of a few birds from the branches overhead.

All right, so at least one semivive appeared to be keeping an eye on the grounds. Silas knew there were probably more; Lucius wouldn't entrust his resting place, and the place where his coven slept, to the watchful eyes of only one semivive. Probably there were cameras as well, although Silas couldn't see any evidence of them at the moment. Still, he had to assume the property had some kind of surveillance system set up, in which case he might have already been spotted. But wouldn't the semivive have been notified if a camera had detected an intruder on the grounds?

Maybe. For all he knew, the semivive making the sweep had only continued so he might collect a few of his compatriots to assist in capturing the interloper. Even semivives like the next-door gardener had described, ones gone dull-eyed from having their spirits subsumed by their vampire masters for years or even decades, knew enough not to tackle a *gula* without a little help from their friends.

Well, whatever they were up to, he'd just have to make sure they didn't catch him.

He moved again, this time running from the stand of trees where he'd been hiding to a low hedge. It wasn't tall enough to conceal him, so he crouched down, peering around one side so he could once again survey his surroundings. Here he saw a pond, and farther beyond that what appeared to be a rose garden. Just at the edge of his vision was a series of shallow steps, leading up to what he presumed was the front entrance of the house.

That wouldn't work. What he needed was a rear entrance, something off the kitchen or what might have been the servants' quarters. At least, he assumed a place of this size had once boasted a sizable staff, even though of course Lucius Montfort would use semivives in those capacities, rather than actual humans. On second thought, maybe looking for the servants' quarters wasn't such a good idea. There could be semivives loitering there, those who weren't on active guard duty.

This was the problem with going in blind, without any advance surveillance. Unfortunately, Silas hadn't had much of a choice. It was a gamble just coming here. Even with Michael St. John's dubious advice to guide him, the chance had always existed that the Mediterranean house had been exactly what it appeared to be. Silas had this one opportunity, and that was it.

His gaze tracked up the side of the house, to the second floor. Most likely the bedrooms were located there. Would Serena be held in one of those rooms? Belatedly, he recalled that he still had the original plans for the house cached on his phone. He got it out of his pocket and navigated to the browser, then pulled up the assessor's information. Yes, it looked as though the place had been built with a central hallway, with two wings branching off that. On the ground floor were the kitchen and dining room, several salons, a library, a smaller game room and breakfast room. The bedrooms occupied the second floor, with the master suite in the east wing.

Silas assumed Lucius must have taken over the master suite, since its scale would suit him. But would he have Serena in there as well? Probably not; vampires were at their most vulnerable while they "slept," and to have a hostage close by who might want to do her captor harm wouldn't make much sense.

However, the plans seemed to indicate that the bedroom next to the master suite was connected to it by an adjoining door, and it did make some sense that Serena would be kept there, close enough for Lucius to intrude on her whenever he desired, but where she could also be locked out when necessary. All Silas had to do was get up there somehow.

He didn't have a rope. What he did have, when he transformed, was a very efficient pair of wings.

Even so, he hesitated. Because he'd never encountered anything like the illusion Lucius had cast over the house to alter its appearance, he didn't know how far that illusion went. Was it like some kind of veil that took effect along the perimeter of the property, or did it affect only the house itself? If the latter, then anyone driving by would see an enormous winged monster flying up and over the building.

He'd have to go closer to the front of the house, which actually faced the arroyo rather than the street. No onlookers should be able to see him from that vantage point, and from there he could access one of the second-story windows. It didn't matter if it was the room where Serena was being held, as long as he could get to her quickly. In his *gula* form, he could move very fast indeed. Not as fast as a vampire, but then, he wouldn't be outrunning vampires, only semivives.

Gravel crunched again, and he crouched as low as he could, then peeked around the hedge. A different semivive, this one taller than the last, rounded the pond and then continued on his way, apparently oblivious to the intruder lurking only a few yards past the path he was on now. Silas waited until those footsteps had faded as well, then darted from his cover, pulling off his jacket as he did so. A moment later, he'd removed his T-shirt as well. The last thing he wanted was to leave a set of shredded garments lying on the ground, obvious evidence that a Watcher had trespassed here.

After this point, he knew he wouldn't have much cover. He would have to run, and take to the air as he went.

By now the transformation required very little effort, hardly more than the flick of a mental switch. He'd trained to do this, learned how to make his mind flip over to that other state, bringing forth the creature who dwelt within the very cells of his body.

As he ran, wings sprouted from his back, their huge leathery span beating against the damp air, propelling him upward. The ground dropped away, and he was flying, his jacket and shirt clutched in one hand as he maneuvered toward the east wing and one of the windows there.

Too late he saw the camera mounted above that window. Well, they would have known he was here as soon as he crashed through the glass, and so he didn't hesitate, but barreled through the casement, holding up his free arm to shield himself from the flying debris. His *gula* skin was thicker than human skin, and so the flying shards of glass and splinters of wood were only minor irritants to be brushed aside and ignored.

He hit the floor and rolled, then stood. The room was empty, although the bed was rumpled, a leatherbound book with gilt lettering lying there open and face down, as if whoever was reading it had been interrupted not too long ago.

Jane Austen. *Northanger Abbey.*

This must be where they'd held Serena. He could sense her, caught a faint lingering sweetness on the air, as if from the shampoo she used.

The door stood open. He hurried out into the hallway, wings furled tightly against his body so he could fit through the narrow entrance. Then he stopped dead, for Serena stood there toward the end of the hall, eyes wide and frightened, her arms held by a pair of blank-faced semivives, even as she struggled against them.

"Silas!" she screamed. "Run!"

He opened his mouth to reply, but in the next instant one—no, two...three—bolts of excruciating pain hit him in the back, lancing fire through his entire body. Then another, and another.

*Tasers,* he thought, with what remained of his consciousness. Blackness encroached at the edge of his vision, and he dropped to his knees, even as his fingers groped for the knives hidden in his pockets.

The last thing he saw was Serena's tear-filled eyes. He fell into them, and oblivion claimed him.

## CHAPTER SEVENTEEN

AT FIRST I DIDN'T KNOW WHAT WAS GOING ON, WHY several semivives had come to my room to hustle me away. As far as I knew, my plan to deceive Lucius was working. The night before, he'd walked me to my room after dinner, and kissed me again. I let him. He needed to believe that I'd succumbed, that I wasn't going to fight him anymore. Only I knew I'd continue to fight him in every way I could...when he wasn't looking.

I'd been so afraid he would try to push his way into my bed, make me prove my loyalty, but he didn't. Oh, he was the perfect gentleman, wishing me a good night and saying that we could talk more the next evening. What he intended by that performance, I wasn't sure. To lull me into a false sense of security? There was a joke. I knew I would never be secure anywhere around him.

All the same, I was glad of that small reprieve. I had to hope that my luck would continue the next night as well. As Silas had once told me, vampires played the long game. Waiting a few nights to get me in the sack probably wasn't too big a deal to someone who'd lived for hundreds of years.

I'd made myself sleep, and when I woke up, I showered and got dressed and did all the things ordinary people did to get ready for their day. That morning a semivive brought me breakfast—a real breakfast of eggs and bacon and toast, all of it well-prepared, the eggs over medium, just the way I liked them. Afterward, I brushed my teeth and refreshed my lip gloss, and sat down on the bed to read more Jane Austen. What else was I supposed to do? Another escape attempt was out of the question. I had to play along, and wait for an opening.

But a little after noon, just as I was thinking that it was almost getting time for lunch, two semivives came to my door. I didn't see a tray, or any other indication that they were going to bring me my midday meal.

Instead, one of them came over to the bed and plucked the book from my hands, then set it down on the coverlet. "Get up," he said.

"What?" I asked, bewildered by his behavior.

"You will come with us."

The other semivive grabbed me by the arm and pulled me off the bed, while his companion came around and took my other arm. Startled—and worried, because I knew none of the vampires could be awake at this hour, and so it couldn't have been any of them giving orders—I struggled in their grip, asking what the hell they were doing.

They ignored me and pulled me out of the room, and dragged me partway down the hall. Then I realized that several more semivives stood opposite us in the corridor, just past the door to my room. Each one of them held a Taser gun.

Oh, no.

A shadow moved past the window—a shadow with large, bat-like wings.

Somehow, against all odds, Silas had found me. But Lucius Montfort's minions knew my guardian was here, and now they lay in wait for him.

And there wasn't a goddamn thing I could do about it.

A sickening crunch of glass from inside my bedroom, and then Silas burst into the hallway in *gula* form, orange-copper eyes glaring with rage and worry. All I could do was scream at him to run, but my warning was useless, as it came far too late to prevent what happened next. The semivives fired their Tasers, hitting him multiple times, sparks flying, that massive body of his felled by all those shocks so he collapsed face first on the floor.

Then he changed. As soon as he lost consciousness, his body returned to its human form, the cruel hooks of the Tasers caught in the smooth skin of his back.

I made an incoherent cry of horror and began to move toward him, but the semivives holding me caught me before I'd taken a single step.

"No," said one of them. "He is no concern of yours. We will deal with him."

They dragged me away, screaming my denial, protesting that I needed to stay with him. Why I screamed, I didn't know. It wasn't as if there was anyone in the house who would come to my aid. But my rage and my worry were so great, I didn't really stop to think. I needed to cry my despair to the universe...even though I knew it would do nothing to get me or Silas out of this situation. No, he'd come to help me, and now he was a prisoner as well.

The semivives took me downstairs, to the same salon where Lucius had forced brandy between my lips. They bound me to the same heavy chair and left me there in the semidarkness; the heavy drapes were shut, and so the only light I could see was the half-hearted illumination that trickled in from the hallway.

I pulled against the ropes holding me in place, but, just as the last time, the semivives had done a very good job of tying me up. The chair rocked beneath me, and I settled down, knowing my struggles might knock the whole damn thing over if I wasn't careful. My current situation wasn't comfortable, but it would be orders of magnitude worse if I toppled the damn chair and me along with it. Then I'd be stuck lying on the floor until Lucius came to fetch me, which would be hours and hours from now.

Instead, I sat there and did my best not to cry. My imagination kept conjuring worse and worse fates for Silas. If he were lucky, he would only be locked up, but what if Lucius' minions had decided it was better to get rid of the troublesome *gula* once and for all?

I tried to reassure myself that they wouldn't take such drastic measures without first consulting Lucius. No, they must be holding him until their master awoke, which meant Silas had to be captive somewhere in this enormous mansion. Did it have a cellar? Probably, even though such things were rare in Southern California. Older houses were more likely to have some kind of a basement, though, and a huge, ostentatious structure like this would have been built for people with money, which meant—at least in the circles where I'd grown up—you tended to have a wine cellar.

All right, so I could mostly make myself accept the idea that Silas hadn't been summarily executed. That didn't mean Lucius wouldn't get rid of him as soon as he awoke from his daytime slumber. I had to stop Lucius from enacting his revenge, but how? I was walking a very narrow line here. If I defended Silas too vehemently, then the vampire master would know for sure that my sudden change of heart had been merely a sham. But if I acted as if I didn't care, then Lucius would surely get rid of the man I loved, since in the vampire's eyes, Silas was not merely an intruder and an enemy, but a rival as well.

God, I didn't know what to do. One misstep, and I could be sealing both my and Silas' fates.

The excruciating hours ticked past. Because I'd been given a decent breakfast, I wasn't nearly as hungry as I'd been the day before. However, about two hours into my ordeal, my bladder started complaining. All I could do was ignore it as best I could, and hope that Lucius would come here as soon as he woke up and was informed by his semivives about what had happened.

I was literally grinding my teeth, jaw clenched against the discomfort, when I heard the door open and swift footsteps cross the floor. Seconds later, strong, pale fingers were working away at the ropes that held my wrists to the chair.

"My darling," Lucius said. "I must apologize for the behavior of my servants."

"Oh, God," I blurted out. "I've never been so happy to see anyone in my life."

Which wasn't entirely a lie. Even Lucius Montfort's face was welcome if it meant I could get out of this torture chamber of a chair.

His silvery eyes lit up in what I thought might have been the first genuine expression of happiness I'd ever witnessed in him. "You are not hurt?"

"No," I replied. "But I need you to point me toward the nearest bathroom."

"Across the hallway, three doors down," he said as he knelt and undid the ropes that held my ankles to the legs of the chair.

"Thank you," I said breathlessly as I got up and bolted from the room. Not to escape, but just to get to the damn bathroom before my bladder exploded.

When I emerged a few minutes later, Lucius waited for me in the hallway. "Come along, Serena. You've had quite a shock."

I didn't argue, or struggle when he put his hand on my elbow and guided me down the corridor. Not to the salon where I'd been held captive all those hours, but another room I'd never seen before, this one obviously some kind of a sun porch, the walls all made of glass. In the daytime, it must have been a cheerful spot, with its light oak furniture and plants all around, but now I could see very little beyond the glass except the gloom of the garden, only faintly illuminated by landscape lights placed here and there.

Off in one corner stood a bistro set, two chairs and a small counter-height table. On the table was a pitcher of water and several glasses. Lucius poured some for me and then handed me the glass.

Now that I didn't have to worry about my bladder betraying me, I realized how thirsty I really was. I gulped down almost the entire contents of the glass, and Lucius refilled it.

"Again, my apologies," he said, once I felt somewhat restored and had set my glass back down on the table. "I had given my servants instructions as to what they should do in the event of a security breach. However, I had forgotten to update them as to how they should treat you in case one of the *gula* did enter the property. Matters between us moved rather swiftly yesterday."

"It's all right," I told him, even though it really wasn't. "I survived." Then, because I had to know, even if the question made Lucius newly suspicious of me, I asked, "What happened to Silas?"

"He is still alive, if that is what you are inquiring," Lucius replied, his tone deceptively casual. "Does it matter?"

"Of course it matters," I said indignantly. "Look, Lucius, just because things have...changed...between the two of us, that doesn't mean I want anything bad to happen to Silas. I still care about him. Only...."

"'Only'?" Lucius repeated, eyebrows lifting slightly.

"Only not in the same way. But that doesn't mean he isn't still an honorable man."

"My dear, he's not a man at all."

*Oh, and you are?* But of course I didn't say that. I forced myself to reach over and take the vampire's hand, to feel his cold fingers beneath mine, so different from the heat of Silas' touch. "You know what I mean."

"Yes, I suppose so."

Maybe it would have been better to leave it alone,

but I needed some kind of assurance that Silas would remain alive, that Lucius simply hadn't killed him yet because he hadn't thought of the best way to go about the process. "What are you going to do with him?"

Lucius gave me a considering look. "Well, I suppose that depends on you, Serena."

I didn't much like the sound of that remark. "On me?"

"Yes. If everything continues to go well—if you truly mean to be with me, to introduce me to your brother so we might enter into a mutually beneficial relationship—then I will keep your *gula* alive. As a favor to you, and nothing more."

What could I do except agree? I couldn't allow anything to happen to Silas. Perhaps he would think the cost too high, but I didn't agree. Besides, I still couldn't believe that Jackson would have anything to do with Lucius Montfort and his machinations, no matter what my visions might have told me.

"Of course, Lucius," I said calmly. "I wouldn't think of doing anything else."

Painfully, Silas opened his eyes. At first he couldn't see much of anything, but as his vision adjusted to the dim lighting, he realized he must be in the cellar beneath the house—racks of dusty wine bottles lined the walls, which were of rough concrete, like the floor. The illumination, such as it was, came from an emergency fixture over the door. At the moment, it gave off a faint reddish light, just enough so he wasn't in complete darkness. For a regular person, it might not have been enough, but even when Silas wasn't in *gula* form, he could still see better in the dark than any human.

A set of heavy iron manacles had been fitted to his legs, to his wrists. He could move around, but he wouldn't get very far. If he tried, he might be able to reach one of the wine racks, but knocking it over would do him no good and only make a hell of a mess.

Speaking of messes….

He wanted to scrub his hand over his face in frustration, but he knew that would only result in smacking himself with the chains that bound him. At least he'd been given a chair to sit on, albeit one that was bolted to the floor, so he couldn't use it as a weapon against anyone who came down here to check on him.

And Serena? Silas didn't want to think about what might be happening to her right now. True, Michael St. John had said that Lucius wanted her, and so she might not have come to any physical harm. But the mere thought of the vampire touching her, trying to make her his….

Red-hot rage boiled through him. Silas hauled on the chains with all his might, even though he knew that wouldn't do any good. All he accomplished was to abuse muscles that already ached from the assault by those multiple Tasers. He could transform, but the manacles at his wrists and ankles were tight enough as it was. In his larger *gula* form, they would surely tear into his flesh. Besides, while he was much stronger as a *gula*, he didn't know if he would be strong enough to rip the chains' bolts from the wall. All he would likely accomplish would be to injure himself further.

The door creaked open, and a tall, dark figure entered the cellar. Silas narrowed his eyes in an attempt to see who the visitor might be. Not Lucius, that much was obvious; even the dim lighting would have shown the master vampire's pale hair, and this person appeared to be dark. One of the semivives?

As the stranger approached, Silas realized it was Michael St. John. The vampire paused a few feet away—safely out of reach—and crossed his arms. "So, it looks like you figured out what I was telling you. I didn't expect you to screw it up so badly, though."

Silas wanted to argue, but the truth was, he *had* screwed up. Once he realized the property really did hide Lucius Montfort's mansion, he should have gone back to his truck and called for reinforcements. But he'd been so eager to rescue Serena, so sure he could handle it, that he'd blundered right into a trap.

No wonder the Conclave had wanted to give him a dressing-down over getting involved with her. A Watcher should never allow himself to become emotionally involved, especially with the very person he was assigned to protect.

"Why are you here, St. John?" Silas asked, not bothering to keep the edge from his voice. "Come to gloat?"

"No," the vampire replied. "You probably don't believe me, but I wanted you to rescue Serena. She doesn't deserve to have Lucius Montfort breathing down her neck."

"Has he — ?"

"No. At least, not that I'm aware of. Only a matter of time, though. I have no doubt that he's using you as leverage. So she'll probably have to sacrifice herself to keep you alive."

The very thought of the master vampire touching Serena, making love to her, was enough to make Silas strain against his bonds once again. The manacles bit so hard into his wrists that they cut through the skin, blood beginning to well up under the unforgiving metal.

Michael St. John's gaze flickered toward the bloody mess, but otherwise he didn't react. That had to have taken a great deal of restraint, because usually vampires couldn't keep themselves away from fresh blood. He went on, "I'll do my best to keep an eye out for Serena. Who knows — maybe an opportunity will present itself to get her away from Lucius."

"You'd defy him like that? He would snap your neck."

"Would that be any great loss?" St. John offered Silas a bitter smile. "I'm finding that this whole vampire thing isn't quite what it's cracked up to be. Anyway, I'd better go. Just try to keep calm, and don't give Lucius a reason to kill you."

With that parting shot, the vampire was gone. The door must have opened and shut, but Michael St. John had moved so quickly that Silas didn't even see him leave.

Did he dare to hope that he had an ally here? He might as well...hope was the only thing he had at the moment.

Lucius didn't waste any time. He had some food brought for me, and some more water, but after I'd eaten the sandwich and apple—no takeout tonight—he handed my phone over to me.

For a moment, I stared at it blankly. Then I realized he must have had not-Brian fetch it from my condo. "What am I supposed to do with this?"

"Call your mother. Your sister's funeral is tomorrow, and the reception tomorrow night. I want to make sure I will be at that reception."

He made it sound so simple. I cleared my throat, then said, "You do realize that everyone thinks I've been kidnapped." I didn't bother to add that it was only the truth—he *had* kidnapped me, after all. Since I was trying to stay on his good side, though, bringing up inconvenient facts probably wasn't a very good idea.

The faintest lift of his shoulders, as if my concerns didn't count for much. "Yes, and I have a solution, one that will explain where you have been…and will also explain why you and I are together."

"I'm all ears."

Apparently ignoring the sarcasm in that comment, he said, "People would have seen us speaking with one another at your sister's reception. You will simply tell your mother that you had an immediate connection with me, and that caused you to quarrel with your sister. Wishing to get away for a few days and clear the air, you accepted my invitation up to my retreat in the mountains—a retreat with no real cell phone reception. On coming back down the mountain, you got all the calls you missed while you were out of town, and learned of your sister's tragic death. Hence, the reason why you are only calling now."

What a load of…. "I'm not sure my mother is going to buy that."

"Why not?"

"Because I'm not the sort of person who ups and disappears. Even if I'm angry about something. My mother knows that as well as anyone else."

Lucius didn't seem perturbed by my explanation. "Everyone does things that are out of character from time to time. Besides, your family already thinks you are a little…off…to borrow a phrase. You should be able to persuade her." His brows drew together, and the glint from those silver eyes suddenly seemed a little sharper. "Make the call."

No way out. I had to do as he asked, and sound convincing. Silas' life hung in the balance. Problem was, my mother would surely start poking holes in that story the second I opened my mouth. But there wasn't much I could do about that, except stay sharp and try like hell to keep her from cornering me. I had to make sure Lucius was at that reception the next night, or risk harm to the man I loved.

Before I could lose my nerve, I entered the code to unlock the phone, then went to my contacts list and pushed the entry for the phone at the house. Yes, there was a chance my mother might be out, in which case I'd try her cell next, but since Vanessa's funeral was the next day, I really didn't see my parents going out on the town tonight.

The phone rang twice, three times. I'd taken note of the time on the home screen of my cell phone, so I knew it was seven thirty-two. They were probably in the middle of dinner. I guessed that Jackson and his family were there, too, all of them trying to cope with their grief.

Then my mother's voice, sounding incredulous. "Serena?"

Of course she would have seen my information on the caller I.D. "Yes, Mom, it's me."

A long, deadly pause, followed by, "Where have

you been? Don't you know that the whole world's been looking for you?"

A slight exaggeration, but I certainly wasn't going to call her on it. "Mom, I just found out—about that, and…and about Vanessa. I've been out of town."

"Out of town where? You never leave the house!"

"I…that is…." The words trailed off as I sent a helpless glance over at Lucius. He sat there quietly, watching me, and made a sort of *go on* motion with one pale, elegant hand. "Up in the mountains. He and I went up to his retreat there, and my cell phone didn't work, so—"

"He who?" she demanded. "Serena, you're not making any sense."

"Lucius Montfort," I said desperately.

Another one of those heavy pauses. When she spoke again, my mother sounded incredulous. "You mean your sister's new investor?"

"Yes. She, well, she wasn't very happy about it. We had an argument. So I decided to check out for a while. I had no idea of anything that was going on. I'm sorry."

In the background, I heard my father's voice say, "Who is it?" and my mother respond in a sort of hissing whisper, "It's Serena."

A bit of a clacking sound, as if my father had plucked the receiver out of my mother's hand against her wishes and it had banged against his watch, or maybe his wedding ring. "Serena? You're all right?"

For some reason, hearing my father's voice, the obvious concern and relief in it, made me want to break into sobs. I couldn't, though. Not with Lucius Montfort sitting a few feet away and listening to the entire exchange. "I'm fine. It's like I was telling Mom —I met someone, and we took off for a few days. I figured it wouldn't be a big deal. My editing job had been postponed, and you were out of town, and—"

"Wait," he broke in. My father had the kind of voice that people listened to and obeyed, deep and resonant. "Who is this someone?"

"Lucius Montfort. Vanessa's investor. We met at her fashion show. He's just as shocked by what happened as everyone else is. I—I mean, he would like to come to the reception tomorrow night to pay his condolences. If that's all right."

"Of course."

I couldn't exactly be relieved, since attending the reception was part of Lucius' master plan. But at least I wouldn't have to argue about it. If my father had agreed, that was the end of the matter. My mother bossed the rest of us around, but she was too traditional to go up against my father's wishes...at least publicly.

"Thanks, Dad."

"You're sure you're all right?"

God knows what he'd heard in my voice. "Yes. It's just—I'm trying to come to grips with all this. I feel so awful about disappearing...."

326 | CHRISTINE POPE

"It's fine. We're just glad that you're safe, and so glad that you'll be with us tomorrow. The service is at four, but be at the house by two-thirty so we can all drive together."

"Sure," I said automatically. "I will."

"Where are you now? Are you home? Maybe you should come over now and stay the night."

Oh, no, that wouldn't work at all. I began to shake my head, then realized of course my father couldn't see me. "No, I'm not at home. I'm—I'm at Lucius' place in…." I stopped there and glanced over at him, not sure whether he wanted me to say where he lived. But he nodded, and I realized he wanted me to tell them he was in San Rafael, because that would make him seem more respectable to them. "In San Rafael. I didn't want to be alone after…well, after I heard the news. His driver will bring me over tomorrow."

That improvisation got me an approving look from Lucius. I knew he wouldn't let me out of the sight of his semivives, so having one of them act as his driver made sense. And of course that would only make his estimation go up with my parents. If you had a driver, you usually weren't playing in the minor leagues.

"If you're sure—"

"I'm sure, Dad. I'll be there. What time does the reception start?"

"Six-thirty. That will give us all enough time to drive back from Forest Lawn."

And it would be after sundown. Not by a lot, but

enough that Lucius wouldn't have a problem venturing out into the world. "Okay. I'll let Lucius know. And I'll be at the house at two-thirty." Because I could hear my mother in the background, murmuring that she wanted to talk to me again, I said hastily, "I have to go. But I'll see you tomorrow."

I ended the call, then flipped the little switch on the side of the phone to turn off the sound. That way, even if my mother kept calling back, I wouldn't have to deal with it. I knew I'd be walking into a shitstorm the next day, so I wanted a little peace now.

Not that I would really have much peace tonight, either. Lucius reached out and took my hand, drawing me to him. "Was that so difficult?"

"Not as bad as I'd thought it would be," I admitted. His arm went around me, and I had to force myself not to stiffen. "But I'm going to catch holy hell from my mother tomorrow. Giving me a hard time will help to distract her from the reality of burying her daughter."

"I am sorry about that," Lucius said, his voice soft. One hand touched my hair, smoothing it away from my face.

Somehow I doubted it. Tristan and Leticia were a subject I wanted to deal with later, though. I had fantasies of driving a stake through both of their black hearts, but at least they'd made themselves scarce lately. I hadn't seen either of them during the past twenty-four hours. "About that, though," I began, and he lifted an eyebrow.

"What is it?"

"I'll have to go shopping tomorrow. I don't have anything suitable for wearing to a funeral."

For a second his brow puckered, but then he seemed to relax, saying, "Of course. I'll send one of my semivives with you. You won't have to go too far, I trust?"

"No," I replied. "Just to the Macy's over on Lake Street. I should be able to find something there."

"Good. Then that won't be a problem." His arms tightened around me, and I worried that he would try to kiss me. Right then, I just didn't know if I could pretend to enjoy his caresses. Hearing my parents' voices had rattled me more than I wanted to admit.

But he let me go, his expression one of concern. Completely false, I was sure. He wanted to play at being the thoughtful lover, probably so he could perfect the act before he had to show it off in front of my parents and the rest of my family and friends.

Actually, I was fine with that. Anything to give me a bit of a reprieve, a little time to gather myself.

The next day, I would have to bury my sister.

# CHAPTER EIGHTEEN

LUCIUS HAD NOT-BRIAN ACT AS MY CHAUFFEUR FOR my shopping trip to Macy's. His little joke, I assumed, but also protective cover. Who better to take me to get a dress than my gay neighbor? I actually hadn't seen him at all the past few days, probably because he had to be pretending that everything was fine, and life continuing just as it always had. Once again, I wondered how long it would take for Lewis to realize that his partner was now someone very different.

Since he hadn't been a semivive for very long, not-Brian didn't have that dead-eyed expression yet. In fact, he seemed almost cheerful, praising me for "coming to my senses" and accepting his master as my new companion.

"It's all for the best," he chirped as he swung into the parking garage at Macy's.

Somehow, I refrained from hitting him in the head with my purse.

If it had been merely my own safety on the line, I would have attempted to get help while I was at the store, maybe by telling the saleswoman who was helping me find a dress that I needed to duck out on the man who'd come with me. I could have bolted out the back, caught a cab, had it take me to my parents' house, where I could have told them the real story and prayed that they wouldn't think I'd lost my mind.

But with Silas as hostage, I didn't have that luxury.

Instead, I tried on several dresses, and chose one I thought would be most appropriate—a black sheath with three-quarter-length sleeves and a wide boatneck collar. Very Jackie-O. My mother would definitely approve. Plain black pumps with thin heels, also quite retro. I didn't worry about jewelry; I had the silver hoops I'd been wearing when I was taken, and they'd do. I wasn't trying to impress anyone. I just didn't want to make a fashion gaffe that might set my mother off.

Afterward, not-Brian took me back to the mansion, where I changed and primped—again, because I knew it was expected that I present as perfect a façade as possible. I'd already wept for Vanessa, so I thought I'd probably be able to hold it together, to squeeze out just the one or two decorous tears I was allowed for a public display.

When I left my room, however, I was startled to

see not-Brian waiting for me. He held a slim black box in his hand and extended it toward me. "You should wear this," he said. "Your mother will expect to see it."

I recognized the box at once—it was the one that held the white gold Longines watch that had been my twenty-first birthday present. "Thank you," I replied as I took the box from him. For some reason, I was unexpectedly moved. I hadn't expected a semivive to think of such a small but important detail. Was it possible that more of his personality remained locked inside there than I'd thought?

As much as I wanted to, I knew I didn't dare ask. Right now, Lucius—and by extension, his minions— thought I was on their side. Too much probing would make it seem as if I thought the semivives needed to be saved.

In silence, I opened the box and extracted the watch, then fastened it around my wrist.

"I'll take that," said not-Brian, reaching for the now-empty box. "The car is waiting for you outside."

I took in a breath. Right then, I didn't know which ordeal I dreaded the most, the funeral itself, or the reception afterward, where I would be expected to introduce Lucius to my family. But I couldn't back out. I had to go along with the master vampire's wishes, or Silas' life would be forfeit.

The watch told me it was a little before two. I had a bit of time to spare. A notion struck me then.

"I want to see him," I told not-Brian.

"See who?"

"Silas. I've done everything that Lucius asked, and I'll continue to do so. But I think it's only fair that I should be able to see Silas and make sure he's safe."

Not-Brian's eyes narrowed. The expression was very unlike the real-life Brian, reminding me that even if he might seem something like his old self from time to time, he certainly wasn't my friend. "I don't think that's a good idea."

"You can stand there and watch me talk to him," I said. "It's not like I'm going to be passing secrets or trying to bust him out of wherever you're keeping him. I just want…proof of life, so to speak."

A long pause. Was I making things difficult for not-Brian, asking for something that definitely wasn't on the program? I didn't know how much autonomy of thought the semivives were allowed, but surely they had to make some decisions on their own, if for no other reason than having masters who were out of commission during the daylight hours.

At last he said, "All right. Just a minute. Then you're going out to the car."

Relief surged through me. "That's fine. Thank you."

He gave an offhand shrug, and led me down the hallway and to the stairs. Once we were on the ground floor, we passed the living room and the library and the game room, and kept going into the kitchen, which looked to me big enough to support a medium-sized restaurant.

On one wall of the kitchen was a door. Not-Brian opened it and guided me down a narrow, dark flight of steps, into what was clearly the wine cellar. We came around a corner, and there was Silas.

I wanted to cry out in dismay but somehow managed to stop in time, knowing that I couldn't show myself to be sympathetic to the captive. But....

He was chained to the concrete floor by a set of heavy manacles, his legs and wrists both restrained, although he sat on a chair, one that I realized had also been bolted to the floor—probably so he couldn't use it as a weapon. His chest was bare and smudged with dirt and sweat, and his heavy hair stuck to his cheeks and forehead. The worst, though, were his eyes, hollow with anger and pain.

Those dark eyes met mine, and widened. "Serena?" His voice was a cracked whisper; I didn't see any water nearby. Bastards.

"Yes, it's me. I'm—I'm fine."

His mouth compressed as he seemed to take in my appearance. "You look...good."

"I'm going to my sister's funeral."

"Ah." That was all, but I could hear the condemnation in his voice, that I should be standing here all shiny and polished, just as much Lucius' slave in my own way.

God, I wished I could tell him the truth, but I

didn't dare reveal anything of what I was up to. Not with not-Brian standing there and taking in everything I did and said.

"He needs water," I said in an undertone. "I understand why you had to lock him up, but would it kill you to get him something to drink?"

"I'll be sure to take care of it," the semivive responded, with something dangerously close to a smirk. Clearly, Silas' current condition didn't bother him in the slightest.

If I stayed any longer, I'd be sure to betray just how much it bothered me. Although I hated to leave Silas in such a state, I knew he would only remain alive for as long as Lucius believed I had switched allegiance. At least now I knew that my lover was alive, that the master vampire hadn't been lying about that one all-important thing.

"I've seen enough," I told not-Brian, and turned on my heels and went back up the stairs.

After that, I was taken out the side entrance, where Lucius' sleek charcoal-gray Mercedes waited for me under a porte-cochère. At the sight of the car, a shiver went down my spine. The last time I had seen it, the Mercedes had been sitting in the driveway of my sister's house in West Hollywood; not-Brian had driven me to Macy's in his own Audi, keeping up the façade that everything was still normal in his world.

Also waiting with the car was the brown-haired semivive I'd seen earlier patrolling the grounds.

Apparently, he fulfilled even more duties than I had originally thought.

"Ms. Quinn," he said politely as he opened the rear door for me.

It seemed I was getting the royal treatment, now that the semivives thought I was their master's chosen one. I managed to smile and then got in. The leather upholstery was soft and supple, but I didn't pay much attention to my surroundings. I'd spent most of my life in and around vehicles like this one.

The driver slid into his seat and started the car. Then, the ride so smooth I could hardly tell we were moving at all, he headed down the driveway and out onto the street. Part of me wanted to grab the door handle so I could hurl myself out onto the asphalt, but I knew attempting to escape would only sign Silas' death warrant. I had to pretend that I was exactly where I wanted to be.

So I stared at the expensive houses passing by and twisted my hands in my lap. As we jogged across the Colorado Boulevard bridge and dropped south so we could take California Boulevard to cut over to San Marino, my gut clenched tighter and tighter. It was one thing to have spoken with my parents on the phone the day before. At least then a safe distance existed between us. But now I would have to face them, would have to spew more lies and try to defend behavior that I would have thought indefensible if I'd witnessed it in anyone else. I couldn't tell them the truth, that I'd been held captive by a scheming vampire this entire week.

Oh, well. If I'd survived my week with Lucius Montfort, I could survive what was coming next.

At the entrance to my parents' property, the semi-vive driver stopped next to the keypad for the gate and sent me a questioning glance over his shoulder.

"Five-eight-three-two-six," I said wearily. There, now Lucius would know exactly how to gain access to their house. Not that he would do something so gauche. He thought he had me right where he wanted me, and so he had no need to resort to brute-force tactics.

We went through the now-open gate and followed the long, curving driveway to the house. Several other cars were already parked there, the usual assortment of Mercedes and BMWs, Audis and Range Rovers. Family members, and some of my parents' closest friends, I assumed. A much bigger crowd would assemble here later, but this service at Forest Lawn was for those who'd known Vanessa best.

A lump began to form in my throat, but I choked it back. I had to stay as calm and collected as I could. "Lucius will be meeting me here later," I told the semi-vive driver as he pulled up behind a Range Rover that was so new, it still had dealer plates. "You won't need to wait for me."

"I know," he said. "I'll get the door for you."

I made myself wait in the back seat while he put

the car in park, then circled around the rear and opened the door for me. He offered a hand, but I ignored it. There were limits to how far I intended to take this charade.

There wasn't any indication that this was a house in mourning—no wreath on the door, no curtains pulled shut. My parents weren't into those sorts of outward displays. Since I didn't live here anymore, I didn't let myself inside. Instead, I rang the doorbell and waited.

Only a moment later, the door opened. To my relief, it was my father who stood there. Dealing with my mother from the very outset would have been a struggle.

"Serena," he said, and held out his arms.

I went into them, let him hug me. Overall, we weren't a very demonstrative family, but these weren't ordinary circumstances. It felt good to have my father embrace me, for me to breathe in the faintest hint of Armani cologne. The scent reminded me of home.

"We'll be setting out in a few minutes," he said after he let me go. "We're just waiting for your Aunt Laurie and Uncle Adam. They're running a little late, but they called to let us know they should be here in about ten minutes."

That made sense. Laurie was my mother's younger sister, and she and her husband lived down in Rancho Bernardo, in San Diego County. They had quite a hike to get here, even when using the less-traveled toll roads rather than the mess that was I-5. "Jess isn't coming with them?" I asked, inquiring about my cousin, who was a few years younger than I and going to school at UC San Diego.

"No. She already had a school trip scheduled in Baja and couldn't get away." As usual, my father's tone was pleasant enough, but I thought I detected a note of disapproval in it. I got the impression that he thought my cousin should have canceled her trip.

Maybe so, but I wasn't going to worry about it. I had enough worries of my own to deal with.

"Anyway, we're all in the living room. I know Jackson will be glad to see you." My trepidation must have been clear in my face, because my father added in an undertone, "Your mother won't make a scene. I'm not saying she won't want to talk about what happened at a later time, when you can have some privacy, but she's not going to make trouble today."

"Thanks, Dad," I said quietly. And I meant it. Not that I was looking forward to a dressing-down at some undisclosed future date, but at least I would be able to get through this nightmare of a day without worrying about my mother telling me what a selfish brat I had been.

We went into the living room, where everyone had questions in their eyes but were polite and respectful, greeting me, offering their condolences. Jackson hugged me tightly, and so did his wife Bethany. Their children as well, all three of them looking very pale and solemn. My brother also looked as if he wanted to talk to me in private, but he only said that he was glad I could be there with everyone.

And then my missing aunt and uncle appeared, and after another round of out-of-character hugs, the group of us, numbering around twenty-five, got into their respective vehicles and headed out for the long drive to Forest Lawn. Rose Hills was probably slightly more convenient, but Quinns had been buried at Forest Lawn in Glendale ever since the family had come to Southern California.

I was sure my mother would launch into me as soon as we were all alone in the Audi SUV they'd bought the year before, despite what my father had just told me. Apparently he'd put the fear of God in her, though, because all she said was, "I knew you'd wear those silly earrings. Take these instead."

She reached back to hand me a pair of diamond studs set in white gold. A far better match for the Longines watch I wore, but still, I had to shake my head mentally at her caring about such a stupid detail. God forbid I should be seen in front of her friends and family while wearing a pair of thirty-dollar silver hoops.

In silence, I removed the hoops and then slipped the diamond studs into my ears. It wasn't worth arguing about. That was the story of my life, really— deciding which battles to fight. With my mother, it was never easy. I dropped the hoops into my purse and forced myself not to roll my eyes.

None of us spoke on the way out to the cemetery. Or rather, my mother made a few inconsequential remarks about how she was glad the rain had held off, and expressing her worries that the caterers wouldn't have everything set up by the time we got back to the house, but we didn't really talk.

Just as well. There were so many things I couldn't say to either of my parents.

The rain might have been keeping away, but the day was still gray, although not very cold. I followed the group of mourners into the mausoleum, to the crypt where my grandparents and great-grandparents —and now my sister—slept.

Closed casket, for which I was eternally grateful. I didn't think I could bear to look down into Vanessa's still face, artificially preserved by the mortician's art. I feared I would see accusation there, blame for bringing Lucius Montfort and his unholy disciples into her orbit. I couldn't even deny it. No, I certainly hadn't attracted the vampires' attention on purpose, but I also couldn't deny that if it hadn't been for me, my sister would still be alive.

Why did tears burn so much more when you couldn't let them fall?

I stood there and listened to the minister talk about Vanessa's talent and spirit and brilliance, and how the world would be a much darker place without her. No arguments from me. The sun wouldn't set for several hours, but right then I felt as though I were shrouded in night, carrying a blackness with me I could never dispel.

Afterward, we all walked away, still quiet, leaving her to her endless sleep. I didn't want to think of my bright, mercurial sister's body inside that casket, gradually falling into decay. Although, strangely, part of me was glad. At least she was truly dead, not undead. This wasn't like some vampire movie where the victim would sit up in her coffin and go raging about the countryside once all the mourners were gone. That wasn't how you became a vampire in real life. The master vampire had to intend to make you one of his own, or else you would be dead in the ordinary way, with no chance of return.

The sun had slipped behind the hills by the time we got back to the car. Uneasy, I stared out at the gathering darkness. In less than an hour, the daylight would be gone altogether, and Lucius would be free to leave his black-curtained bedroom and come in search of me.

I swallowed. Yes, I'd already gotten permission for him to attend the reception, and yet I quailed at the thought of introducing him to my family, to my brother. Once I had taken that step, there was no going back. I could only plunge forward into the future, and hope that I might be able to change it somehow.

The caterers were putting the finishing touches on the spread in the dining room as we all returned. My mother immediately went to inspect everything, no doubt glad of the chance to put her grief aside and focus on something infinitely more prosaic, more manageable.

For myself, I could only be relieved when one of the waiters offered me a glass of white wine. I sipped it gratefully, hoping it would help to ease some of the tension that had wound my neck and back so tight. A glance down at my watch told me it was six-fifteen.

Lucius might be here very soon.

But then the first of the other guests began to arrive — Vanessa's assistants, fellow designers, friends and models and account executives and lord knows what else. My parents' house was very large, but the crowd was big enough that it spread out into the living room and the family room, and the covered patio beyond that. This had all been anticipated, and so all those areas had been tastefully decorated with floral arrangements and large framed photos of Vanessa, but still, I began to be somewhat over-whelmed. My solitary life of the past few years hadn't prepared me to be surrounded by hundreds of people, most of whom wanted to share condolences with me, or hug me and exclaim over how much I looked like my sister.

I'd just snagged another glass of wine from the tray of a passing waiter when I heard Lucius' voice in my ear. "My dear, you do rather look like you want to bolt."

I startled, although not badly enough that I spilled any of my wine. There he stood only a foot away, impeccable in a charcoal gray suit and pale gray shirt. The tie at his throat was black and red and silver, held in place with a white gold and ruby pin.

Incongruously, I was almost relieved to see him. Why, I couldn't really say, except that at least he was someone who knew all the secrets I was hiding.

Well, all but one.

"I'm not much for crowds," I said.

"Actually, neither am I. But we'll be home soon enough."

I didn't much like the way he referred to his mansion as "home," especially with the intimation that it was now my home as well.

His silver eyes glinted at me, as though daring me to protest. When I remained silent, he went on, "How was the service?"

"Horrible," I said shortly.

"These things are difficult. I understand."

I looked past him to see my parents approaching, and stiffened. He gave a brief glance over one shoulder, then smiled at me, as if trying to offer reassurance. I knew better, though. There was nothing remotely reassuring about Lucius Montfort.

My turn to smile, however much it pained me. "Mom, Dad," I said. "This is Lucius Montfort."

"Very good to meet you," my father said, and extended a hand.

"Very pleased to meet you as well," Lucius replied. "And you, Mrs. Quinn."

"Barbara," she said, dark eyes assessing, taking in the expensive bespoke suit, the quiet elegance of the tie pin. If it weren't so painful, it would have been almost amusing to watch the way she relaxed slightly once she'd taken his measure. This wasn't some scruffy interloper, someone not worthy of her precious daughter. In her eyes, Lucius must have appeared nearly perfect, if it weren't for the way we'd disappeared together this past week. I had no doubt she'd soon overlook that transgression, however, given the chance.

If she only knew what he really was.

"A tragedy," Lucius murmured. "I was very much looking forward to working with your daughter. Hers was the kind of talent that doesn't come along very often."

"Yes, we are very proud of what Vanessa accomplished," my father said. "At this point, we can only hope that the authorities find her murderer, and bring him to justice."

"Of course," the vampire replied. His expression was dead sober, revealing nothing except genuine regret at Vanessa's loss.

I had to take a sip of wine then. Otherwise, the compulsion to blurt out that two of his compatriots were my sister's true murderers would have been almost overwhelming.

After exchanging a few more paeans to my sister's talent, my parents excused themselves and went off to circulate in the crowd. Lucius waited until they were safely out of earshot, then said, "It's killing you, isn't it?"

"What's killing me?" I responded innocently.

"Not being able to tell them the truth." He drank some of his wine. "About everything."

If I protested too much, he would know I was lying. I lifted my shoulders and took a sip of wine, then said, "I will admit that it is rather difficult."

"You are doing splendidly." A smile, and he reached out with his free hand so he could briefly touch my arm. To an onlooker, the gesture would have looked like the most innocent of caresses, but I knew he'd done so to emphasize his control over me. "And you look splendid, too. You bought that dress this morning?"

"Yes."

"It's very becoming. You are definitely the most beautiful woman here."

"What, even with all these models everywhere?"

"They are empty. You, my dear, have suffered and prevailed. Your beauty lies in much more than your face, lovely as it is."

If Silas had been saying such things to me, I would have flushed with pleasure. As it was, all I could do was summon a wan smile. I didn't want Lucius Mont-fort paying me compliments. Already I found it more and more difficult to determine whether he meant any of what he said, or whether this supposed devotion of his was only another trick to play with my head.

"Serena!"

Damn it. There was my brother Jackson approaching. I didn't see any sign of Bethany or the kids, and I guessed my sister-in-law was probably off with them somewhere, doing her best to keep them amused, probably with food. Lord knows there was a bewildering variety available. My mother never did anything by halves.

This was why I was here, why Lucius stood by my side, comfortable as though he was meant to be there. I'd promised this introduction, and now I knew I had to honor that promise. It was the only way to keep Silas alive. Never mind that once my brother and the master vampire met, we'd be firmly set on the path that led to the two of them working together, of the world changing forever.

A world where I was Lucius' plaything.

I swallowed, and did my best to smile, to look as if I was glad my brother had sought me out. Lucius stood at my side, expectant, a glow of satisfaction entering his eyes. No going back now.

"Jackson," I said firmly, "I'd like you to meet Lucius Montfort."